GREYHOUND
FOR BREAKFAST

James Kelman was born in Glasgow in 1946. His books include *Not not while the giro*, *The Busconductor Hines*, *A Chancer*, *Greyhound for Breakfast*, which won the 1987 Cheltenham Prize, and *A Disaffection*, which won the James Tait Black Memorial Prize and was shortlisted for the Booker Prize. His most recent novel, *How late it was, how late* won the 1994 Booker Prize. James Kelman lives in Glasgow with his wife and two daughters.

ALSO BY JAMES KELMAN

An old pub near the Angel, and other stories
Three Glasgow Writers (with Tom Leonard and Alex Hamilton)
Short Tales from the Nightshift
Not not while the giro, and other stories
The Busconductor Hines
Lean Tales (with Agnes Owens and Alasdair Gray)
A Chancer
A Disaffection
Hardie and Baird & Other Plays
The Burn
Some Recent Attacks: Essays Cultural and Political
How late it was, how late
The Good Times

James Kelman

GREYHOUND
FOR BREAKFAST

V

VINTAGE

Published by Vintage 1999

4 6 8 10 9 7 5 3

Some of these stories have appeared in the following publications:
*Cencratus, Eboracum, Edinburgh Review, Filter, The Glasgow
Review, Identities, New Statesman, Not Poetry, Scottish Short
Stories, Some Say, Writers-in-Brief*

'Old Francis' first appeared in *TriQuarterly*, a publication
of Northwestern University.

First published in Great Britain in 1987
by Secker & Warburg

Minerva edition published in 1996

Vintage
Random House, 20 Vauxhall Bridge Road, London SW1V 2SA

Random House Australia (Pty) Limited
20 Alfred Street, Milsons Point, Sydney
New South Wales 2061, Australia

Random House New Zealand Limited
18 Poland Road, Glenfield, Auckland 10, New Zealand

Random House South Africa (Pty) Limited
Endulini, 5A Jubilee Road, Parktown 2193, South Africa

The Random House Group Limited Reg. No. 954009
www.randomhouse.co.uk

A CIP catalogue record for this book
is available from the British Library

ISBN 0 7493 8616 9

Printed and bound in Great Britain by
Cox & Wyman Limited, Reading, Berkshire

CONTENTS

OLD FRANCIS

HE WIPED the bench dry enough to sit down, thrust his hands into his jacket pockets and hunched his shoulders, his chin coming down onto his chest. It was cold now and it hadnt been earlier, unless he just wasnt feeling it earlier. And he started shivering immediately, as if the thought had induced it. This was the worst yet. No question about it. If care wasnt taken things would degenerate even further. If that was possible. But of course it was possible. Anything was possible. Everything was possible. Every last thing in the world. A man in a training suit was approaching at a jog, a fastish sort of jog. The noise of his breathing, audible from a long way off. Frank stared at him, not caring in the slightest when it became obvious the jogger had noticed and was now a wee bit self-conscious in his run, as if his elbows were rotating in an unnatural manner. It was something to smile about. Joggers were always supposed to be so self-absorbed but here it seemed like they were just the same as the rut, the common rut, of whom Francis was definitely one. But then as he passed by the bench the jogger muttered something which ended in an 'sk' sound, perhaps 'brisk'. Could he have said something like 'brisk'? Brisk this morning. That was a fair probability, in reference to the weather. Autumn. The path by the side of the burn was deep in slimy leaves, decaying leaves, approaching that physical state where they were set to be reclaimed by the earth, unless perhaps along came the midgie men and they shovelled it all up and dumped it into the midgie motor then on to the rubbish dump where they would sprinkle aboard paraffin and so on and so forth till the day of judgement. And where was the jogger! Vanished. Without breaking stride he must have carried straight on and up the slow

[1]

winding incline towards the bridge, where to vanish was the only outcome, leaving Francis alone with his thoughts.

These thoughts of Francis's were diabolical.

The sound of laughter. Laughter! Muffled, yes, but still, laughter. Could this be the case!! Truly? Or was it a form of eternal high jinks!!

Hearty stuff as well. Three blokes coming along the path from the same direction the jogger had appeared from. They noticed Francis. O yes, they soon spotted him. They couldnt miss him. It was not possible. If they had wanted to miss him they couldnt have. And they were taking stock of him and how the situation was in toto. They were going to get money off of him, off of. One of them had strolled on a little bit ahead; he was wearing a coat that must have belonged to somebody else altogether, it was really outlandish. Francis shook his head. The bloke halted at the bench and looked at him:

You got twenty pence there jim, for the busfare home?

Francis was frowning at the bloke's outfit. Sorry, he said, but that's some coat you're wearing!

What?

Francis smiled.

Funny man.

Sorry, I'm no being sarcastic.

A funny man! he called to his two companions. He's cracking funnies about my coat!

Surely no! said this one who was holding a bottle by its neck.

Aye.

That's cheeky! He swigged from the bottle and handed it on to the third man. Then he added: Maybe he likes its style!

The first bloke nodded, he smiled briefly.

And he wants to buy it! Heh, maybe he wants to buy it! Eh, d'you want to buy it?

Frank coughed and cleared his throat, and he stared at the grass by his shoes, sparish clumps of it amid the muddiness, many feets have stood and so on. He raised his head and gazed at the second man; he was dangerous as well, every bit as dangerous. He noticed his pulse slowing now. Definitely, slowing. Therefore it

[2]

must have been galloping. That's what Francis's pulse does, it gallops. Other cunts's pulses they just fucking stroll along at a safe distance from one's death's possibility. What was he on about now! Old Francis here! His death's possibility! Death: and/or its possibility. Was he about to get a stroke? Perhaps. He shook his head and smiled, then glanced at the first bloke who was gazing at him, and said: I didnt mean you to take it badly.

What?

Your coat. Frank shrugged, his hands still in his pockets. My comment . . . he shrugged again.

Your comment?

Aye, I didnt mean you to take it badly.

I never took it badly.

Frank nodded.

The second bloke laughed suddenly. Heh by the way, he said, when you come to think about it, the guy's right, your fucking coat, eh! Fucking comic cuts! Look at it!

And then he turned and sat down heavily, right next to him on the bench; and he stared straight into his eyes. Somebody whose body was saturated with alcohol. He was literally smelling. Literally actually smelling. Just like Francis right enough, he was smelling as well. Birds of a feather flock together. And what do they do when they are together? A word for booze ending in 'er'. Frank smiled, shaking his head. I'm skint, he said, I'm out the game. No point looking for dough off of me.

Off of. There it had come out again. It was peculiar the way such things happened.

The two blokes were watching him. So was the third. This third was holding the bottle now. And a sorry sight he was too, this third fellow, a poor looking cratur. His trousers were somebody else's; and that was for fucking definite. My my my. Frank shook his head and he called: Eh look, I'm no being sarcastic but that pair of trousers you're wearing I mean for God sake surely you could do a wee bit better, eh?

He glanced at the other two: Eh? surely yous could do a wee bit better than that?

What you talking about? asked the first bloke.

[3]

Your mate's trousers, they're fucking falling to bits. I mean look at his arse, his arse is fucking poking out!

And so it was, you could see part of the man's shirt tail poking out! Frank shook his head, but didnt smile. He gestured at the trousers.

He is a funny man right enough! said the second bloke.

Instead of answering him the first bloke just watched Frank, not showing much emotion at all, just in a very sort of cold manner, passionless. If he had been unsure of his ground at any time he was definitely not unsure now. It was him that was dangerous. Of the trio, it was him. Best just to humour him. Frank muttered, I'm skint. He shrugged and gazed over the path towards the burn.

You're skint.

Frank continued gazing over the path.

It's just a couple of bob we're looking for.

Sorry, I really am skint but.

The second bloke leaned closer and said: Snout?

Frank shook his head.

You've got no snout! The bloke didnt believe him. He just didnt believe him. He turned and gave an exaggerated look to his mates. It was as if he was just not able to believe it possible. Frank was taken aback. It was actually irritating. It really was. He was frowning at the fellow, then quickly he checked what the other one was doing. You never know, he might have been sneaking up behind him at the back of the bloody bench! It was downright fucking nonsensical. And yet it was the sort of incident you could credit. You were sitting down in an attempt to recover a certain inner equilibrium when suddenly there appear certain forces, seemingly arbitrary forces, as if they had been called up by a positive evil. Perhaps Augustine was right after all? Before he left the Manicheans.

Twenty pence just, said the first.

Frank shook his head. He glanced at the bloke. Look, I'm telling you the truth, I'm skint.

You've got a watch.

What – you kidding! Frank stared at him for a moment; then he sniffed and cleared his throat, gazed back over the path.

[4]

He has got a watch, said the second bloke.

And now the third stepped across to the bench, and he handed the bottle to the first. Frank had his hands out of his pockets and placed them onto his kneecaps, gripping them, his knuckles showing white.

Did you miss your bus? asked the first.

Did you miss your bus! laughed the second.

And the third bloke just stared. Frank stared back at him. Was he the leader after all? Perhaps he was the one he would have to go for first, boot him in the balls and then face the other pair. Fucking bastards. Because if they thought he was going to give them the watch just like that then they had another think coming. Bastards. One thing he was never was a coward. Bastards, he was never fucking a coward. He flexed his fingers then closed them over his kneecaps again, and he sighed, his shoulders drooping a bit. He stared over the path. It was as if they were aspects of the same person. That was what really was the dangerous thing.

The second bloke was speaking; he was saying, I dont think he even goes on public transport, this yin, I think he's a car-owner.

A car-owner! Frank grinned. I'm actually a train-owner! A train-owner! That was really funny. One of his better witticisms. A train-owner. Ha ha. Frank smiled. He would have to watch himself though, such comments, so unfunny as to approach the borderline.

What borderline? One of irrationality perhaps. A nonsensicality. A plain whimsy. Whimsy. There was a bird whistling in a tree nearby. D d d dooie. D d d dooie. Wee fucking bird, its own wee fucking heart and soul. D d d dooie. What was it looking for? It was looking for a mate. A wee female. A wee chookie. Aw the sin. My my my. My my my. And yet it was quite upsetting. It brought tears to the eye. If Frank could just heave a brick at the tree so it would get to fuck away out of this, this vale of misery. God. I need a drink, said Frank to the first bloke. He gestured at the bottle: D'you mind?

The man handed him the bottle.

The second looked at him, biding his time, waiting to see the outcome.

And the third bloke put his hands into his trouser pockets and strolled across the path, down to the small fence at the burn, where he leant his elbows.

The noise of the water, the current not being too strong, a gush more than anything, a continuous gushing sound, and quite reassuring. This freshness as well, it was good. The whole scene in fact, was very peaceful, very very peaceful; a deep tranquillity. Not yet 10 o'clock in the morning but so incredibly calm.

There was no label on the bottle. Francis frowned at this. What happened to the label? he asked.

It fell off.

Is it hair lacquer or something?

Hair lacquer! laughed the second bloke.

It looks like it to me, replied Francis.

You dont have to fucking drink it you know!

Francis nodded; he studied the bottle. The liquid looked fine – as much as it was possible to tell from looking; but what was there could be told about a drink by looking at the outside of its bottle? He couldnt even tell what colour it was, although the actual glass was dark brownish. He raised the neck of the bottle, tilted his head and tasted a mouthful: Christ it was fiery stuff! He shook his head at the two blokes, he seemed to be frowning but he wasnt. WWhhh! Fucking hot stuff this! he said.

Aye.

Francis had another go. Really fiery but warming, a good drink. He wiped his mouth and returned the bottle. Ta, he said.

I told you it was the mccoy, said the second bloke.

Did you?

Aye.

Mm. It's fucking hot, I'll say that!

Know what we call it?

Naw.

Sherry vindaloo!

Francis smiled. That was a good yin, sherry vindaloo. He'd remember it.

The first bloke nodded and repeated it: Sherry vindaloo.

The second bloke laughed and swigged some, he walked to hand it to the third who did a slightly peculiar thing, it was a full examination; he studied the bottle all round before taking a sip which must have finished it because the next thing he was leaning over the fence and dropping the bottle into the burn. Francis glanced at the first bloke but didnt say anything. Then he shivered. It was still quite cold. High time that sun put in an appearance, else all would be lost! Francis grinned. The world was really a predictable place to live in. Augustine was right but wasnt right though obviously he wasnt wrong. He was a good strong man. If Francis had been like him he would have been quite happy.

The first bloke was looking at him. You'll do for me, he said.

What was that?

I said you'll do for me.

Francis nodded. Thanks. As long as you didnt take offence about that comment.

Och naw, fuck.

Francis nodded. And thanks for the drink.

Ye kidding? It's just a drink.

Aye well . . .

The bloke shrugged. That's how we were wanting to get a few bob, so's we could get a refill.

Mm, aye.

See your watch, we could get no bad for it.

Frank nodded. There was no chance, no fucking chance. Down by the fence the second bloke was gazing at him and he shifted on his seat immediately so that when he was looking straight ahead he was looking away from the three men. He didnt want to see them at the moment. There was something about them that was frightening. He was recognizing in himself fear. He was scared, he was frightened; it was the three men who were frightening him, something in them together that was making him scared, the sum of the parts, it was an evil force. If he just stared straight ahead. If he stayed calm. He was on a bench in the park and it was 10 a.m. There was a jogger somewhere. All it needed was somebody to touch him perhaps. If that happened he would die. His heart would stop beating. If that happened he would die and revelation. But if he just got up. If he was to just get up off of the bench and start walking slowly and deliberately along in the opposite direction, to from where they had come. That would be fine if he could just do that. But he couldnt, he couldnt do it; his hands gripped his kneecaps, the knuckles pure white. Did he want to die? What had his life been like? Had it been worth living? His boyhood, what like was his boyhood? had that been okay? It hadnt been too bad he hadnt been too bad, he'd just been okay normal, normal, the same as anybody else. He'd just fallen into bad ways. But he wasnt evil. Nobody could call him evil. He was not evil. He was just an ordinary person who was on hard times who was not doing as well as he used to and who would be getting better soon once things picked up, he would be fine again and able to be just the same, he was all right, he was fine, it was just to be staring ahead.

A HISTORY

WHEN FROM OUT of the evening the quiet reached such a pitch I had to unlock the door and wander abroad. At this time the waves ceased pounding the rocks and the wind entered its period of abeyance. Along the shore I travelled very casually indeed, examining this, that and the other, frequently stooping to raise a boulder. That absurd and unrealized dream from childhood, that beneath certain boulders . . .

I was going south to south east, towards the third promontory. It was where I could take my ease at times such as this. A fine huddle of rocks and stone. There were three little caverns and one larger one, a cave; this cave would presently be dry. It always afforded a good shelter. From it I could gaze out on the sea. I withdrew my articles from my coat pocket, a collection of shells. Even now I retained the habit, as though some among them would prove of value eventually. I leaned close to the entrance of the cave and chipped them out in a handful, not hearing any splash due to the roaring of the waves. Yet there too had been a striped crab shell of a sort I was unfamiliar with, about five inches in diameter. I kept an assortment of items at home to which this crab shell might have proved a fair addition. In all probability, however, the stripes had simply been a result of the sea's turmoil. Or perhaps it had been wedged in between two rocks for several centuries. I doubted my motives for having thrown it away. But I had no history to consider. None whatsoever. I had that small collection of things and too the cottage itself, its furnishings and fittings, certain obvious domestic objects. But be that as it may not one of these goods was a history of mine. My own history was not in that cottage. If it could be trapped anywhere it would not be there. I felt that the existence of a dead body would alter things. Previous to this I had come upon a dead body so I did have some knowledge. It had been a poor thing, a drowned man of middle age, a seaman or fisherman. I made the trip to the village to convey the information then returned to the cottage to await their arrival. I had carried the body into there and placed it on the floor to safeguard against its being carried back out on the tide. The face was bearded, no boots on the feet though a sock remained on the left foot. A man in the sea with his wits about him, ridding himself of the boots to assist the possibility of survival. He would have had a family and everyday responsibilities whether to them or to his shipmates; that amazing urge to survive which is doomed. He would have been dead in twenty minutes, maybe less. If I had been God I would have allowed him to survive for twenty hours.

But now here I was. And could it be described as good, this lack of damp, not being chilled to the bone; even a sensation of warmth. All in all I was wishing I had kept a hold of the shells and that striped one of a crab, and I would then have been very content indeed, simply to remain there in the cave, knowing I would only have to travel such and such a distance back to the cottage.

THE ONE WITH THE DOG

WHAT I fucking do is wander about the place, just going here and there. I've got my pitches. A few other cunts use them as well. They keep out my road cause I lose my temper. I've got two mates I sometimes meet up with to split for a drink and the rest of it. Their pitches are out the road of mine. One of them's quiet. That suits me. The other yin's a gab. I'm no that bothered. What I do I just nod. If anybody's skint it'll be him. He's fucking hopeless. The quiet yin's no bad. I quite like the way he does it. He goes up and stares into their eyes. That's a bit like me except I'll say something. Give us a couple of bob. The busfare home. That kind of thing. It doesnt fucking matter. All they have to do is look at you and they know the score. What I do I just stand waiting at the space by the shops. Sometimes you get them with change in their hands; they've no had time to stick it back into their purses or pockets. Men's the best. Going up to women's no so hot because they'll look scared. The men are scared as well but it's no sexual and there's no the same risks with the polis if you get clocked doing it. Sometimes I feel like saying to them give us your jacket ya bastard. It makes me laugh. I've never said it yet. I dont like the cunts and I get annoyed. Sometimes I think ya bastard ye I'm fucking skint and you're no. It's a mistake. It shouldnt fucking matter cause you cant stop it. There's this dog started following me. It used to go with that other yin, the quiet cunt. It tagged behind him across in the park one morning and me and the gab told him to fucking dump it cause it must belong to somebody but he didnt fucking bother, just shrugs. One thing I'm finding but it makes it a wee bit easier getting a turn. But I dont like it following me about. I dont like that kind of company. I used to have a mate like that as well, followed me about and that and I didnt like it. I used to tell him to fuck off. That's what I sometimes do with the dog. Then sometimes they see you doing it and you can see them fucking they dont like it, they dont like it and it makes them scared at the same time. I'd tell them to fuck off as well. That's what I feel like doing but what I do I just ignore them. That's what I do with the dog too, cause it's best. Anything else is daft, it's just getting angry and that's a mistake. I try no to get angry; it's just the trouble is I've got a temper. That's what the gab says as well, your trouble he says you've got a fucking temper, you're better off just taking it easy. But I do take it easy. If they weigh you in then good and if they dont then there's always the next yin along. And even if you dont get a turn the whole fucking day then there's always the other two and usually one of them's managed to get something. That's the good thing about it, having mates. What I dont understand I dont understand how you get a few of the cunts going about in wee teams, maybe four or five to a pitch, one trying for the dough while the rest hang about in the background. That's fucking hopeless cause it just puts them off giving you anything and sometimes you can even see them away crossing the street just to keep out the way, as if they're fucking scared they're going to get set about if they dont cough up. It's stupid as well cause there's always some cunt sees what you're up to and next thing the polis is there and you're in fucking bother. What I think I think these yins that hang about in the background it's cause they're depressed. They've had too many knockbacks and they cant fucking take it so what they do they start hanging about with some cunt that doesnt care and they just take whatever they can get. If it was me I'd just tell them to fuck off; away and fuck I'd tell them, that's what I'd say if it was me.

OF THE SPIRIT

I SIT here you know I just sit here wondering what to do and my belly goes and my nerves are really on edge and I dont know what the fuck I'm to do it's something to think about I try to think about it while my head is going and sometimes this brings it back but only for a spell then suddenly I'm aware again of the feeling like a knife in the pit of my guts it's a worry I get worried about it because I know I should be doing things there are things needing doing I know I know I know it well but cant just bring myself to do them it isnt even as though there is that something that I can bring myself to do for if that was true it would be there I would be there and not having to worry about it at this stage my muscles go altogether and there's aches down the sides of my body they are actual aches and also under my arms at the shoulder my armpits there are aches and I think what I know about early-warning signs the early-warning signal of the dickey heart it feels like that is what it is the warning about impending strokes and death because also my chest is like that the pains at each side and stretching from there down the sides of my body as if I'm hunched right over the workbench with a case of snapped digestion the kind that has dissolved from the centre but still is there round the edges and I try to take myself out of it I think about a hundred and one things all different things different sorts of things the sorts of things you can think about as an average adult human being with an ordinary job and family the countless things and doing this can ease the aches for a time it can make me feel calm a bit as though things are coming under control due to thinking it all through as if really I am in control and able to consider things objectively

[13]

as if I'm going daft or something but this is what it's like as if just my head's packed it in and I'm stranded there with this head full of nothing and with all that sort of dithering it'd make you think about you've got it so that sometimes I wish my hands were clamps like the kind joiners use and I could fasten them onto the sides of my head and then apply the thumbscrews so everything starts squeezing and squeezing

I try not to think about it too much because that doesnt pay you dont have to tell me I know it far too well already then I wouldnt be bothering otherwise I wouldnt be bothering but just sitting here and not bothering but just with my head all screwed up and not a single idea or thought but just maybe the aches and the pains, that physicality.

RENEE

I HAD landed in a position of some authority offering scope for advancement. A storekeeper. I kept records of food for the stores of food I had authority of. The Foodstore was a fairly large smallroom. I had no assistants. Those in superior positions held little or no authority over me. I was belonging to the few able to match figures on paper with objects on shelves and was left alone to get on with it.

Members of the kitchenstaff came to obtain grub and it was down to me to check they were due this grub. If so I marked it all in a wee notebook I kept hidden in a concealed spot. The chap I succeeded was at that moment serving a bit of time as an effect of his failure to conceal said notebook. He left the fucker lying around for any mug to find. And eventually someone pulled a stroke with cases of strong drink, and this predecessor of mine wound up taking the blame.

The kitchenstaff consisted of females most of whom were Portuguese but though I found them really desirable they seemed to regard Scotchmen with disfavour. And the rest of the British for that matter. They spoke very little English. I could manage La Muchacha Hermosa in their own language but it got me nowhere. Alongside them worked a pair of girls from somewhere on the southeastern tip of England, one in particular I was disposed towards. The other was not bad. I had to carry on the chat with both however because generally speaking this always transpires in such circumstances viz when you are on your tod and have nobody to help out in 4somes. Obviously I had no desire to escort both on a night out. But neither did I wish to ask one lest the other

[15]

was hurt. What a mug! Never mind. It could have gone on for ages but for the intervention of the Portuguese. At long last they successfully conveyed to me that a certain girl from the southeastern tip of England wouldnt take it amiss if I was to dive in with the head down. Joan was her name; she seemed surprised when I asked her out but she was pleased. We walked down to the local pictures after work. The Odeon. People considered it a dump but I didnt; it showed two full-length feature films while the flash joints up west were charging a fortune for the privilege of seeing one.

My relations with the other girl declined palpably which was a bit of a pity because I quite liked her. She began visiting the Foodstore only when absolutely necessary. Then soon after this Joan was becoming irritated all the time. To some extent I couldnt blame her. My financial situation was hopeless and the very ideas of equality and going dutch were anathema to her. The upshot was the Odeon three weeks running. She hated it. That last conversation was totally ridiculous, me standing about humming and hawing and trying to assume a woebegone countenance. She said nothing but her face inflamed, she was quite passionate in some ways. The bloody Odeon again, she muttered and set off marching down the Gray's Inn Road.

I strode after her. But not too quickly because I was having to figure out a speech. By the time I had counted through the last of my coins and paid for the two tickets she was through in the foyer at the end of the sweeties' queue. She paid a fortune for chocolate but the thought of assisting me with the tickets never crossed her mind. And neither did the thought of walking off and leaving me – anything was better than spending the night indoors back at the female hostel where she stayed with her pal.

I waited for her to stick the sweeties and so on into her handbag then paused as she stepped past me and into the hall, where I handed the tickets to the aged usherette who was also from Scotland and occasionally gave me a cheery smile.

It was supposed to be hazardous for single women alone in the Odeon but to me that was extremely doubtful, perhaps if they'd had a halfbottle of rum sticking out their coat pockets. I never saw any bother. Just sometimes it was less than straightforward distinguishing the soundtrack from the racket caused by a few dozen snoring dossers. By the time we reached the seats the speech was forgotten about and we settled down to watch the movie. Later I slipped my arm about her shoulders and that was that, and we nestled in for a cuddle. On the road home afterwards we continued on past the local pub, straight to the female hostel. We stood in at the entrance out from the worst of the wind. There was no chance of her smuggling me inside. The place was very strict about that. Men were not wanted at all costs. She had hinted once or twice about my getting her into my own quarters. But it was not possible. In fact – well, the rumour circulating amongst the kitchenstaff at that precise moment concerned myself; they were saying I used the Foodstore as a sort of home-from-home to the extent that I actually slept in it. It was the main joke and I helped it along, telling them I was having a coloured television installed, plus a four-poster bed and a small portable bar, the usual sort of nonsense. The truth of the matter is that I *was* sleeping in the place; but nobody knew for sure and none had the authority to enter the Foodstore unless I was with them, this last being a new condition of the post because of the plight of my predecessor. Two keys only existed: one was held by myself while the other was kept in the office of the security staff. That was in case of emergencies. But I reckoned that with me being there on the premises most of the time there would be very little scope for 'emergencies'. I had overheard a couple of those in superior positions refer to the plight of my predecessor as an 'emergency'. The idea of becoming one myself was not appealing. But as long as the Foodstore remained under my control I had grounds for optimism; for the first time in a long while I was beginning to feel confident about the future. Even so, just occasionally, I could suddenly become inveighed by a sense of panic and if outside of the Foodstore I had to rush straight back to ensure everything was okay, that I hadnt forgotten to lock the bloody door. That Saturday night I started getting fidgety with Joan.

It was getting on for midnight according to her watch and I had visions of folk stealing in and filling swagbags full of grub and strong drink. And also there was an underlying suspicion that all was not well between Joan and myself, a sort of coldness, even a slight impatience. Eventually I asked her if anything was up but she said there wasnt then told me she had been invited to a good party the following night and would it be okay if she went. Of course it was okay. I quite fancied going myself. Good parties are uncommon. Especially in London. Things have a habit of going badly. I told Joan that but she said it would probably be alright, it was taking place in the home of the big brother of a former boyfriend. That sounds great, I said.

What d'you mean jock? she said.

Nothing.

Joan was good at kidding on she didnt notice things, my sarcasm was one of them. And five minutes later I was striding back down the road and sneaking in past the security office and down the long dark corridors to the Foodstore.

I didnt see her the next day but she sent a note via one of the Portuguese women, just to say she would meet me at the lounge door of the local pub at 8 that evening. It was after 9 when she arrived and I was into my third pint. She apologized. She was looking really great as well and there was a perfume she had on that was something special. Then too the material of her dress; I touched the side of her arm and there seemed to be a kind of heat radiated from it. Or else the Guinness was stronger than usual. And I kept having to stop myself from touching the nape of her neck. I noticed the landlord of the pub glancing at me in a surreptitious fashion as if fearing I might do something that would embarrass us all.

Joan kept looking at her watch until I swallowed down the last of the beer and collected my tobacco tin and matches. It was cold and blowy, and nobody was about. Nor were there any buses in view. It was as well to start walking. Joan wasnt too pleased; each time a taxi passed she made a show of looking to see if it was for hire. Eventually we reached Chancery Lane tube station.

As it transpired the party was not too bad at all, plenty of food and stuff. Joan's pal was there too but she seemed to be ignoring us. I lost sight of her amid the people who were bustling about dancing and the rest of it. Joan as well, eventually I lost sight of her. I went into a wee side room next to the kitchen, opened a can of beer and sat on a dining chair. A fellow came in who was involved with another of the girls from the hostel; he supported Charlton Athletic and we spoke about football for a time, then women. His girlfriend was older than him and it was causing problems with her parents or her roommates or something. His voice grated on me and it was as if he was just kidding on he was a Londoner. He kept on yapping. I began to wonder if maybe it was a plot of some sort to detain me.

Shortly before midnight a girl told me to go along to the end bedroom on the first floor. Joan was there. She nodded me inside but bypassed me, shutting the door behind me; and there was her pal, Renee was her name, she was sitting on the edge of the bed crying her eyes out. I took my tin out to roll a smoke then put it away again. She knew I was there. I stepped across and touched her shoulder. Okay? I said.

She shook the hand off. She had stopped crying but was trembling a little. I rolled a smoke now and offered her it but she didnt smoke. She dried her nose with a tissue. I laid my hand on her arm and asked if she was feeling any better. When she didnt answer I said: Will I tell Joan to come in?

No, she replied. She sniffed and dried her nose again. I stood smoking while she continued to sit there staring at the floor.

Do you want me to leave? I said.

Yes.

Joan had gone. Downstairs in the main dancing room I found her doing a slow one with this monkey dressed in a cravat and strange trousers. Over she came, she was frowning. Jock, she said, how's Renee? is she alright?

I think so. What was up with her?

She paused a moment then shrugged briefly, glanced away from me. Look jock, she said, I better finish the dance with David.

Oh good. Ask him if he's selling that cravat.

It wouldnt suit you, she muttered, and off she went. A loud dancing record started and other people got up onto the floor. I returned to the wee side room. The Charlton Athletic supporter was sitting on the floor with another guy; they both watched me enter. That was enough. Cheerio, I said.

It was time to get back to the Foodstore. I went into the kitchen first though and lifted a handful of cocktail sausages, wrapped them in a napkin and stuck them into my pocket and also as well a halfbottle of gin. Out in the hall I bumped into a couple at the foot of the stairs. I asked them if Renee was still in the end bedroom but they didnt seem to understand what I said.

Closing the front door after me I waited a moment in the porch, then I opened the gin and swigged a mouthful. It was really fucking horrible and didnt even taste like gin. I set off walking. Along the street and round from Basset Road I saw Renee away about fifty yards off, standing at an empty taxi rank. A man approached her and looked as if he was trying to chat her up. She stood stiffly, gazing directly to the front. He stepped towards her and she said something to him. Hey Renee! I shouted. Hey . . . I trotted along the road and the man walked smartly off in the opposite direction.

Renee was frowning, and she looked at me. He thought I was a prostitute, she said, he asked me how much I charged . . . She turned and stared after him but he had vanished.

Dont worry, I said, that kind of thing happens all the time. London. You waiting for a taxi?

Yes. She stepped back the way and continued speaking without looking at me. I shouldnt've come. I had a headache most of the day. I just shouldnt've come. I wasnt going to. I changed my mind at the last minute.

It was rubbish anyway, I said. Looked as if it was going to be good at the start and then it wasnt.

She nodded. Where's Joan?

Joan . . . I shrugged. I pressed the lid off the tobacco tin but put it back on and brought out the gin instead. She didnt want any of it. She rubbed her forehead. If you've got a sore head, I said, this night air'll clear it. Eh, come on we'll walk for a bit.

She continued to stand there.

It's quite a nice night.

Jock, I just want to go home.

I know, but just . . . a lot of queeries hang about here you know – we'll probably pick up a taxi quite soon. Eh? hey . . . I brought out the cocktail sausages, unwrapped the napkin, passed her a couple. Then we carried on, eating as we walked. I began telling her about some sort of nonsense connected to the Foodstore to which she made no comment though she was quite interested. Then she started talking about her life, just general stuff to do with her family back home in this southeastern tip of England which is apparently very green. Joan was her best pal and they had come up from there together. This was their first job and they were supposed to be sticking it out till something better turned up. Meantime they were supposed to be saving for this great flat they planned on acquiring. Has it got all mod cons? I said.

Pardon?

I shook my head but when she saw me smiling she started smiling as well. And she added, Sometimes you're funny jock.

I am not always sure about women, about what exactly is going on with them. This was just such an occasion. But I knew it was okay to put my arm round her shoulders. She continued talking about the hostel then about the kitchen and the Portuguese women whom she liked working beside because they were always having a laugh. And then I knew about the blunder I had committed; it was Renee I was supposed to have asked out back at the beginning, not Joan. It was basic and simple and everything was explained. I was glad she wasnt looking straight at my face.

A taxi trundled past. We were walking quite the thing though and scarcely noticed till it was out of earshot. Beyond Marble Arch the wind had died and it was not a bad night considering it was still only March. We had the full length of Oxford Street ahead of us but it was fine, and the shop windows were there to be looked into. I took Renee's hand and she smiled as if she had just remembered something funny; it had nothing to do with me.

When we arrived at the hostel she didnt want to go in. We moved into the space to the side of the entrance and started kissing immediately. And the way her eyes had closed as she turned her face to meet me, a harmony. I asked if it was definitely out of the question to smuggle me inside.

Honestly jock.

Are you sure?

There's just no way.

I was breathing her perfume, the point behind her ear. She had her coat open and my jacket was open, our arms round each other's waist. I had been hard since stepping into the space, and Renee was not backing away from it. We continued kissing. She definitely did not want to go in and up to her room, and it was because of Joan. She'll be there in the morning, said Renee, and I wont bear to look at her. Not now.

That was that. I opened my tin and rolled a cigarette. She was waiting for me to make things happen. Eventually I said, Listen Renee, the trouble with the place I stay in, it's 8 bloody beds to a room and that I mean you cant even get leaving a suitcase because somebody'll knock it. No kidding.

She pulled away to look at me properly. I brought out the gin, offered her a swig, took one myself when she declined. There was an all-night snackbar across at the Square and I asked if she fancied a cup of coffee. She shrugged. The two of us came out onto the pavement, walked for a couple of minutes together without speaking. Then we had our arms round each other again and we walked that way that the bodies link, the thighs fast together, the feet keeping pace and so on. At last I said, Right: how would you like to find out where I really stay?

I didnt look at her. But when she made no answer I did, and I could see she was trying not to smile. What's up? I asked.

Oh jock!

What?

[22]

She shook her head, lips tightly shut; but not able to stop smiling now.

I dont stay in the Foodstore if that's what you're thinking.

Yes you do.

What?

You do jock.

Naw I dont.

Oh well then I'm looking forward to meeting your landlord! And she laughed aloud.

I chipped away the cigarette and had another swig of gin, gestured with it to her but she shook her head. You're wrong, I said.

Am I!

Well you're no, but you are.

Oh, I see. Renee shook her head: All the kitchenstaff know!

They dont.

Jock, they do.

They fucking dont! I'll tell you something, it was me started the rumour in the first place.

You?

Aye, of course.

But the Portuguese women all laugh about it jock.

Aye okay, but it's like a double bluff; when it comes right down to it they dont really believe it.

Joan does.

Joan . . .

It was her that told me.

Oh christ. I took out my tin and rolled another fag immediately. Look, I said, Renee I mean the only reason I do it's because of the thieving that goes on in there. You cant turn your back. Christ, you know what like it is!

She didnt answer.

As far as I'm concerned I'm only going to stay there till I make sure I'm no going to get fucking set up – cause that's what they're trying to fucking do, and I'm no kidding.

There's no need to swear about it.

Sorry.

[23]

Anyhow, you dont have to worry.

What?

About who knows; it's only the kitchenstaff, and they wont say anything.

How do you know?

They wont.

What a life!

Jock, dont worry.

I wonder how the hell they found out.

Renee chuckled. Maybe you were snoring!

She seemed to take it for granted I could smuggle the two of us inside with the greatest of ease, and showed not the slightest interest in how it was to be accomplished. I led her round into the narrow, enclosed alley at the back of the building and told her to wait at a special spot. She smiled and kissed my nose. Renee, I said, you're actually crazy, do you know that?

Not as crazy as you. She raised her eyebrows.

It was never easy getting inside the building at night and that was another reason why I didnt go out very often. The security man on nightshift was from Yorkshire and me and him got on quite well together. Usually the way I managed things was to chap the window of his office and go in for a cup of tea and a chat. He assumed I was just stopping off on my road home and when I said goodnight he paid no further attention, never for one moment even dreaming I would be sneaking back beneath the window and along the corridor to the rear staircase. Tonight he kept me yapping for more than twenty minutes. I left him seated at his desk, twiddling the tuner of his transistor radio; he spent most of the night trying for a clear sound on the BBC World Service.

She stepped forwards from the shadows when I appeared at the window. We were both shivering with nervousness and it made it the more awkward when she clambered up and over the sill. I snibbed the window afterwards. That was the sort of thing Yorky would have discovered routinely. We went quickly along and down to the basement, and along to where the Foodstore was situated beyond the kitchen and coldrooms. Once inside I locked the door and stood there with my eyes shut and breathing very harshly.

Alright? she said.

Aye.

She smiled, still shivering. Can you put on a light?

No, too risky. Sometimes I use a candle . . . I crossed the narrow floor and opened the shutters; the light from the globes at either end of the alley was barely sufficient to see each other by. I opened them more fully.

God, she said, it cant be very nice staying here.

Well, it's only temporary remember . . . I brought out the rags and sacking from the teachests, fixed us a place to sit down comfortably. It was always a warm place too. She unbuttoned her coat. I opened the halfbottle and this time she took a small mouthful of the gin. We leaned our backs against the wall and sighed simultaneously, and grinned at each other. This is actually crazy, I said.

She chuckled.

Perishable items? I said.

Pardon?

I've got milk stout and diabetic lager and butter and cheese and stale rolls, plus honey and some cakes from yesterday morning. Interested?

No thanks.

More gin?

She shook her head in a significant way and we smiled at each other again, before moving closely in together.

The daylight through the window. I blinked my eyes open. My right arm seemed to be not there any longer, Renee was lying on it, facing into the wall. I was hard. I turned onto my side and moved to rub against her; soon she was awake.

When eventually I was on top and moving to enter her she stared in horror beyond my head, and then she screamed. Through the window and across the alley up in the ground-floor window a crowd of female faces, all gesticulating and laughing. The

Portuguese women. I grabbed at the sacking to try and cover the two of us. Renee had her head to the side, shielding her face in below my chest. Oh jock, she was crying. Oh jock.

Dont worry, dont worry.

How long've they been watching!

It's alright, dont worry.

Oh jock, oh jock . . .

Dont worry.

Shut the shutters, please.

I did as she asked without putting on my clothes first. I quite enjoyed the exhibitionist experience of it. Renee dressed without speaking. I tried to talk her into coming down to Kings Cross for a coffee so we could discuss things but she shook her head and mumbled a negative. She was absolutely depressed. I put my hands on her shoulders and gazed into her eyes, hoping we would manage to exchange a smile but there was nothing coming from her. It had just turned 7 a.m. I'm going to go home, she said. She lifted her bag and waited for me to unlock the door, and she left saying, Bye jock.

It was time for me to leave as well. This had been a warning. I gathered the chattels immediately and filled a plastic bag with perishables. I got my all-important notebook from its concealed spot, just in case of future emergencies, and left, leaving the key in the lock.

FIFTY PENCE

THE OLD woman opened her eyes when the gas-light flickered, but soon closed them again. The boy was squinting at the football news on the back page, trying to find something new to read. He let the newspaper fall onto his lap and lifted the tongs. He released the catch and wangled the points round a large coal lying in the shovel and carefully placed it on the spare fire in the grate. The old woman regarded him gravely for a moment. When he smiled back her forehead wrinkled in a taut kindly expression. Her gaze roamed upwards to the clock then her eyelids closed over.

He glanced at the clock; 8.40. He should have been home by now. The poker was lying near his foot inside the fire-surround. He wanted to rake among the ashes to see if anything red remained. Perhaps there would be enough to kindle the lump and save the fire, perhaps the new lump was too big to catch light. The rustle as he turned a page of the paper seemed to reverberate around the narrow, high-ceilinged kitchen. There was nothing to keep him. His parents would be annoyed. The bus journey home took nearly an hour and during the long winter nights they liked him to be in bed by 10 o'clock. They would guess he was here.

He got to his feet, stretched. The movement roused the old woman; she muttered vaguely about apples being in the cupboard. He drank a mouthful of water straight from the brass tap at the sink then returned to his chair.

The fire looked dead. Lifting the poker suddenly he dug right into the ashes. The old woman bent forwards and took the poker from him without comment. Gripping it with her right hand she moved her left deftly in and out the coals. Finally she balanced the new lump on smaller pieces, her thin fingers indifferent to any heat which may have remained. The poker was put back in position; handle on the floor with its sooty point projected into the air, lying angled against the fender. Wiping her fingertips on her apron she walked to the door and through to the parlour.

Neither spoke when she came back. She sat on her wooden chair and stared into the fire. Cloying black smoke drifted from the new lump. It crackled.

A little after 9.45 she looked up on hearing the light rap on the outside door. The boy stirred from his doze. He made to rise and answer but relaxed when she indicated he should remain where he was.

The outside door opened and closed, and muttering as the footsteps approached. She came in first and he followed, he appeared to be limping slightly. Mumbling incoherently and did not notice his grandson. She walked across to the sink and filled the kettle and set it on the oven gas to make a pot of tea. The boy wondered if she knew what his grandfather was saying to her. He called a greeting. The old man turned slowly and stared at him. The boy grinned but the old man turned back and resumed the muttering. His grandmother seemed not to notice anything odd about it. As the old man spoke he was scratching his head. There was no bunnet. The bunnet was not on his head.

The muttering stopped. The old man stared at the woman then at the boy. The boy looked helplessly at her but she watched the man. The expression on her face gave nothing away. Her usual face. Again the boy called a greeting but the old man turned to her and continued his muttering. The tone of his voice had altered now; it was angry. She looked away from him. When her gaze fell on him the boy tried to smile. He was aware that if he blinked, tears would appear in his eyes. He smiled at her.

Ten shillings I'm telling you, said the voice.

The boy and his grandmother looked quickly at the old man.

Ten shillings Frances, he said. The anger had gone from his voice. As if noticing the boy for the first time he looked straight at him. For several seconds he stood there, watching him, then he turned sharply back to face his wife. Ach, he grunted.

She was standing holding the apron bunched in her fists.

Shaking his head the man attempted a step towards her but he fell on the floor. He sat up for a moment then fell sideways. The boy ran across crying it was okay – it was okay.

His grandmother spoke as he bent down over the old man. He fell down, she said. He fell down.

She knelt by him on the linoleum and together they tried to raise him to his feet but it was difficult; he was heavy. The boy dragged over a chair and they managed to get him up onto it. He slumped there, his head lolling, his chin touching his chest.

He lost money, said the old woman. He said he lost money. That was what kept him. He went looking the streets for it and lost his bunnet.

It's okay Grannie, said the boy.

It kept him late, she said.

After a moment the boy asked if they should get him changed into his pyjamas and then into bed but she did not reply. He asked again, urgently.

I'll get him son, she said eventually. You can get away home now.

He looked at her in surprise.

Your mum and dad will be wondering where you've got to, she added.

It was pointless saying anything more. He could tell that by her face. Crossing to the bed in the recess he lifted his coat and slipped it on. He opened the door. When he glanced back his grandmother nodded. She was grasping her husband by the shoulders, propping him up. He could see the old man looking at her. He could see the big bald patch on the head. His grandmother nodded once more. He left then.

EVEN MONEY

It was a bit strange to see the two of them. She was wee and skinny with a really pecked-out crabbit face. He was also skinny, but shifty looking. Difficult to tell why he was shifty looking. Maybe he wasnt. Aye he was, he was fucking shifty looking and that's final. He was following her. He could easily have caught up with her and introduced hisself but he didnt, he just followed her, in steady pursuit, at a safe distance. And that is the action of a shifty character. The fact that a well-thumbed copy of the *Sporting Life* poked out from his coat pocket is neither here nor there. Being a betting man myself I've always resented the shady associations punters have for non-bettors. Anyhow, back to the story, the distance between the pair amounted to twenty yards, and there is an interesting point to discuss. It is this: the wee woman actually passed the man in the first place and may have seen him. She could have nodded or even spoken to him. But she did seem not to notice him. Because of that I dont know whether she knew him or not. And it is not possible to say if he knew her. He looked to be following her in an off-hand kind of fashion. When she stopped outside the post office he paused. In she went. But just as you were thinking, Aw aye, there he goes . . . Naw; he didnt, he just walked on.

HOME FOR A COUPLE OF DAYS

THREE RAPS at the door. His eyes opened and blinked as they met the sun rays streaming in through the slight gap between the curtains. 'Mister Brown?' called somebody – a girl's voice.

'Just a minute.' He squinted at his wristwatch. 9 o'clock. He walked to the door and opened it, poked his head out from behind it.

'That's your breakfast.' She held out the tray as if for approval. A boiled egg and a plate of toast, a wee pot of tea.

'Thanks, that's fine, thanks.' He took it and shut the door, poured a cup of tea immediately and carried it into the bathroom. He was hot and sweaty and needed a shower. He stared at himself in the mirror. He was quite looking forward to the day. Hearing the girl's accent made it all even more so. After the shower he started on the grub, ate all the toast but left the egg. He finished the pot of tea then shaved. As he prepared to leave he checked his wallet. He would have to get to a bank at some point.

The Green Park was a small hotel on the west side of Sauchiehall Street. Eddie had moved in late last night and taken a bed and breakfast. Beyond that he was not sure, how long he would be staying. Everything depended.

He was strolling in the direction of Partick, glancing now and then at the back pages of the *Daily Record*, quite enjoying the novelty of Scottish football again. He stopped himself from smiling, lighted a cigarette. It was a sunny morning in early May and maybe it was that alone made him feel so optimistic about the future. The sound of a machine, noisy – but seeming to come from far away. It was just from the bowling greens across the street, a loud lawn-mower or something.

He continued round the winding bend, down past the hospital and up Church Street, cutting in through Chancellor Street and along the lane. The padlock hung ajar on the bolt of the door of the local pub he used to frequent. Farther on the old primary school across the other side of the street. He could not remember any names of teachers or pupils at this moment. A funny feeling. It was as if he had lost his memory for one split second. He had stopped walking. He lighted another cigarette. When he returned the lighter and cigarette packet to the side pockets of his jacket he noticed a movement in the net curtains of the ground floor window nearby where he was standing. It was Mrs McLachlan. Who else. He smiled and waved but the face disappeared.

His mother stayed up the next close. He kept walking. He would see her a bit later on. He would have to get her something too, a present, she was due it.

Along Dumbarton Road he entered the first cafe and he ordered a roll and sausage and asked for a cup of tea right away. The elderly woman behind the counter did not look twice at him. Why should she? She once caught him thieving a bar of Turkish Delight, that's why. He read the *Daily Record* to the front cover, still quite enjoying it all, everything, even the advertisements with the Glasgow addresses, it was good reading them as well.

At midday he was back up the lane and along to the old local. He got a pint of heavy, sat in a corner sipping at it. The place had really changed. It was drastic – new curtains!

There were not many customers about but Eddie recognized one, a middle-aged man of average build who was wearing a pair of glasses. He leaned on the bar with his arms folded, chatting to the bartender. Neilie Johnston. When Eddie finished his beer he walked with the empty glass to the counter. 'Heavy,' he said and he pointed at Neilie's drink. The bartender nodded and poured him a whisky. Neilie looked at it and then at Eddie.

'Eddie!'

'How's it going Neilie?'

'Aw no bad son no bad.' Neilie chuckled. The two of them shook hands. 'Where've you been?'

'London.'

'Aw London; aw aye. Well well.'

'Just got back last night.'

'Good . . .' Neilie glanced at Eddie's suit. 'Prospering son eh?'

'Doing alright.'

'That's the game.'

'What about yourself? still marking the board?'

'Marking the board! Naw. Christ son I've been away from that for a while!' Neilie pursed his lips before lifting the whisky and drinking a fairly large mouthful. He sniffed and nodded. 'With Sweeney being out the game and the rest of it.'

'Aye.'

'You knew about that son?'

'Mm.'

'Aye well the licence got lost because of it. And they'll no get it back either neither they will. They're fucking finished – caput! Him and his brother.'

Both of them were silent for a time. The bartender had walked farther along and was now looking at a morning paper. Neilie nudged the glasses up his nose a bit and he said, 'You and him got on okay as well son, you and Sweeney, eh?'

Eddie shrugged. 'Aye, I suppose.' He glanced at the other men ranged about the pub interior, brought his cigarettes and lighter out. When they were both smoking he called the bartender: 'Two halfs!'

'You on holiday like?' said Neilie.

'Couple of days just, a wee break . . .' he paused to pay for the two whiskies.

Neilie emptied the fresh one into the tumbler he already had. 'Ta son,' he said, 'it's appreciated.'

'You skint?'

'Aye, how d'you guess! Giro in two days.'

'Nothing doing then?'

'Eh well . . .' Neilie sniffed. 'I'm waiting the word on something, a wee bit of business. Nothing startling right enough.' He pursed his lips and shrugged, swallowed some whisky.

'I hope you're lucky.'

[33]

'Aye, ta.'

'Cheers.' Eddie drank his own whisky in a gulp and chased it down with a mouthful of heavy beer. 'Aw Christ,' he said, glancing at the empty tumbler.

'You should never rush whisky son!' Neilie chuckled, peering along at the bartender.

'I'm out the habit.'

'Wish to fuck I could say the same!'

Eddie took a long drag on the cigarette and he kept the smoke in his lungs for a while. Then he drank more beer. Neilie was watching him, smiling in quite a friendly way. Eddie said, 'Any of the old team come in these days?'

'Eh . . .'

'Fisher I mean, or Stevie Price? Any of them? Billy Dempster?'

'Fisher drinks in T. C.'s.'

'Does he? Changed days.'

'Och there's a lot changed son, a lot.'

'Stevie's married right enough eh!'

'Is that right?'

'He's got two wee lassies.'

'Well well.'

'He's staying over in the south side.'

'Aw.'

A couple of minutes later and Eddie was swallowing the last of his beer and returning his cigarettes and lighter to the side pockets. 'Okay Neilie, nice seeing you.'

Neilie looked as if he was going to say something but changed his mind.

'I'm taking a walk,' said Eddie.

'Fair enough son.'

'I'll look in later.' Eddie patted him on the side of the shoulder, nodded at the bartender. He glanced at the other customers as he walked to the exit but saw nobody he knew.

It was good getting back out into the fresh air. The place was depressing and Neilie hadnt helped matters. A rumour used to go about that he kept his wife on the game. Eddie could believe it.

There was a traffic jam down at Partick Cross. The rear end of a big articulated lorry was sticking out into the main road and its front seemed to be stuck between two parked cars near to The Springwell Tavern. The lines of motors stretched along the different routes at the junction. Eddie stood at the Byres Road corner amongst a fair crowd of spectators. Two policemen arrived and donned the special sleeves they had for such emergencies and started directing operations. Eddie continued across the road.

In T. C.'s two games of dominoes were in progress plus there was music and a much cheerier atmosphere. It was better and fitted in more with the way Eddie remembered things. And there was Fisher at the other end of the bar in company with another guy. Eddie called to him: 'Hey Tam!'

'Eddie!' Fisher was delighted. He waved his right fist in the air and when Eddie reached the other end he shook hands with him in a really vigorous way. 'Ya bastard,' he said, 'it's great to see ye!' And then he grinned and murmured, 'When did you get out!'

'Out – what d'you mean?'

Fisher laughed.

'I'm being serious,' said Eddie.

'Just that I heard you were having a holiday on the Isle of Wight.'

'That's garbage.'

'If you say so.'

'Aye, fuck, I say so.' Eddie smiled.

'Well, I mean, when Sweeney copped it . . . Then hearing about you . . . Made me think it was gen.'

'Ah well, there you are!'

'That's good,' said Fisher and he nodded, then jerked his thumb at the other guy. 'This is Mick . . .'

After the introductions Eddie got a round of drinks up and the three of them went to a table at the wall, the only one available. An elderly man was sitting at it already; he had a grumpy wizened face. He moved a few inches to allow the trio more space.

There was a short silence. And Eddie said, 'Well Tam, how's Eileen?'

'Dont know. We split.'

'Aw. Christ.'

'Ah,' Fisher said, 'she started . . . well, she started seeing this other guy, if you want to know the truth.'

'Honest?' Eddie frowned.

Fisher shook his head. 'A funny lassie Eileen I mean you never really fucking knew her man I mean.' He shook his head again. 'You didnt know where you were with her, that was the fucking trouble!'

After a moment Eddie nodded. He lifted his pint and drank from it, waiting for Fisher to continue but instead of continuing Fisher turned and looked towards the bar, exhaled a cloud of smoke. The other guy, Mick, raised his eyebrows at Eddie who shrugged. Then Fisher faced to the front again and said, 'I was surprised to hear that about Sweeney but, warehouses, I didnt think it was his scene.'

Eddie made no answer.

'Eh . . . ?'

'Mm.'

'Best of gear right enough,' Fisher added, still gazing at Eddie.

Eddie dragged on his cigarette. Then he said, 'You probably heard he screwed the place well he never, he just handled the stuff.'

'Aw.'

'It was for screwing the place they done him for, but . . .' Eddie sniffed, drank from his pint.

'Aye, good.' Fisher grinned. 'So how you doing yourself then Eddie?'

'No bad.'

'Better than no bad with that!' He gestured at Eddie's clothes. He reached to draw his thumb and forefinger along the lapel of the jacket. 'Hand stitched,' he said, 'you didnt get that from John Collier's. Eh Mick?'

Mick smiled.

Eddie opened the jacket, indicated the inner pocket. 'Look, no labels.'

'What does that mean?'

'It means it was fucking dear.'

'You're a bastard,' said Fisher.

Eddie grinned. 'Yous for another? A wee yin?'

'Eh . . . Aye.' Fisher said, 'I'll have a doctor.'

'What?'

'A doctor.' Fisher winked at Mick. 'He doesnt know what a doctor is!'

'What is it?' asked Eddie.

'A doctor, a doctor snoddy, a voddy.'

'Aw aye. What about yourself?' Eddie asked Mick.

'I'll have one as well Eddie, thanks.'

Although it was busy at the bar he was served quite quickly. It was good seeing as many working behind the counter as this. One of things he didnt like about England was the way sometimes you could wait ages to get served in their pubs – especially if they heard your accent.

He checked the time of the clock on the gantry with his wristwatch. He would have to remember about the bank otherwise it could cause problems. Plus he was wanting to get a wee present for his mother, he needed a couple of quid for that as well.

When he returned to the table Fisher said, 'I was telling Mick about some of your exploits.'

'Exploits.' Eddie laughed briefly, putting the drinks on the table top and sitting down.

'It's cause the 2,000 Guineas is coming up. It's reminding me about something!'

'Aw aye.' Eddie said to Mick. 'The problem with this cunt Fisher is that he's loyal to horses.'

'Loyal to fucking horses!' Fisher laughed loudly.

'Ah well if you're thinking about what I think you're thinking about!'

'It was all Sweeney's fault!'

'That's right, blame a guy that cant talk up for himself!'

'So it was but!'

Eddie smiled. 'And Dempster, dont forget Dempster!'

'That's right,' said Fisher, turning to Mick, 'Dempster was into it as well.'

Mick shook his head. Fisher was laughing again, quite loudly.

'It wasnt as funny as all that,' said Eddie.

'You dont think so! Every other cunt does!'

'Dont believe a word of it,' Eddie told Mick.

'And do you still punt?' Mick asked him.

'Now and again.'

'Now and again!' Fisher laughed.

Eddie smiled.

'There's four races on the telly this afternoon,' said Mick.

'Aye,' said Fisher, 'we were thinking of getting a couple of cans and that. You interested?'

'Eh, naw, I'm no sure yet, what I'm doing.'

Fisher nodded.

'It's just eh . . .'

'Dont worry about it,' said Fisher, and he drank a mouthful of the vodka.

'How's Stevie?'

'Alright – as far as I know, I dont see him much; he hardly comes out. Once or twice at the weekends, that's about it.'

'Aye.'

'What about yourself, you no married yet?'

'Eh . . .' Eddie made a gesture with his right hand. 'Kind of yes and no.'

Fisher jerked his thumb at Mick. 'He's married – got one on the way.'

'Have you? Good, that's good.' Eddie raised his tumbler of whisky and saluted him. 'All the best.'

'Thanks.'

'I cant imagine having a kid,' said Eddie, and to Fisher he said: 'Can you?'

'What! I cant even keep myself going never mind a snapper!'

Mick laughed and brought out a 10-pack of cigarettes. Eddie pushed it away when offered. 'It's my crash,' he said.

'Naw,' said Mick, 'you bought the bevy.'

'I know but . . .' He opened his own packet and handed each of them a cigarette and he said to Fisher: 'You skint?'

Fisher paused and squinted at him, 'What do you think?'

'I think you're skint.'

'I'm skint.'

'It's a fucking dump of a city this, every cunt's skint.'

Fisher jerked his thumb at Mick. 'No him, he's no skint, a fucking millionaire, eh!'

Mick chuckled, 'That'll be fucking right.'

Eddie flicked his lighter and they took a light from him. Fisher said, 'Nice . . .'

Eddie nodded, slipping it back into his pocket.

'What you up for by the way?'

'Och, a couple of things.'

'No going to tell us?'

'Nothing to tell.'

Fisher winked at Mick: 'Dont believe a word of it.'

'It's gen,' said Eddie, 'just the maw and that. Plus I was wanting to see a few of the old faces. A wee while since I've been away, three year.'

'Aye and no even a postcard!'

'You never sent me one!'

'Aye but I dont know where the fuck you get to man I mean I fucking thought you were inside!'

'Tch!'

'He's supposed to be my best mate as well Mick, what d'you make of it!'

Mick smiled.

Not too long afterwards Eddie had swallowed the last of his whisky and then the heavy beer. 'That's me,' he said, 'better hit the road. Aw right Tam! Mick, nice meeting you.' Eddie shook hands with the two of them again.

Fisher said, 'No bothering about the racing on the telly then . . .'

'Nah, better no – I've got a couple of things to do. The maw as well Tam, I've got to see her.'

'Aye how's she keeping? I dont see her about much.'

'Aw she's fine, keeping fine.'

'That's good. Tell her I was asking for her.'

'Will do . . .' Eddie edged his way out. The elderly man shifted on his chair, made a movement towards the drink he had lying by his hand. Eddie nodded at Mick and said to Fisher, 'I'll probably look in later on.'

A couple of faces at the bar seemed familiar but not sufficiently so and he continued on to the exit, strolling, hands in his trouser pockets, the cigarette in the corner of his mouth. Outside on the pavement he glanced from right to left, then the pub door banged behind him. It was Fisher. Eddie looked at him. 'Naw eh . . .' Fisher sniffed. 'I was just wondering and that, how you're fixed, just a couple of quid.'

Eddie sighed, shook his head. 'Sorry Tam but I'm being honest, I've got to hit the bank straight away; I'm totally skint.'

'Aw. Okay. No problem.'

'I mean if I had it . . . I'm no kidding ye, it's just I'm skint.'

'Naw dont worry about it Eddie.'

'Aye but Christ!' Eddie held his hands raised, palms upwards. 'Sorry I mean.' He hesitated a moment then said, 'Wait a minute . . .' He dug out a big handful of loose change from his trouser pockets and arranged it into a neat sort of column on his left hand, and presented it to Fisher. 'Any good?'

Fisher gazed at the money.

'Take it,' said Eddie, giving it into his right hand.

'Ta Eddie. Mick's been keeping me going in there.'

'When's the giro due?'

'Two more days.'

'Garbage eh.' He paused, nodded again and patted Fisher on the side of the shoulder. 'Right you are then Tam, eh! I'll see ye!'

'Aye.'

'I'll take a look in later on.'

'Aye do that Eddie. You've actually just caught me at a bad time.'

'I know the feeling,' said Eddie and he winked and gave a quick wave. He walked on across the street without looking behind. Farther along he stepped sideways onto the path up by the Art Galleries.

There were a lot of children rushing about, plus women pushing prams. And the bowling greens were busy. Not just pensioners playing either, even young boys were out. Eddie still had the *Record* rolled in his pocket and he sat down on a bench for a few minutes, glancing back through the pages again, examining what was on at all the cinemas, theatres, seeing the pub entertainment and restaurants advertised.

No wind. Hardly even a breeze. The sun seemed to be beating right down on his head alone. Or else it was the alcohol; he was beginning to feel the effects. If he stayed on the bench he would end up falling asleep. The hotel. He got up, paused to light a cigarette. Along Sauchiehall Street there was a good curry smell coming for somewhere. He was starving. He turned into the entrance to The Green Park, walking up the wee flight of stairs and in to the lobby, the reception lounge. Somebody was hoovering carpets. He pressed the buzzer button, pressed it again when there came a break in the noise.

The girl who had brought him breakfast. 'Mrs Grady's out the now,' she told him.

'Aw.'

'What was it you were wanting?'

'Eh well it was just I was wondering if there's a bank near?'

'A bank. Yes, if you go along to Charing Cross. They're all around there.'

'Oh aye. Right.' Eddie smiled. 'It's funny how you forget wee details like that.'

'Mmhh.'

'Things have really changed as well. The people . . .' He grinned, shaking his head.

She frowned. 'Do you mean Glasgow people?'

'Aye but really I mean I'm talking about people I know, friends and that, people I knew before.'

'Aw, I see.'

Eddie yawned. He dragged on his cigarette. 'Another thing I was wanting to ask her, if it's okay to go into the room, during the day.'

[41]

'She prefers you not to, unless you're on full board.'

'Okay.'

'You can go into the lounge though.'

He nodded.

'I dont know whether she knew you were staying tonight . . .'

'I am.'

'I'll tell her.'

'Eh . . .' Eddie had been about to walk off; he said, 'Does she do evening meals as well like?'

'She does.' The girl smiled.

'What's up?'

'I dont advise it at the moment,' she said quietly, 'the real cook's off sick just now and she's doing it all herself.'

'Aw aye. Thanks for the warning!' Eddie dragged on the cigarette again. 'I smelled a curry there somewhere . . .'

'Yeh, there's places all around.'

'Great.'

'Dont go to the first one, the one further along's far better – supposed to be one of the best in Glasgow.'

'Is that right. That's great. Would you fancy coming at all?'

'Pardon?'

'It would be nice if you came, as well, if you came with me.' Eddie shrugged. 'It'd be good.'

'Thanks, but I'm working.'

'Well, I would wait.'

'No, I dont think so.'

'It's up to you,' he shrugged, 'I'd like you to but.'

'Thanks.'

Eddie nodded. He looked towards the glass-panelled door of the lounge, he patted his inside jacket pocket in an absent-minded way. And the girl said, 'You know if it was a cheque you could cash it here. Mrs Grady would do it for you.'

'That's good.' He pointed at the lounge door. 'Is that the lounge? Do you think it'd be alright if I maybe had a doze?'

'A doze?'

'I'm really tired. I was travelling a while and hardly got any sleep last night. If I could just stretch out a bit . . .'

He looked about for an ashtray, there was one on the small half-moon table closeby where he was standing; he stubbed the cigarette out, and yawned suddenly.

'Look,' said the girl, 'I'm sure if you went up the stair and lay down for an hour or so; I dont think she would mind.'

'You sure?'

'It'll be okay.'

'You sure but I mean . . .'

'Yeh.'

'I dont want to cause you any bother.'

'It's alright.'

'Thanks a lot.'

'Your bag's still there in your room as well you know.'

'Aye.'

'Will I give you a call? about 5?'

'Aye, fine. 6 would be even better!'

'I'm sorry, it'll have to be 5 – she'll be back in the kitchen after that.'

'I was only kidding.'

'If it could be later I'd do it.'

'Naw, honest, I was only kidding.'

The girl nodded.

After a moment he walked to the foot of the narrow, carpeted staircase.

'You'll be wanting a cheque cashed then?'

'Aye, probably.'

'I'll mention it to her.'

Up in the room he unzipped his bag but did not take anything out, he sat down on the edge of the bed instead. Then he got up, gave a loud sigh and took off his jacket, draping it over the back of the bedside chair. He closed the curtains, lay stretched out on top of the bedspread. He breathed in and out deeply, gazing at the ceiling. He felt amazingly tired, how tired he was. He had never been much of an afternoon drinker and today was just proving the point. He raised himself up to unknot his shoelaces, lay back again, kicking the shoes off and letting them drop off onto the floor. He shut his eyes. He was not quite sure what he was going to do. Maybe he would just leave tomorrow. He would if he felt like it. Maybe even tonight! if he felt like it. Less than a minute later he was sleeping.

MANCHESTER IN JULY

I WAS there once without enough for a room, not even for a night's lodgings in the local Walton House. 6/6d it was at the time which proves how fucking recent it was. At the NAB a clerk proffered a few bob as a temporary measure and told me to come back once I had fixed myself up with a rentbook. I got irritated at this because of the logical absurdity but they were not obliged to dish out cash to people without addresses. By the time I had worked out my anger I was skint again (10 fags and some sort of basic takeaway from a Chinese Restaurant). I wound up trying for a kip in the station, then tramped about the 'dilly trying to punt the wares to Mr and Mrs Anybody. When it was morning I headed along and under the bridge to Salford, eventually picking up another few bob in the office across from Strangeways. I went away back there and then and booked in at the Walton for that coming evening, just to be on the safe side.

The middle of July. What a wonderful heat it was. I spent most of the day snoozing full stretch on my back in a grass square adjacent to the House, doing my best to conserve the rest of the bread.

Into the communal lounge about 6.30 p.m. I sat on this ancient leather effort of a chair which had brass studs stuck in it. The other seating in the place was similarly odd and disjointed. Old guys sprawled everywhere snoring and farting and burping and staring in a glassy-eyed way at the television. I had been scratching myself as soon as I crossed the threshold, just at the actual idea of it. Yet in a funny fucking way it was quite comfortable and relaxing and it seemed to induce in you a sort of stupor. Plus it was fine getting the chance to see a telly again. One felt like a human being. I mind it was showing The Fugitive with that guy David Jansen and this tall police lieutenant who was chasing him about the States (and wound up he was the guy who killed Jansen's wife). I was right into it anyway, along with the remaining few in the room who were still compos mentis, when in walks these three blokes in clean boilersuits and they switched it off, the telly. 10 minutes before the end or something. I jumped out the chair and stood there glaring at them. A couple of the old guys got up then; but they just headed off towards the door, and then upstairs to the palliases. It was fucking bedtime! 10.50 p.m. on a Thursday night. It might even have been a fucking Friday.

NOT TOO LONG FROM
NOW TONIGHT WILL BE
THAT LAST TIME

HE WAS walking slowly. His pace quickened then slackened once more. He stopped by the doorway of a shop and lighted a cigarette. The floor was dry, a sort of parquetry. He lowered himself down to sit on his heels, his arms folded, elbows resting on his knees, his back to the glass door.

He could have gone straight home and crept inside and into bed perhaps quietly enough not to disturb her and come morning, maybe that hour earlier than usual, and out and away, before she was awake. But why bother. He could simply not return. In this way they would simply not meet, they would not have to meet. And that would be great. He was not up to it. It was not something he felt capable of managing. It was not something he was capable of. He could not cope with it.

But why bother. If he was obliged to do certain things and then failed to do these things then that was that and nothing could be offered instead. He had always known the truth of that. Always; even though he seemed never to have given it voice. Never; especially not with her. She would never have understood.

And then there were his silences. That inability he had to get out of himself. It was not disgust, not contempt; nothing like that. It was something different altogether. But he had no wish to work out what the hell it was.

He had been trying to adapt for years. And now she was there now lying in bed sleeping or awake, about to become awake, to peer at the clockface, knowing she is not as warm as usual, because of course he is not home yet and the time, and her eyes.

He keeps imagining going somewhere else and taking a room perhaps with full board in some place far away where all the people are just people, people he does not know and has no obligation to speak to. There was something good about that. He inhaled on the cigarette then raised himself up and bent his knees a couple of times, before pacing on. After a time he slowed, but was soon walking more quickly.

FORGETTING TO MENTION
ALLENDE

THE MILK was bubbling over the sides of the saucepan. He rushed to the oven, grabbed the handle and held the pan in the air. The wean was pulling at his trouser-leg, she gripped the material. For christ sake Audrey, he tugged her hand away while returning the saucepan to the oven. The girl went back to sit on the floor, glancing at him as she turned the pages of her colouring book. He smiled: Dont go telling mummy about the milk now eh!

She looked at him.

Aye, he said, that's all I need, you to get into a huff.

Her eyes were watering.

Aw christ.

She looked at him.

You're a big girl now, you cant just . . . he paused. Back at the oven he prepared her drink, lighting a cigarette in the process, which he placed in an ashtray. Along with the drink he gave her two digestive biscuits.

When he sat down on the armchair he stared at the ceiling, half expecting to see it bouncing up and down. For the past couple of hours somebody had been playing records at full blast. It was nearly time for the wean to have her morning kip as well. The same yesterday. He had tried; he had put her down and sat with her, read part of a story: it was hopeless but, the fucking music, blasting out. And at least seven out of the past ten weekdays the same story. He suspected it came from the flat above. Yet it could be coming from through the wall, or the flat below. It was maybe even coming from the other side of the stair – difficult to tell because of the volume, and the way the walls were, like wafer fucking biscuits. Before flitting to the place he had heard it was a

[49]

good scheme, the houses designed well, good thick walls and that, they could be having a party next door and you wouldnt know unless they came and invited you in. What a load of rubbish. He stared at the ceiling, wondering whether to go and dig out the culprits, tell them the wean was supposed to be having her mid-morning nap. He definitely had the right to complain, but wasnt going to, not yet; it would be daft antagonizing the neighbours at this stage.

Inhaling deeply he got up and wiped the oven clean with a damp cloth. Normally he liked music, any kind. The problem was it was the same songs being played over and over, all the fucking time the same songs – terrible; pointless trying to read or even watch the midday TV programmes. Maybe he was going to have to get used to it: the sounds to become part of the general hum of the place, like the cars screeching in and out of the street, that ice-cream van which came shrieking I LOVE TO GO A WANDERING ten times a night including Sunday.

A digestive biscuit lay crunched on the carpet by her feet.

Thanks, he said, and bent to lift the pieces. The carpet loves broken biscuits. Daddy loves picking them up as well. Come on . . . he smiled as he picked her up. He carried her into the room. She twisted her head from side to side. It was the music.

I know, he said, I know I know I know, you'll just have to forget about it.

I cant.

You can if you try.

She looked at him. He undressed her to her pants and vest and sat her down in the cot, then walked to the window to draw the curtains. The new wallpaper was fine. He came back and sat on the edge of the double bed, resting his hands on the frame of the cot. Just make stories out of the picture, he told her, indicating the wall. Then he got up, leaned in to kiss her forehead. I'll away ben and let you sleep.

She nodded, shifting her gaze to the wall.

You'll have to try Audrey, otherwise you'll be awful tired at that nursery.

Sitting down on the armchair he lifted the cigarette from

the ashtray, and frowned at the ceiling. He exhaled smoke while reaching for last night's *Evening Times*. The tin of paint and associated articles were lying at the point where he had left off yesterday. He should have resumed work by now. He opened the newspaper at the sits. vac. col.

The two other children were both boys, in primaries five and six at the local primary school. They stayed in at dinnertime to eat there but normally one would come home after; and if it happened before one o'clock he could send the wee girl back with him to nursery. But neither liked taking her. Neither did daddy for that matter. It meant saying hello to the woman in charge occasionally. And he always came out of the place feeling like an idiot. An old story. It was exactly the same with the headmistress of the primary school, the headmistress of the last primary school, the last nursery – the way they spoke to him even. Fuck it. He got up to make another coffee.

The music had stopped. It was nearly one o'clock. He rushed through to get the wean.

The nursery took up a separate wing within the building of the primary school; only a five-minute walk from where he lived. Weans everywhere but no sign of his pair. He was looking out for them, to see if they were being included in the games yet. He had no worries about the younger one, it was the eldest who presented the problem. Not a problem really, the boy was fine – just inclined to wander about on his tod, not getting involved with the rest, nor making any attempt to. It wasnt really a problem.

The old man with the twins was approaching the gate from the opposite direction; and he paused there, and called: Nice to see a friendly face! Indicating the two weans he continued, The grandkids, what a pair! No twins in the family then all of a sudden bang, two lots of them. My eldest boy gets one pair then the lassie gets another pair. And you know the worrying thing? The old man grinned: Everything comes in threes! Eh? can you imagine it? three lots of twins! That'd put the cat right among the bloody pigeons!

A nursery assistant was standing within the entrance lobby;

once she had collected the children the old man said: Murray's the name, John, John Murray.

Tommy McGoldrick.

They shook hands.

I saw you a couple of days ago, the end of last week . . . went on the old man. I was telling my lassie, makes a change to see a friendly face. All these women and that eh! He laughed, and they continued walking towards the gate. You're no long in the scheme then Tommy?

Naw.

Same with myself, a couple of months just, still feeling my way about. I'm staying with the lassie and that, helping her out. Her man's working down in England temporarily. Good job but, big money. Course he's having to put in the hours, but like I was saying to her, you dont mind working so long as the money's there – though between you and me Tommy there's a few staying about here that look as if a hard day's graft would kill them! Know what I mean? naw, I dont know how they do it; on the broo and that and they can still afford to go out get drunk. Telling you, if you took a walk into that pub down at the shopping centre you'd see half of them were drawing social security. Aye, and you couldnt embarrass them!

They were at the gate. When the old man made as though to continue speaking McGoldrick said, I better be going then.

Right you are Tommy, see you the morrow maybe eh?

Aye, cheerio Mr Murray.

Heh, John, my name's John – I dont believe in the Mr soinso this and the Mr soinso that carry on. What I say is if a man's good enough to talk to then he's good enough to call you by your first name.

He kept a watch for the two boys as he walked back down the road; then detoured to purchase a pie from the local shop, and he put it under the grill to heat up. At 1.20 p.m. he was sitting down with the knife and fork, the bread and butter, the cup of tea, and the letter-box flapped. He had yet to fix up the doorbell.

The eldest was there. Hello da, he said, strolling in.

You no late?

He had walked to the table in the kitchen and sat down there, looking at the pie and stuff. Cold meat and totties we got, he said, the totties were like chewing gum.

What d'you mean chewing gum?

That's what they were like.

Aye well I'd swop you dinners any day of the week . . . He forked a piece of pie into his mouth. What did you get for pudding?

Cake and custard I think.

You think? what d'you mean you think?

The boy yawned and got up from the chair. He walked to the oven and looked at it, then walked to the door: I'm away, he said.

Heh you, you were supposed to be here half an hour ago to take that wean to the nursery.

It wasnt my turn.

Turn? what d'you mean turn? it's no a question of turns.

I took her last.

Aw did you.

Aye.

Well where's your bloody brother then?

I dont know.

Christ . . . He got up and followed him to the door, which could only be locked by turning a handle on the inside, unless a key was used on the outside. As the boy stepped downstairs he called: How you doing up there? that teacher, is she any good?

The boy shrugged.

Ach. He shook his head then shut and locked the door. He poured more tea into the cup. The tin of paint and associated articles. The whole house needed to be done up; wallpaper or paint, his wife didnt care which, just so long as it was new, that it was different from what it had been when they arrived.

He collected the dirty dishes, the breakfast bowls and teaplates from last night's supper. He put the plug in the sink and turned on the hot water tap, shoving his hand under the jet of water to feel the temperature change; it was still a novelty. He swallowed the dregs of the tea, lighted a cigarette, and stacked in the dishes.

A vacuum cleaner started somewhere. Then the music drowned out its noise. He became aware of his feet tapping to the music. Normally he would have liked the songs, dancing music. The wife wouldnt be home till near 6 p.m., tired out; she worked as a cashier in a supermarket, nonstop the whole day. She hardly had the energy for anything. He glanced at the fridge, then checked that he had taken out the meat to defrost. A couple of days ago he had forgotten yet again – egg and chips as usual, the weans delighted of course. The wife just laughed.

He made coffee upon finishing the dishes. But rather than sitting down to drink it he walked to the corner of the room and put the cup down on a dining chair which had old newspaper on its top, to keep it clear of paint splashes. He levered the lid off the tin, stroking the brush across the palm of his hand to check the bristles werent too stiff, then dipped it in and rapidly applied paint to wall. It streaked. He had forgotten to mix the fucking stuff.

Twenty minutes later he was amazed at the area he had covered. That was the thing about painting; you could sit on your arse for most of the day and then scab in for two hours; when the wife came in she'd think you'd been hard at it since breakfast time. He noticed his brushstrokes were shifting periodically to the rhythm of the music. When the letter-box flapped he continued for a moment, then laid the brush carefully on the lid of the tin, on the newspaper covering the chair.

Hi, grinned a well-dressed teenager. Gesturing at his pal he said: We're in your area this morning – this is Ricky, I'm Pete.

Eh, I'm actually doing a bit of painting just now.

We'll only take a moment of your time Mr McGoldrick.

Aye, see I've left the lid off the tin and that.

Yeh, the thing is Mr McGoldrick . . .

His pal was smiling and nodding. They were both holding christian stuff, Mormons probably.

Being honest, said McGoldrick, I dont really . . . I'm an atheist.

O yeh – you mean you dont believe in God?

Naw, no really, I prefer taking a back seat I mean, it's all politics and that, eh, honest, I'll need to get back to the painting.

[54]

Yeh, but maybe if you could just spare Ricky and myself one moment of your time Mr McGoldrick, we might have a chat about that. You know it's a big thing to say you dont believe in God I mean how can you know that just to come right out and – hey! it's a big thing – right?

McGoldrick shrugged, he made to close the door.

Yeh, I appreciate you're busy at this time of the day Mr McGoldrick but listen, maybe Ricky and myself can leave some of our literature with you – and you can read through it, go over it I mean, by yourself. We can call back in a day or so, when it's more convenient and we can discuss things with you I mean it seems like a real big thing to me you know the way you can just come right out and say you dont believe in God like that I mean . . . hey! it's a big thing, right?

His pal had sorted out some leaflets and he passed them to McGoldrick.

Thanks, he replied. He shut the door and locked it. He remained there, listening to their footsteps go up the stair. Then he suddenly shook his head. He had forgotten to mention Allende. He always meant to mention Allende to the bastards. Fuck it. He left the leaflets on the small table in the lobby.

The coffee was stone cold as well. He filled the electric kettle. The music blasting; another of these good dancing numbers. Before returning to the paint he lighted a cigarette, stopping off at the bathroom on his way ben.

SAMARITANS

HEH WHAT d'you make of this man I'm standing in the betting shop and this guy comes over. Heh john, he says, you got a smoke?

A smoke . . .

Aye, he says.

So okay I mean you dont like to see a cunt without a smoke. Okay, I says, here.

Ta.

Puts it in his mouth while I'm clawing myself to find a match.

Naw, he's saying, I dont like going to the begging games . . .

Fair enough, I says, I've been skint myself.

Aw it's no that, he says, I'm no skint.

And out comes this gold lighter man and he flicks it and that and the flame, straight away, no bother. Puffs out the smoke. I'm waiting for the bank to open at half one, he says, I've got a cheque to cash.

Good, I says, but I'm thinking well fuck you as well, that's my last fag man I mean jesus christ almighty.

FOREIGN LANGUAGE USERS

A WISE man resists playing cards with foreign language users. This is a maxim Mister Joseph Kerr should always have been well aware of. So how come he had succumbed to temptation yet again? Because he thought he would take them, that's how. If you had discussed the point prior to play he would have nodded in a perfunctory fashion – that's how much a part of him the maxim was. And yet he still succumbed. Of course. Gamblers are a strange breed. In fact, when he noticed his pockets were empty he frowned. That is exactly what he did, he frowned. Then he stared at the foreign language users who by this time had forgotten all about him. And the croupier was shuffling the deck for a new deal. And yes, she was also concealing her impatience in an unsubtle way, this croupier, and this unsubtlety was her method of displaying it, her impatience.

Mister Joseph Kerr nudged the spectacles up his nose a wee bit, a nervous gesture. His chair moved noisily, causing the other players to glance at him.

But what was he to do now? There was nothing he could do now. No, nothing to be done. It was something he just had to face. And yet these damn foreign language users had taken his money by devices one could scarcely describe as being other than less than fair, not to put too fine a point on things. And how in the name of all that's holy could the fact that it was himself to blame be of any consolation?

He scratched his ear and continued to stand there, by the chair, and then he sighed in an exaggerated manner but it was bitterly done, and he declared how things had gone too far for him now, that he had so to speak come to the end of his tether. The croupier merely looked at him in reply but this look might well have been a straightforward appeal for a new player.

Mister Joseph Kerr shrugged. Then he stood to the side, making space for the new player who moved easily onto the seat. There was a pause. Mister Joseph Kerr had raised his eyebrows in a slightly mocking fashion. He smiled at the new player and touched him on the shoulder, saying how he should definitely pay heed to that which he knew so thoroughly beforehand. The new player glared at the hand on his shoulder. What's the meaning of this? he murmured.

In all probability he too was a foreign language user. Mister Joseph Kerr nodded wearily. Maybe he was just bloody well growing old! Could that be it? He sighed as he strolled round the table, continuing on in the style of somebody heading to an exit. He entered the gents' washroom and gazed at himself in the mirror. It was a poor show right enough, this tired face he saw; and something in it too as if, as if his eyes had perhaps clouded over, but his spectacles of course, having misted over. The thought how at least he was breathing, at least he was breathing, that was worth remembering.

LET THAT BE A LESSON

BETWEEN 12 and 1 o'clock every Sunday the boys met up the field and played football for the rest of the afternoon. They stopped for breaks whenever they felt like it; these they spent lying around smoking and chatting, unless it was raining, in which case they found shelter till it eased off enough to resume. Occasionally when somebody produced a pack of cards the game was forgotten about. Today was like that, plus the rain had become a downpour, looking as if it was on for the day. A few of the boys went home. Ten or so others gathered in the back close of a tenement to continue the cards. Then a man came down the stairs and told them to get to hell out of it. They went slowly, a couple of them staring back at the man till they were outside on the pavement. Matt then let it slip his house was vacant but insisted his maw and da had given him his last warning about bringing people in. He refused to even consider disobeying them. He kept on refusing till finally they offered him a bribe of 10 pence a skull. 'Okay,' he said, 'on condition the game stops whenever I say so.'

They spoke in whispers when he led them upstairs and into his room. The bed was used as the card table, the boys crouching or kneeling roundabout it. The game alternated between brag, pontoon, banker and chase-the-ace. After a couple of hours just five players remained. Arthur had the bulk of the money and his only real rival was Jimmy. The other three were just hanging on by the skin of their teeth. Beside Matt there were Dougie and Eddie: Eddie kept dashing out the house and round the street to his own place where he was thieving money from his grand-father's coat pockets, his mother's purse, his big sister's purse, his young brother's secret bank. The last time he returned it was with a packet of ten cigarettes which he sold to Jimmy for 20 pence more than the retail price. Dougie had been in and out the game at different times since the start, but then he would find a coin from somewhere and buy his way back in. Matt himself had managed to survive by selling pieces on jam for 15 pence, cups of tea for 10. But the clock ticked on and he was beginning to show the strain. Every few minutes he jumped up and rushed ben the living room to look out the window. In fact it was really the bread worrying him the most. A couple of slices just were left and his da would be needing sandwiches for work tomorrow. It would be a total disaster if there was nothing there in the morning.

Jimmy passed a fag to him. He took two deep draws on it, passed it on to Dougie. Eddie was shuffling cards and getting set to deal. 'I want to change the game,' he said.

'No again,' muttered Arthur.

'Brag,' said Matt.

Arthur shrugged. Eddie dealt the cards and the others posted the kitty money. Matt lifted his cards and dropped them at once, there was a noise from outside: his hand went to his face and covered his eyes. Jimmy whispered, 'Fucking hell man . . .'

The front door was opened now and people in the lobby. Matt's parents had friends with them. They could be heard walking down to the living-room then the door clicked shut. Matt glanced about at the others. 'It's alright,' he said, 'Sshh; just keep quiet.' He got up and left the bedroom, closing the door behind himself. Minutes later he was back and he had a radio with him, he turned on some music. 'I told them yous were in and we were listening to records. It'll be alright if we keep it quiet . . .' Matt added, 'They've got a drink in them anyway.'

He knelt down at his place and the game continued, each of the boys making sure the coins did not chink. But less than quarter of an hour later the door banged open and Matt's da was glowering at them. 'Right yous mob,' he said, 'Think we're bloody daft or something!'

Nobody moved.

'Right!' he said, jerking his thumb at the door.

The other four got up onto their feet but Matt looked at the floor and stayed where he was.

'You and all,' cried his da.

Arthur was nearest to the man, he was about an inch taller than him. 'It was just for pennies we were playing Mister McDonald,' he said.

Matt's da frowned at him: 'Think I'm bloody daft?'

'Honest.'

Instead of replying Mister McDonald glared at his son. 'I thought I told you I didnt want you hanging about with this yin?'

Matt sniffed. His face went red.

'Eh? I'm asking you a question.' Mister McDonald jerked his thumb at Arthur and added, 'Thinks he's a flyman so he does!'

'Naw he doesni.'

'Aye he does.' The man glanced from Arthur to Jimmy and the other two boys, then noticed Matt looking at him and he glared: 'What's up with your face?'

'Nothing.'

'I'll bloody nothing you.'

'Da . . .' muttered Matt.

His father stared at him for a moment longer. Then he pulled the door fully open: 'Okay, the lot of yous, ben the living-room!'

'What?' Matt frowned.

'Ben the bloody living-room,' roared his da. The four boys walked out into the lobby immediately and he beckoned Matt onto his feet and waved him out as well. He walked behind them, then stepped in front to open the living-room door. 'In yous get,' he said.

The boys shuffled inside. Matt's maw was sitting chatting with two other women on the settee and a man was sitting on one of the armchairs, glancing at a newspaper and sipping from a can of export beer. When Mister McDonald closed the door and herded the five into the centre of the room his wife whispered loudly, 'In the name of God what's he playing at now!' And she laughed briefly then sipped at a glass of martini.

Matt marched across to her: 'Hey maw what's up with him at all is he cracking up or something?'

Missis McDonald laughed.

'Is he bevied?' asked Matt.

'Oh uh! Imagine saying that about your daddy!'

'It's no bloody wonder the way you bring him up!' called Mister McDonald; he winked at the other man and said, 'Telling you Pat, she lets this boy get away with murder. Right enough, he's her favourite!'

The man grinned.

Mister McDonald slapped his hands together and moved his shoulders, he winked: 'Fancy a wee game of cards?'

'What?'

'Eh? No fancy it?'

'A wee game of cards?'

'Aye, fancy it?'

'Ah well I'm partial to a wee game now and then, I must say.'

Mister McDonald winked again: 'That's the way Pat that's the way.

Missis McDonald said to the two women, 'Are you listening to this!'

'I'm trying no to!' replied one, and she gave Pat a look.

Pat held his hands palms upward and said, 'Just a wee game hen . . .'

'Tch!' She shook her head and reached for a cigarette from an open packet on the coffee table.

Matt gazed at Missis McDonald: 'Maw is he going daft!'

'Hh! I thought you knew that by this time!'

Both men were smiling. Mister McDonald nodded to Pat and he stood up, then he indicated the chairs round the dining table and he said to the boys, 'Okay lads, grab a pew.'

'Naw,' shouted Matt.

'Shut up,' replied his da.

'Maw! Will you tell him!'

'Hh!' His mother raised her eyebrows and she glanced at the other two women: 'Men are so bloody thick arent they!'

'Maw . . .'

Missis McDonald ignored him. She picked a cigarette out from the packet, got her lighter from the table. Matt turned from her. The two men were already seated and taking loose change from their pockets and setting it down at the edge of the table. Some of the coins made a noise and Missis McDonald cried, 'Would you at least have the sense to put down some bloody newspaper!'

'Sorry,' answered her husband, and winked at the other man: 'Newspaper Pat, have we got such a commodity?'

'Da . . .'

'What is it son?'

'Da, we're no playing with you.'

'Aye you are.'

'Naw we're no.'

'Aw sit down and stop moaning . . .' Mister McDonald winked at Pat: 'I wonder who he takes after eh!' He glanced round at Arthur: 'Heh son will you pass that paper there!'

The newspaper was on top of a glass display cabinet and Arthur got it quickly and handed it to the man.

'Now sit down.'

Arthur glanced swiftly at Matt but he sat down. Jimmy and the other two boys did likewise. 'That's better,' said Mister McDonald, spreading pages of newspaper about the table. The other man had taken his cigarettes out and placed one in front of Mister McDonald; he looked at the boys as if about to offer them one as well, but he changed his mind and put the packet away into his side jacket pocket. Matt was still standing midway between the dining table and the settee. His father looked at him and said, 'Where's the cards then?'

'Jesus Christ!' cried Matt.

'Hear that language?' said his maw to the other women; the three of them laughed.

Matt went striding out the room and crashed the door shut. Mister McDonald called to his wife, 'That's bloody ridiculous the way he's acting! Eh?' He glanced at Pat: 'Imagine acting like that in front of visitors but? Eh? In our day? Can you imagine? You'd have got your bloody arse skelped.' He called to his wife: 'That boy, it's a bloody good hiding he needs!'

'Aye well why dont you do it then!'

'Aye I've a good mind to.'

'Good!' She winked at the two women and lifted her glass of martini, reached for the bottle to top it up.

Mister McDonald was lighting the cigarette given to him by Pat. He blew a cloud of smoke at the ceiling, then said: 'Okay. Cards.'

'Eh . . .' Dougie sniffed. 'They're in Matt's room Mister McDonald.'

'Well just go and get them son – naw! Dont . . .' He pushed his chair backwards and leant to the sideboard, pulled out a drawer; he took a pack of cards from it. 'We'll play with the good yins.'

Pat grinned at him. 'I hope they're no marked!'

'You better believe it!' Mister McDonald winked once more, started shuffling the cards. 'What is it we're playing lads?' He looked at Arthur.

Arthur blushed. 'Eh . . .'

'Ponnies?'

'Eh naw eh it was eh, it was eh – brag, it was brag.'

'Brag . . .'

'Aye.'

'Three or four-card?' asked the other man.

'Three. Deuces floating.'

Mister McDonald frowned at Arthur: 'Deuces floating!' He grinned at Pat. 'Deuces floating! Long time eh!'

'Aye you're no kidding! Deuces floating!' Pat glanced across at the three women but they were talking about something and did not notice, and he grinned at Mister McDonald: 'Years since I've played that.'

Mister McDonald shoved the cards to Jimmy. 'Want to get the ball rolling son.'

Jimmy lifted the pack.

'Better shuffle first.' Then he glanced suddenly at Arthur: 'You ready Big Time?'

Arthur did not say anything. His face was red. He saw Eddie looking away and he placed his hands on the edge of his seat and gripped it.

'It's a game I've always liked but, brag . . .' Pat tapped ash into the ashtray; his jacket cuff caught on a page of newspaper and he straightened it carefully. 'What about the post?' he said to Jimmy.

'Two pence.'

Mister McDonald smiled: 'We'll no get rooked at that anyway, eh Pat!'

Pat grinned.

Twenty minutes passed. The door clicked open and Matt appeared. His da called, 'Fancy a game?'

'Nope.'

'It's no a bad game Matt,' said the other man.

Matt nodded. He was holding a packet of cigarettes and a box of matches in his left hand. He displayed it: 'Hey Jimmy you left your smokes in the room.'

Jimmy gazed at him.

He opened the packet and extracted one, put it in his mouth and got out a match, lighted the cigarette, handed Jimmy the packet and matchbox.

His maw had been watching and she laughed. 'See that!' she said to the other women. 'He's a big boy because he smokes!'

Mister McDonald frowned at Matt. 'Is this you smoking in the house?'

Matt ignored the question and said to Arthur: 'How's it going?'

'Okay . . .'

'A wee bit slow mind you,' said Mister McDonald. 'Eh Pat?'

'Well . . . I suppose . . . Maybe if we stopped the deuces floating?'

Mister McDonald nodded then winked. 'I was thinking about a wee game of ponnies.'

'Aw aye. I dont mind.'

'How about it lads?' Mister McDonald had glanced at Dougie and Eddie, and now at Jimmy and at Arthur. But nobody responded. They looked to Matt eventually and he walked across to his maw and whispered something to her.

She paused then called to her husband: 'Right, that's enough.'

'Pardon?'

'Time for the boys to go home for their tea.'

Mister McDonald sniffed; he looked at the boys. 'Have yous to go home for your tea?'

No reply.

'Eh lads? Is it teatime?' He grinned.

Matt shouted, 'Da, they've got to go home!'

'Nobody's asking you.'

Matt glared at his mother who shrugged, turned to the other women and shrugged again. The boy strode out the room. 'Dont bang that door!' cried Mister McDonald. But Matt did bang it, and his bedroom door could be heard banging as well. 'Some temper that boy,' muttered the man.

'See you!' called his wife, 'you're just bloody stupid, so you are!'

'Aw thanks . . .' He winked at the other man. His face became serious and he said to Arthur: 'You can deal son.'

'Eh . . .' Arthur gazed at Jimmy, Dougie and Eddie.

It was Jimmy who spoke. He coughed beforehand, then said, 'Eh Mister McDonald, see at ponnies, what you usually do is dish round the cards first.'

'Mmhh.'

'Because it's the bank. You've got to see who gets it first.'

'Aw.'

Jimmy hesitated and looked at Arthur who was staring at the table, as if he was reading something in the spread newspaper. Mister McDonald shifted on his chair and said to Pat, 'See what I thought, I thought give the boy the bank cause he's won most of the cash.' He pointed at the columns of coins in front of Arthur. 'Know what I mean? I thought it'd give the lads a chance to win something back.'

'I take your point.'

'And it saves time.' He paused, glanced at Arthur: 'No think so son? A wee bit of excitement as well eh!' He rubbed his hands together and smiled. 'Do you no want the bank?'

Arthur shrugged slightly, still staring at the table.

'I mean you dont have to; nobody's forcing you. See I

[66]

thought cause you were winning the most money you wouldnt mind taking it on – eh Pat?'

'Well . . . I suppose . . .' Pat brought out his cigarettes and gave one to Mister McDonald.

'Is it alright if we smoke as well?' Jimmy sniffed.

'Christ son there's nobody stopping you!' Mister McDonald frowned at him. 'What do you mean? For God sake dont tell me yous've been sitting there gasping! I never thought.' He looked at Pat. 'Did you?'

'Naw.'

Mister McDonald frowned at the boys. 'Honest,' he said, 'if yous want to smoke smoke – far be it from me . . .'

Moments after this Arthur was dealing. A couple of rounds later Matt's da put down a £1 note for the bet, and he gave a wink to Pat, then a swift glance across to the settee. He said to Arthur, 'Okay son?'

Arthur looked at Jimmy but said nothing. He dealt the cards and eventually had to twist and was bust. Mister McDonald lifted the winnings and added, 'Hard lines son.'

Arthur nodded. Mister McDonald bet £1 in the next round and he won it; and he won the next one as well. Then the door opened and in came Matt. He walked to the table, positioning himself behind Arthur's chair, not saying anything to anybody. His da had bet another £1 and Arthur was counting out coins to cover it. Mister McDonald needed a twist this time and he got a ten and was bust. Ha ha, said Matt.

'He was due a win,' replied Mister McDonald. 'Eh Pat?'

'He was, aye.'

The cards were dealt for the next round and Mister McDonald grinned and turned his face up. It was an ace. He slapped his hands together, winked at Pat. 'A big bullet,' he said, 'a big bullet.' He brought a £5 note from his hip pocket and laid it down. After several moments silence he said to Pat: 'You having a side bet with me?'

'Eh . . .'

'You canni bet all that anyway,' cried Matt. 'It's no allowed!'

'What?'

'You're no allowed to bet all that on an ace! There's a limit!'

'A limit?' Mister McDonald screwed his face up. 'First I've heard of it. You never said anything about limits Arthur?'

'That's no bloody fair,' cried Matt.

Arthur was gazing down at his money. He had three £1 notes there plus the coins; he started counting the coins.

'Dont,' said Matt. He turned to the settee: 'Hey maw!'

'Tch tch tch.' Mister McDonald shook his head.

'Da's betting a fiver!'

'What!' Missis McDonald stared across. 'Am I hearing right? Ya bloody dumpling!'

Her husband stared at her.

'I'm telling you,' she said, 'a joke's a joke but this's gone far enough.'

'A bet's a bet.'

'A fiver? Dont be so bloody stupid; all you're doing is making a fool of yourself!' She shook her head at the other two women: 'Have you ever heard of anything like this in your life!'

Her husband smiled. He winked at Pat, then called: 'When you make a bet you make a bet. That's what you dont know.'

Missis McDonald stared at him. 'Aw rap up,' she said. 'Come on Arthur put your money away. Yous as well.' She gestured with her right hand at the boys. And after a moment Arthur started putting his money into his pocket.

'So that's it then?' said Mister McDonald. 'You finished?'

Arthur shrugged slightly.

'Tch tch tch.' Mister McDonald said to Jimmy: 'What about you son, you finished as well?'

'It's all finished,' said his wife. 'You spoiled it.'

'I spoiled it!' Mister McDonald chuckled. 'Me?' He said to Pat: 'It was me that spoiled it.'

Missis McDonald said to the boys: 'It's time you were all away.'

Mister McDonald grinned at Matt. 'I think something's bothering your maw son.'

[68]

His wife sighed. She turned to the two women. 'See?' She shook her head and folded her arms, sat back on the settee.

And a moment later Matt nodded at the four boys and they got up from the table and followed him to the door. He led them down the lobby, standing aside to let them out onto the landing. 'See yous the morrow,' he muttered, shutting the door.

GOOD INTENTIONS

WE HAD been sceptical from the very outset but the way he set about the tasks suited us perfectly. In fact, it was an eye-opener. He would stand there with the poised rifle, the weather-beaten countenance, the shiny little uniform; yet giving absolutely nothing away. His legs were bandy and it produced a swaggering stance, as though he had no time for us and deep down regarded us as amateurs. But we, of course, made no comment. The old age pensioner is a strange beast on occasion and we were well acquainted with this, perhaps too well acquainted. In the final analysis it was probably that at the root of the project's failure.

CUTE CHICK!

THERE USED to be this talkative old lady with a polite English accent who roamed the betting shops of Glasgow being avoided by everybody. Whenever she appeared the heavily backed favourite was just about to get beat by a big outsider. And she would always cry out in a surprised way about how she'd managed to choose it, before going to collect her dough at the pay-out window. And when asked for her nom-de-plume she spoke loudly and clearly: Cute Chick!

It made the punters' blood run cold.

THE SMALL FAMILY

I SUPPOSE it is best not to say what the name of the station was but if I mention it was the one that got 'swallowed' up then the majority of folk familiar with the old subway system will have a fair idea of the one in question. Although lying underground it was one of those which seemed very close to the surface in a strange sense. Actual daylight always appeared to be entering though from where I don't know and people somehow assumed the outer layer of corrugated roofing explained everything. I also remember when I was a boy I was absolutely fascinated by the inordinate amount of dripping. Water seemed to come from anywhere and everywhere. As a result, I was ready and willing to believe anything. Especially was I willing to believe that the tunnel beneath the Clyde was full of rotting timbers and set to collapse at any moment. This was the yarn told me by my older brother. I doubt whether the fact that it actually was a yarn fully dawned on me for a further decade.

Those familiar with the station must readily recall its peculiar hallmark, a weird form of illusion; its main ground resembled a large mound or hill and from the bottom of the long flights of stairs intending travellers would find themselves 'walking up' a stiffish gradient along the platform. Such a gradient was a physical absurdity of course but this did not stop visiting travellers from experiencing the sensation. I have to confess that I was as guilty as the next regular in the enjoyment I gained from observing the unwary.

Another hallmark of the station, though the term is somewhat inappropriate, was the Small Family. As far as many people are concerned when we speak of the station we are speaking of them, the Small Family, but I am not alone in the belief that had the peculiar 'mound' or 'hill' not existed then the Small Family would have associated itself with another station. Individually members of the family were not especially small, rather was the phrase applied as a simplified form of reference by the regulars which in the first instance must have derived from the little mother. There was no father, no male parent, and the female – the little mother – was very small indeed, birdlike almost. Yet be that as it may this tiny woman most certainly was a parent who tended her young come hell or high water.

Of the four children in the family group I chiefly recall the eldest, a large boy or young man. He had the appearance of being big and strong but at the same time with a form of 'lightness' of the brain, a slightly brutish quality. I once heard a traveller describe his walk as 'thick' and this to my mind was very apt indeed. The other children were aged from infancy to pubescence but at this juncture I am unable to recollect their sexes; they would walk to the front of the mother with the large boy bringing up the rear, often carrying a long stick which he let trail on the ground.

When regulars spoke of the Small Family they did so in a wryly amused fashion. In those days an odd camaraderie existed between us. I am of the opinion that this was the case because of the tacit assumption that in stations like ours the queerest occurrences might take place right beneath one's nose but that in the very act of perception the substance of such an occurrence would have slipped, as it were, 'round a corner'. I should point out that I am very aware of the pitfalls in nostalgia. But I doubt whether it is necessary to state that the Small Family in itself was never a source of amusement to us. The truth of the matter is that we regulars admired if not marvelled at them. Above all did we esteem the little mother. In conversation with an old friend recently we were discussing this; he made the strong point that simply to have been a parent of the large boy would have tested a man's resources. This is not, of course, in any sense, to excuse the absence of a male parent; it was intended as a testimony to the character of the tiny woman. In those days things were more tough than they are now and she could not have had an easy time of it. My friend reminded me that the family seemed to earn their living by gathering and that often they were to be seen carrying large bundles of soft goods. It is possible they may have kept a stall in one of the lesser street markets in the area to the south of the Tron.

I told my friend of a dream I used to have in which the large mound or hill in the station had become hollow and was fashioned out as a makeshift home for the Small Family. Inside it the floors were carpeted and the kitchen contained every domestic and labour-saving convenience. The rationale of the dream is fairly obvious but my friend also pointed to an element of reality insofar as the back end of the mound would have afforded a degree of shelter. He also reminded me that any form of shelter was always welcome in the old station because of the tremendous rushes of air. This most definitely was the case and of the more amusing side-effects of the illusion, as experienced by visiting travellers, perhaps the most striking was the sensation that true equilibrium would be achieved only by crawling on all fours.

I had wanted to speak to my friend of an incident that occurred many many years ago. In matters like this it is far better to move straightaway to the core of the subject otherwise we run the risk of losing our way. My desire was basic, to have the subject aired. It is my opinion that to air a subject, to present the question, is to find oneself on the road to solution. I may well be wrong. In itself the incident is of no major significance, neither then or now. But it is one that remains to the forefront of my memory and has done for more than thirty years. It concerns my own children.

I have had five children, the eldest of whom is a daughter. At the time I speak she was 9 or 10 years old but even then had looks of a striking quality. She also regarded herself as quite grown up, as quite the young lady. I must confess that both myself and my wife regarded the girl in a similar light which is not at all uncommon, she being the eldest of the five.

The day of the incident was a Sunday and my wife was not feeling a hundred percent; she decided to remain home with the youngest two while I set off with the other three on a visit to an elderly relation. All children loved the old subway system and mine were no different. Even yet I can recall their excitement as we tramped downwards, down the long flights of stone steps, thoroughly enjoying the onrush of air, the strange smells and echoing sounds. Once onto the platform we 'ascended' the large mound or hill to stand hand in hand, peering into the blackness of the tunnel, awaiting the arrival of the next train.

In our group as a whole I should say there had been close on twenty folk, and by 'group' I simply refer to those on the platform who were intending passengers, as opposed to the Small Family. They had appeared suddenly, from nowhere it seemed. I myself travelled but rarely on Sundays and I confess to rather a shock on discovering they were here in the station on that day as though it were any other. The other travellers must have been experiencing an unease similar to my own. Not to put too fine a point on it there most certainly was a general strain, and we stood as though rooted to the spot. But gradually I became aware of a pressure on my hand. It was being caused by the child whose hand I held and she in turn was being affected by the child whose hand he was holding who in turn was being affected by my eldest daughter's hand. My eldest daughter was very uncomfortable indeed, but not agitated and by no means in any distress. It was the large boy, he was staring at her. He had halted at the rear of his family and was standing stockstill, staring at her in an entirely un-selfconscious manner. It was the most peculiar thing. I see the moment clearly and distinctly and the two figures are in isolation. Beyond that is a blur, until I hear my daughter's voice:

'Dad, I want to put her on the mantelpiece!' and she pointed to someone in their group, either a child or I suppose, perhaps, the tiny woman.

There are many aspects of this incident I regard as worthy of comment, as worthy of discussion. Over the years I have dwelt on the matter periodically but without ever allowing it to become an obsession. I would like, however, to speak of it with my friend. I have wanted to do so for quite some time but the subject I find difficult to approach, that is, the core of the subject for I find it all too easy to discuss topics peripheral to it.

As the years pass I have become close to overwhelmed by an ever-increasing burden of guilt. There is no one cause. I think that if I could isolate different events, the experiences I derived from them, if I could bring these out into the open then perhaps I would be on the road to assuaging such feelings and ridding myself of the burden. I am also aware that the sensation of guilt – even chronic guilt – is part and parcel of the ageing process and in neither case does a cure exist. Ultimately, however, to have said that is to have said very little.

END OF A BEGINNING

RODDY CLOSED the door and bounded upstairs to the kitchen. 7.30 – surely the place would be empty. Open door is a good sign. One empty kitchen! He whistled as he poured the contents of the tin of minced beef into his new saucepan. First Friday night in London and free. Free. Nobody at all. Nobody knows. I know nobody but the silent landlord and his noisy children. Can return at all hours without reproach or guilt. No angry or martyred parent. Not one single solitary person but whom I may meet tonight. Alone and almost in Soho.

He carefully mussed his hair in front of the cracked mirror that balanced on a shelf. Hearing the saucepan begin to sizzle on the black stove he remembered coffee. He turned the gas down low and returned to his room for the large jar of Nescafé.

Such a small room for the money, plus slot electricity. One mouldy Hank Jansen found under mattress next to an ancient sock. Clean sheets and almost clean floor though not enough for bare feet. Dressing table painted flat green with barber's surplus mirror joined on by unscrew nails. Deep armchair sagging in centre caused by too many overweight bums. Old stiff newspapers with dust and hairs imprinted between pages, found under dark greasy cushion. One grey-green crust of bread discovered wedged between bed-leg and wall. Left wedged.

Lucky to find any place let alone Number 7, Ashdown Ave., Kilburn. Mother would surely take to fellow lodgers. Thick as thieves with silent landlord complete with hanging braces and unshaven chin. Deeply love the rich Sligo tongue and manners. Roddy smiled briefly.

Dear Mother,

Regret to inform you that Mr Murphy's gangerman would not start me this morning or yesterday morning. Appeared to be in some doubt as to whether I could last a morning.

Your slight of son,
Roddy.

Dear Son,

Please come home. All is forgiven if you mend your ways but if not please come home.

Love
Mother.

He lifted a plate and cup from the table, laid out the butter and the loaf of french bread, and bounded back upstairs to the kitchen. Still empty! He put on a kettle of water to boil, stirred the minced beef. A tin of peas would have been a good idea. When the food was ready he poured it onto the plate and carried the saucepan to rinse under the tap at the sink. Suddenly the door banged open and in lurched a big heavy man carrying a pile of fish and chips wrapped in a mixture of brown paper and newspaper. Roddy called hello but no response. He continued rinsing the saucepan. The man had slumped onto a chair and put the fish and chips down on top of a wooden cupboard.

Why does he come in here to eat? Surely be much more comfortable in his own room? Roddy glanced at him sideways. A red faced man in his late fifties or sixties. Straight to the pub from the building site. One of Murphy's men? Flannel grey suit with the trouser bottoms stuffed into a pair of wellington boots covered in caked mud. Huge hand shoving the battered fish into his mouth. God! Should be in his room to eat. Unless – unless it is not allowed. God! Should have inquired from the silent landlord! The man will know. Ask him.

But the older man munched on, oblivious to Roddy's voice. 'I beg your pardon,' he said again, much louder than before.

'Whaa . . .' The older man raised his shaggy eyebrows. A large chip teetered between his thumb and forefinger.

'Can one eat in one's room?'

'Ehh?'

'Is one allowed to?'

The top part of the chip keeled over and landed on the floor but he did not seem to notice as he lowered the remainder carefully into his mouth.

'Are you allowed to eat in your room?' cried Roddy.

'Whaa'' The older man glared as he bent to retrieve the fallen bit of chip, and he nearly toppled over. He glared at Roddy again and started to struggle to his feet. 'Cheeky . . . What you saying!' he shouted.

'Nothing, nothing. You're misunderstanding!' Roddy began to panic and stepped back the way leaning against the sink.

The older man made a growling sound as he rose from the chair and the cuff of his sleeve seemed to catch the edge of the paper holding the fish and chips and it all capsized onto the floor beside the chair. The man roared in anger. 'Yaaaa!' he shouted.

'What's wrong?' cried Roddy. 'Look, you've dropped your dinner!'

The man's eyes were red and wide and he looked wildly about the kitchen. 'I'll fix the bastard!' he shouted as his gaze settled on a long bread knife at the rear of the cupboard and he grabbed at it.

'No no!' screamed Roddy, 'I simply asked . . .'

But the man lumbered towards him, staggering from side to side, the long bread knife held in one hand while the other was raised as if to balance himself.

'Nooo!' screamed Roddy with both his arms up aloft and his body bent as far back as it could go across the sink.

The older man lunged with the knife but he struck it into the front of the sink and he staggered and just managed to correct himself. 'I'll . . .' he roared, 'I'll . . .'

'NO!' shouted Roddy, twisting himself away.

But the man had steadied himself on the sink and he lunged again with the knife, this time the blade went right into Roddy's stomach.

'AAhhh,' he cried, 'Ahhh . . .' And he fell back the way.

The older man seemed to totter on because of the force of the strike and then he too fell and lay sprawled on the floor.

Roddy was sitting at an angle with his back to the wall, his eyes open but glazed, one hand held the handle of the knife and the other was on the floor, and the blood was coming out.

LEADER FROM A
QUALITY NEWSPAPER

It MIGHT well be wondered why certain hints
of infinity are likely to knock folk back on their
uppers. The answer lies not in hypocrisy but in
genuine self doubt. Given the general mysti-
fication which hangs shroud-like from our
shoulders we should not cry out when down falls
the sword of an acquaintance. It is, after all, the
sort of occurrence we are to be secure upon.

A SUNDAY EVENING

SHE WAS annoyed with him; she couldnt say exactly why she was annoyed with him but she was. She watched him as he leaned back on the couch, his head resting against its back, his legs stretching out towards the fireplace. Then she shook her head and returned to the kitchen to see if the water was boiling. It wasnt, and she walked to the window and stared out. Night. A month ago it would've been day. What had happened to the summer. The sound of the water approaching boiling point. She checked the tealeaves were in the teapot. And voices from the front room; he had switched on the wireless. The sandwiches. Quickly she got the margarine and the cheese from the refrigerator, the bread from the bread bin, seeing the amount of crumbs inside – she shouldve cleaned it out. She buttered the bread and she sliced the cheese, but not uniformly, each slice being totally different from the one previous; thick ends and thin ends, and one slice so thin it became nothing at all. She juggled them onto the bread, trying to capture an even thickness on his. Lettuce in the bowl. But she left it there, and it would have needed a wash under the tap. When she had filled the teapot she returned to the window. There were no sounds from outside, not even from animals. Animals. Dogs or cats. A Sunday evening; there wouldnt be any drunks, just silence and maybe a car. Normally she enjoyed the silence of being on the top flat; and the silence of late summer evenings was best; during winter and late autumn she preferred noise. Why was that. But if it was anything it was nothing worth bothering about. The refrigerator vibrated and cut off suddenly. It would reach a peak then cut off suddenly, only noticeable that instant prior to cutting off. It had to do with thermostatic control, a thing which worked on its own, as part of the machinery. The tea wouldnt have infused properly yet, she got a teaspoon from the cutlery drawer and stirred it, and poured it into the mugs. The sandwiches were on a plate and she carried it and his mug of tea ben the front room. He was gazing at the picture on the wall above the mantelpiece, listening or not listening to the wireless. A discussion. All those in favour and all those against. The chairman or presenter of the programme was chuckling about something – a moot point. A moot point. What was a moot point. Did moot mean appropriate. An appropriate point. She passed him the mug and placed the plate on the small table between the couch and the chair she usually sat on, then returned to the kitchen. She would liked to have paused here, by the window, sipping her tea. There could be something, a sound perhaps, a thing of interest, thing of marked interest, something to give cause for thought. What thing could it be. A sound perhaps. She would know it, the sound, as soon as she heard it. But the thought would not be worth bothering about. Not unless the sound it derived from was especially striking. If it was especially striking, totally unfamiliar. Not to the point of uniqueness for that really wasnt possible. Just a strange sound, a strange noise; something to set the hairs on end. What could that be. A sudden scream. Murder being committed – violence, in the home. The sound of violence erupting, below, in the flat downstairs. She raised the mug to her lips, and sipped; the tea without milk or sugar. She preferred it this way although he preferred milk, but no sugar either, he preferred it with milk and no sugar. She should be going to the front room. If she didnt go soon he might be wondering what was up. Unless he didnt notice. He would notice. She sipped her tea. He just wouldnt find it something to be really wondering about. She would be in the bathroom or something, something else, something straight-forward. She was walking to the door, and she switched out the light, then entering the front room and shutting the door after her, and walking to the chair she sat on. He had eaten his sandwich and this left hers on the plate. She would lift it and eat it. She continued to sip tea from her mug. From the wireless an outbreak of applause, for one of the speakers; and the chairman laughed and asked a question which followed on from the point made by the last speaker. She glanced to see that he really was listening, and intently – staring at the fireplace, his look somehow quite lively, not a stare, just a look, looking directly to the fireplace to have his eyes open for the purpose of attention, concentration on the speakers; perhaps had he closed his eyes his attention would wander, he might doze off. He was reaching for the plate, as though about to eat the sandwich but he paused and he glanced at her; he was drawing her attention to it, indicating it, the sandwich, that it was still there. Why was it still there? What was the meaning of that? Why was she not eating her sandwich instead of just sitting there sipping tea? Maybe she didnt want it and this was why it was lying there. Unless it was for him. Maybe she had made him two. She wasnt feeling like eating, or perhaps she ate hers in the kitchen, before coming through to sit down. Why should she have done that? Absent-minded maybe. She had made the one sandwich then started eating it while doing the next, and had finished it; so she'd had to make herself another one just in case. Just in case. In case of what. In case he thought something. What could he have thought. He could've thought why has she made me one and not made one for herself. Why did she eat that one and not this one. Daft, but the kind of thing people ended up thinking when something like that happened – a simple event, the eating or not eating of a sandwich. The speaker on the wireless programme was laughing. Why was he laughing. Because he was getting paid a lot of money. This is why people on the wireless laughed, they were getting paid lots of money. He glanced at her. She wasnt listening to the programme anyway, she never bothered. She found programmes like this one unbelievable. And although she never said so she was probably always wondering why he did listen, why he did listen. What was the point in it, of listening to them. They were always unsatisfactory. Nothing was ever said on them that could be taken down and used in evidence because they never gave anything away, nothing; always it got lost amid the general air of smugness, underlined by the way the presenter was laughing all the time. What was he laughing about. Because they were all in it together and getting paid lots and lots of money. Everything went in circles. And she could just sit there, not taking part, her mind gone, abstracted miles away – a voyage to unknown parts; only brought back to reality by the occasional sips from her mug of tea. She had probably just forgotten about the sandwich. And if he reminded her about it, what would she do. She could smile, she could smile and lift it right away. But she wouldnt. She was a bit annoyed at him. She wouldnt smile therefore. Unless she was so far away that she would've forgotten all about it. He glanced at her briefly, she was staring at the fireplace.

BENSON'S VISITOR

EVERY SUNDAY afternoon he appeared. The patient who had the first bed on the left at the ward entrance always heralded his arrival with the cry: 'It's Benson's visitor!' But he never acknowledged this cry. He was aware some might think him deaf. He stood on the threshold peering down both sides of the ward for ten to fifteen seconds, perhaps to see if Benson was still there and if so whether he had been shifted to a different bed as sometimes happened. If everything was as it should be he stared at the highly polished floor and walked steadily down the right-hand passage, to the bottom end, and from there across to Benson's bed at the end of the left-hand row. At the beginning he had nodded and occasionally greeted other patients but over the years he had ceased doing this and nowadays he could scarcely bear to look at patients other than Benson. And if Benson was awake he found it increasingly difficult to look at him. He used to smile in a friendly manner at the nurses but they barely noticed his presence. If ever he put a question such as 'Not so good today, is he?' the most they would give was a yes or no but sometimes not even that, as if they had not heard him speak at all even. The new nurses were better but gradually they became used to things and acted no differently from the others. Hardly anyone else ever visited the ward and those who did seldom stayed for more than quarter of an hour and they spent most of that gazing vacantly about the ward. On occasion they would stare across as though looking at Benson whereas it seemed obvious they were looking at his visitor. There was one time Benson's visitor saw somebody leave an article on the chair beside the bed of the patient he had been sitting at. He was not sure what to do about it. Eventually, after the person had departed, he walked across and uplifted the article and quickly rushed out to return it. But the person acted in a peculiar way and pretended not to recognize the object. Benson's visitor took it into the Sister's office and attempted to explain what had happened but the Sister was impatient and did not show any interest in the matter at all. She waved him away. He put the article back onto the chair and tried not to think about it. Next Sunday of course the chair was empty and no-one ever referred to either it or the incident ever again. This was many months ago, prior to the arrival of the patient on the left at the ward entrance. And yet, there was something about this patient that made Benson's visitor think that he knew of the affair.

Benson had been a member of the ward longer than anyone else. His visitor accompanied the wheelchair that transported him there. Although the nurse had observed him following she said nothing, merely indicated a large placard pinned to the wall. The placard gave the visiting times. Benson's visitor stared at it for a long while, until the sound of the creaking wheelchair had died away. He missed the subsequent Sunday because of it. It was a feeling he had not cared for.

This afternoon Benson lay snoring fitfully but peacefully. His visitor stared at the slack mouth and the way the chin drooped. When the bell rang Benson's eyes opened. The gaze settled on his visitor who hastily looked down at the floor. Benson's head began to move back and forth against the piled pillows as though to alleviate an itch. His eyes remained on his visitor for a period, then they closed. His visitor's sigh was quite audible. After a moment he stooped to lift his hat and shabby briefcase from where they had been lying. Across the way an older nurse arranged flowers in a vase. She did not notice his approach. He moved to the right side of her at the precise second she moved to the left. He hesitated and she turned swiftly and strode along and out of the ward. There were no other people about except patients and they all seemed to be sleeping. Then another visitor appeared in the doorway. Benson's visitor returned slowly to where he had been sitting and he returned the briefcase and hat to where they had been lying, and he sat down carefully. Shortly afterwards he was aware of a muffled conversation coming from somewhere to his rear but he was not able to look round to see. A voice called: 'It's Benson's visitor!' and gave an abrupt laugh.

He stared at the floor for a long time. Gradually he wanted to see what was happening around him and he raised his head. Benson stared at him. He glowered at him. 'Who are you?' he groaned.

His visitor smiled weakly.

'I don't know you.'

His visitor inclined his head and stared at the floor beneath the bed.

'Is he visiting me? I don't know him from Adam!'

Footsteps approached. He estimated at least two people.

'I don't know him. Who is he?' cried Benson. 'Who are you?'

'Not so good today, is he?' said his visitor. Two nurses were looking at him and he smiled faintly at them. His heart thumped. Then the nurses looked at the patient with concern and one of them said:

'He's your visitor.'

His visitor nodded his head but without daring to look at him.

But Benson cried, 'I don't know him from Adam. Why is he sitting at my bed?'

The older nurse smiled down on him. 'Come now,' she said, 'you mustn't embarrass your visitor.'

'He's your visitor!' smiled the younger nurse.

'Who is he?' groaned Benson, attempting to raise himself up by the elbows as though for a fuller look at him. But the older nurse snapped:

'Come along now lie down!'

The patient lay back down immediately and stared sideways away from both his visitor and the two nurses, the younger of whom glanced at her colleague and then said to Benson's visitor, 'Who are you?' And she smiled as though to soften matters.

Benson's visitor jumped. Somebody else had arrived suddenly. It was the Sister.

'Benson's visitor . . .' began the younger nurse.

'Of course it's Benson's visitor,' she said, 'What's going on here?'

'Who is he?' murmured Benson.

'Oh you know fine well,' replied the Sister.

'Who are you . . .' Benson murmured.

His visitor smiled at the Sister. He wondered whether the other visitor and any of the patients were listening. He thought he should say something. He cleared his throat but was not able to speak. At last he managed: 'Not so good . . .'

The Sister was speaking in a low unhurried voice to the two nurses who responded as to a direct command, but none noticed Benson's gasp, and his eyelids closed.

The older nurse said to his visitor, 'You better go now, visiting's over.'

He nodded and gripped his hat and briefcase, got off the chair and walked from the ward without glancing back. Out along the lengthy corridor the younger nurse appeared from behind a pillar. 'Are you a relative?' she asked.

'You must have a record,' he said.

'Come along now you won't be on it. You won't be there.' She shook her head at him.

A wave of nausea hit him and he wanted down onto the floor, down onto the floor until it passed. Somebody was holding him by the arm. It was the other nurse, and behind her stood the other patient with a worried frown on his forehead. His hat and briefcase were leaving him, the hat having fallen perhaps but the briefcase from out of his hand. And the younger nurse steadied him. 'Come along now,' she was saying.

The older nurse smiled. 'That's the ticket,' she said.

GOVERNOR OF
THE SITUATION

I HATE this part of the city – the stench of poverty, violence, decay, death; the things you usually discern in suchlike places. I dont mind admitting I despise the poor with an intensity that surprises my superiors. But they concede to me on most matters. I am the acknowledged governor of the situation. I'm in my early thirties. Hardly an ounce of spare flesh hangs on me – I'm always on the go – nervous energy – because my appetite is truly gargantuan. For all that, I've heard it said on more than one occasion that my legs are like hollow pins.

THE BAND OF HOPE

OANNY WAS getting pushed by some cunt, right on the shoulder, pushing him. Cut it out, he grunted then opened his eyes. Fat Stanley was grinning down at him. Alec's done the business, he was saying, Come on! Wake up!

The chemmy had finished right enough, the chairs been shifted back from the big horseshoe table and everybody stood about the place chatting. Across at the empty fireplace Alec was in company with a couple of people. Oanny closed his eyes again but opened them immediately. Fat Stanley had said he would be back in a minute and was making his way towards the serving hatch in the snacks area, walking in that funny way he had, as if wanting not to be seen but knowing he was going to get found out. He paused to say something to Alec and then to Victor – Victor with the fag dangling from the corner of his mouth, on the fringes of the company as usual and trying hard to look lackadaisical about everything, but anybody who knew him could tell his nerves were just as shot to fuck as ever.

The smell of soup.

Last orders had already been given in to Ellen and some of the guys were sitting with their bowls, dipping in slices of unbuttered bread, slurping quickly in case the saturated bits fell onto the table top. The place was full of tables. The horseshoe one where the chemmy was played but a great many weer ones too, and not all of them were circular. In the snacks area two huge bench-type tables stood side by side and about forty or more bodies could have sat roundabout in comfort. Not a single table was covered. They all looked ancient. Initials, slogans and dates and stuff had been knifed into them, grime was embedded in the carvings. If you dug in a fingernail it would bring out thick lengths of it. An in-joke circulated: if you were described as 'definitely hungry' it meant you had been spotted eating a chunk of bread after it had fallen onto the top of the table.

Oanny was raking about in the pockets of his coat and jacket. Glancing beneath the table he saw a can of lager. It was open. He lifted it and gave it a shake, then swallowed the dregs without checking to see if it had been used as a makeshift ashtray. He shuddered and smacked his lips, wiped the corners of his mouth with his hand, began searching through his pockets again. It attracted Victor's attention and he signalled he was needing a smoke. Victor frowned and kidded on he did not understand but then he drew a few steps over to him and muttered, You've fucking got some.

Naw I've no.

Aye you have.

Oanny resumed the search. He discovered a crushed packet in the hip pocket of his trousers. It was an unusual place to have put it. He shrugged and smiled briefly, flourishing the packet for Victor's benefit, but Victor just looked away and returned to the empty fireplace. Ah fuck you too, grunted Oanny, taking out a cigarette. He had to straighten it before getting it alight.

Eventually the other three arrived back at the table together. When he gestured at the packet they each helped himself to a cigarette – even Fat Stanley although he was supposed to have stopped. Nobody spoke. Oanny sniffed through one nostril and made a display of peering at the ex-railway clock on the wall which had not ticked for years.

A sound came from Fat Stanley. And he seemed to be making a great effort not to smile. That way he puffed on the fag without inhaling. What a waste. Imagine giving your last fag to a cunt like him! Typical.

It dawned on Oanny: some kind of conspiracy was on the go. Alec had started smiling but not at anybody in particular. Fucking carry on. Oanny shook his head and grunted unintelligibly.

What's up with you? asked Alec.

What's up with me? Nothing up with me.

Glad to hear it . . . A moment later Alec began to footer with the tip of his cigarette, showing great concentration, whistling under his breath. And Victor had turned his head away. Christ! Oanny shook his head again and said:

Okay. How much?

What?

Fine, aye, you've made me ask.

Ask what? said Alec. What you talking about?

Aw forget it, forget it.

Naw, I thought you said how much or something . . . Alec's forehead creased. Fat Stanley was now openly grinning. And Alec added: How much for what?

Oanny glared at him. The doggie in the fucking window! He dragged deeply on his cigarette and shifted on his chair, staring in the direction of the serving hatch in the snacks area. Any of yous got a drink left? he muttered.

You've done it all! replied Victor.

Aw aye, aye, I've done it all, on my tod, aye, I swallowed the whole fucking lot.

Near enough.

Oanny turned and he stared at Victor.

Naw, said Alec, if you hadnt fallen asleep you'd have seen for yourself.

Thanks.

Alec's right, murmured Victor.

Is he? Aw good. Good for Alec. I'm glad to hear it. Who's fucking talking to you anyway? It's Alec I'm talking to, no fucking you. Alright? Oanny frowned across at Alec: All I asked was how much we lifted.

Fair enough. And all I'm asking is how much you put in the kitty?

What? Oanny sat back in the chair. How much had he put in the kitty? He stopped himself searching his pockets again. How much had he put in the kitty? In the kitty? How much? What kind of a fucking question was that? He glanced sideways at Alec. It could not be a real question. Surely no. He scowled and made as though to say something but his attention was diverted by Fat Stanley who had begun wheezing in that way he had.

Eh? asked Alec.

Oanny looked at him and grinned. Fuck off!

The other three laughed loudly. But it subsided soon and Alec lifted the crushed cigarette packet and attempted to get it standing upright. He tried again, watched by the other three. He began smiling. Fat Stanley was also smiling. Oanny snorted: I was beginning to think you'd lost your touch!

Were you! Alec grinned.

Can you blame me? I mean when was the last time you got us a turn?

Fuck the last time Oanny this is this time.

Aw aye, I know.

Victor nodded. You want to have seen it Oanny we cleaned the fucking school.

What?

Magic by the way. I've no seen anything like it for ages.

Every hand he was getting, continued Fat Stanley. Naturals all the time. Must've done near a 10-timer!

Eight just, said Alec.

Jesus! Oanny shook his head, smiled.

Two hundred and twenty . . . Alec sniffed, inhaled and exhaled smoke.

Ho! Ya beauty! Oanny slapped the palms of his hands together, his eyebrows raised. But before anything further was said a minor disturbance broke out at the serving hatch. Somebody was bawling about soup. A drunk. Ellen had reached through from the kitchen, placing four bowls on the counter. That soup's already ordered! she was shouting and then she slammed down the hatch. The drunk still stood there staring at the bowls of soup then staring at the folk sitting nearest him. One of them was Tommy Rollo, the guy who managed the place and dealt the cards. Away home son, he said.

Naw, said the drunk. It's no fucking right so it's no. I was wanting soup and she wouldnt give me it and then . . . He waved his hand at the four bowls, just as Fat Stanley and Victor appeared at his elbow.

Pardon me, said Fat Stanley while he lifted two of the bowls and passed them to Victor, lifted the other two for himself. The pair of them returned the way they had come.

It's no fucking right, muttered the drunk.

Mind your language, said Tommy Rollo.

The kitchen door opened and Ellen came out, pulling on her coat over her shoulders.

Heh missis, said the drunk, a bowl of soup eh?

Away and get your bloody wife to make it. What do you think I'm just here to cater to the likes of you! Ellen glared.

He looked at her. Aw hen, he said, no need for that.

She shook her head.

Look son, called Tommy Rollo, we're no in the mood. Ellen stops when the cards stop. You should know that by now.

A few of the men at the two bench-type tables muttered their agreement. Ellen had walked to sit down on the chair next to Rollo and he poured her a glass of gin from a half bottle of Gordon's. The drunk waited a moment then walked in a purposeful stride to the exit. As soon as he had gone an elderly man in a khaki-coloured trenchcoat cried: That was telling him Ellen!

She ignored him. She sipped at the gin, snapped open her handbag and got a tipped cigarette out, gave herself a light.

*

The rain was no longer falling when they came downstairs and out through the close onto the pavement but the ground was still wet and there were many puddles around. Considering the time of night the city was busy. But it was a Friday and young folk were heading home from the dancing or whatever. Few taxis were available and almost everybody seemed to be heading in the direction of George Square. From here the all-night buses departed hourly.

The Square itself was brightly lit. The Christmas decorations had yet to be dismantled. There was a lot of hustle and bustle. Queues of folk lined the different bus stops; some were in uniform, mainly transport workers going home off backshift. A couple of guys were touting razor blades and other things, plus the newpaper vendors. Girls stood alone, in couples, in groups, as also the youths watching them – some speaking in really loud voices. Now and again policemen strolled by in pairs, gloved hands behind their backs, occasionally pausing to chat to bus inspectors. A newspaper vendor exchanged words with Tommy Rollo and Ellen and he gave them a *Daily Record* without taking money for it. When Alec bought one he winked and said, I thought you'd have landed in Majorca by this time!

Alec smiled slightly, glanced at the headlines before folding the paper away into his side coat pocket. As they continued along the newspaper man called: Yous going up the Duke?

Aye! replied Fat Stanley.

Maybe see yous later on!

No if we see you first, grunted Oanny.

Fat Stanley grinned. He's no that bad, he added.

Fucking idiot, muttered Oanny.

Alec had stepped on a bit and was walking with Rollo and Ellen. They cut down a side street and about twenty yards along a cobbled lane. It was quite dark, light glinting on the cobbles occasionally. Rollo pressed the doorbell and the chime rang out inside. When the door opened the guy behind it greeted Rollo and Ellen and smiled at Alec: Long time no see!

He ignored Fat Stanley and Victor. But when he noticed Oanny bringing up the rear he beckoned to him and whispered, The least bit of argy bargy and you're out the fucking door.

What . . .

You heard.

Oanny squinted at him. He saw Alec inside the lobby gesticulating at him and he shrugged and strolled past the doorman, accompanying Alec down the corridor and into the main gaming area of the club, but he continued on alone, into the wee room where the coffee and food were to be had. There was nobody inside it. He moved to one of the tables towards the centre, and he sighed as he sat down.

*

With the carpets and general decoration, plus the green baize on the tables, there was little resemblance between the Duke and the last place. But at one time you could have bought a full meal up there as well. Ellen kept complaining that the profit she made on the soup and bread barely repaid her outlay but maybe if she tried a wee bit harder, put on a variety – a plate of egg and chips for instance would not take much sweat – then she would get a better turn out it. And anyway, how much did it actually cost to set up a few big pots of soup! Pennies. The place had definitely deteriorated and it was Rollo himself who had to accept most of the blame. Rumour had it his licence was not going to be renewed and this was given as the reason how come he was no longer bothering. If it had been Oanny's club he would have turfed out the riff-raff right away, and that was just for starters. Rollo never seemed to worry about the number of dossers who used the place. They only turned up for a heat and a bowl of soup and to see what the fuck they could beg on the side. What amused Oanny was the way they all materialized just in time for the last couple of hands at chemmy, especially if there had been the one big winner like this evening. This was because usually a big winner chipped a couple of quid – a fiver sometimes – into the centre of the horseshoe table once the play had finished. Rollo took the dough and he dealt a card to everybody standing round the table, first jack lifted the money. It was supposed to go to a genuine loser but half the time some fucking wino ended up getting it. Now apart from giving somebody the taxi-fare home the thing had another purpose, it was to stop the big winners getting pestered by guys looking for the busfare. It worked to some extent but subtleties like this never bothered the real down-and-outs – especially when it was a stranger had won most of the dough, it was like flies round shite watching them. People could get desperate. And walking home was like that when it was the middle of winter, fucking murder polis so it was. Oanny hated being in that situation and it did not happen too often. His habit was to fall asleep shortly after arrival in Rollo's and when he woke up the losers were usually hanging about giving their post-mortems on the night's play. It was rare for him not to have kept the busfare once the kitty had been collected. It was even more rare for him to be tempted into having a go himself on the table. To tell the truth, punting was beginning to bore him. If Alec was going through a bad spell he would pass the cards on to somebody else to play for a while. Oanny used to be the second string. But not any longer. And because Fat Stanley showed his excitement too much Alec had started passing the cards onto Victor. This was right up Victor's alley. But what Alec never seemed to appreciate was that the cunt was every bit as excitable as Fat Stanley, he just did not seem to show it too much. But if you knew him; if you knew him you could see he was a bundle of shakes and twitches.

Oanny rose from his chair a little, enough to see through the glass partition, but it was difficult to distinguish things. No sounds from the gaming section reached into here either. But he could see that only one game of poker was in progress. That was good. Settling onto the chair again he lifted the teacup and stared into it, drank down what was left in it. He brought the halfbottle of vodka out from his inside coat pocket and poured himself another, adding a wee drop of lemonade from the bottle he had lying on the table. What a carry on everything was! He shook his head.

You talking to yourself?

It was the doorman. He must have come in on his tiptoes. He was staring at Oanny and had not spoken as he had as a joke. You're sitting there talking to yourself, he said.

Am I?

Aye.

That's good.

Some people wouldnt think so.

Ach away and give us peace!

Peace? If you wanted peace you wouldnt be sitting about here at all hours!

Oanny frowned at him but then he gestured with the halfbottle: Want a voddy?

Naw, I dont want a voddy.

Good! The fucking price your man charges! What a carry on – a fiver? For a fucking halfbottle!

Well if you dont fucking like it!

Oanny shook his head. He glanced about, opened the new packet of cigarettes and he offered one to the doorman as an afterthought. Each lighted his own. Then Oanny swallowed too big a mouthful of the alcohol and he shuddered and dragged immediately on his cigarette, keeping the smoke down inside his lungs for a longer period than normal.

He put the bottle back in the inside pocket again. He would have to forget about it being there otherwise he could end up doing it in, without even noticing! He shook his head and glanced up. But the doorman had vanished.

He got to his feet, intending to go through and see what was what in the poker but he went for a piss instead. On the return he stopped by the small group of spectators but when Victor chanced to look across he kept on walking, back into the snacks room and onto the same chair as before.

It was enough to have shown his face, just so they would know he was still compos mentis. And anyway, what was the point in spectating? It was only a game of stud and he knew that inside out and back to front. It was a good skilful game mind you – but so was chess, and Oanny would not have watched that either. He knew Alec was doing okay, just seeing Victor's face was enough. Although it was one of those wee surprising things about life that occasionally Oanny could get feelings. It was the same when he was married. He always seemed to know in advance when something was going to happen. It annoyed Doreen. She used to fucking blow her top! Oanny grinned. But it was true, he could get these feelings. In punting it had to do with luck and hunches and that kind of thing. You could sense something was going right. You walked up to back your dog and suddenly you knew it made no difference which one you selected because whatever it was it would fucking guy in, it was a stonewall certainty. Your luck was in and that was that.

And vice versa as well of course. There were times nothing went right. You punt a dozen odds-on chances in a row and each one of them would fucking run backwards. Your luck was out, end of story. The shrewd thing was to get that feeling and use it properly, know when it was best to call a halt, or best to stay with it to the very last. The way Alec was going for instance he had to stay with it and then know that exact moment to get up and call it quits. That was the hard part.

Oanny crushed out the cigarette he had been smoking and folded his arms, leaning them on the edge of the table. It was typical how Victor was the one to see him look in on the game. George Raft with the dirty shirt. What was interesting was how come he had managed to wangle himself in on the company. He just seemed to turn up one time and tag along. Then suddenly he was there every Friday night, up in the usual place at Ashfield. Nobody even knew where the fuck he lived. Maybe he was dossing. He knew an awful lot of the riff-raff. So did Oanny right enough! But you could not help getting to know them when you saw them once or twice every week. Even if you never acknowledged them they still liked to say hello, just to kid on they knew you, in case they wanted to nip you for a couple of bob in the future. Bastards. That was a good point about Victor, you had to admit it, he was not a beggar. That was one thing you had to admit. But where did he stay? Imagine not even knowing where the cunt stayed! And there was no way of finding out, not unless you just came right out and asked him. And how could you do that? Some sort of conversation would have to be on the go first of all and Victor never got involved in conversations, especially not with Oanny. What a carry on it was.

*

Fat Stanley grinned as he sat down facing him across the table. He nodded at the halfbottle of vodka: Any of it left?

What . . .

The vodka, any of it left? Fat Stanley grinned.

Aye . . .

It's for Alec. Fat Stanley watched Oanny pour some into another cup and add a fair proportion of lemonade. When Oanny was putting the halfbottle away into his inside coat pocket the other man added, Eh – what about Victor, should we give him one as well?

I suppose so . . . Oanny shook his head, reached for another cup and poured in a tiny amount and then added a good proportion of lemonade, and muttered, The cunt'll no notice anyway! He glanced at Fat Stanley: You should've told him to come and get it himself!

Ach Oanny, you know what like he is!

Aye, no fucking brains!

Fat Stanley chuckled. Naw, he said, but he likes watching the game.

I know he likes watching the game Stanley. Well I'll tell you, he can watch it till fucking doomsday for all the good it'll do him cause he'll never make a fucking poker player. I mean you ever seen him fucking twitching! Poker by fuck! Couldnt play ludo that cunt!

Ah he's no that bad.

Your trouble is you're too soft.

Fat Stanley raised his eyebrows and smiled while lifting the two teacups. No coming ben? he asked.

In a minute.

It's good. Some rare hands coming out.

Oanny shrugged. Either we win or we dont, it's as simple as that Stanley. Who's all playing?

McArthur and big Dessy, Billy Hendrie, the Ragman . . .

Oanny nodded. How's Alec doing anyway?

Och up and down, up and down.

Early days. Only takes a couple of good pots and we'll be well away.

Fat Stanley smiled. Coming then?

In a minute.

Right you are . . . He headed back through towards the gaming area. After a moment Oanny took the halfbottle out again and he checked the amount remaining. He continued to read the label then sniffed and returned it into the inside pocket. He lighted another cigarette and exhaled onto the table-top, scattering crumbs from the surface.

*

The sound of people talking quite loudly; somebody laughing. The poker had finished. And the main lighting was now on in the gaming area. Alec was a winner. Oanny would have bet money on it. He was standing central to the company and although he was not speaking the ones who were made a point of including him in the general conversation. When Oanny appeared a few of them had exchanged greetings with him. He took out the cigarettes and offered them about. The manager of the club was a guy in late middle age by the name of James Millar. He had nodded to Oanny without any comment, friendly enough but keeping his distance. Now he signalled to the doorman and together they left to stick on some coffee and knock up a few sandwiches. When the kitchen door shut the Ragman said, Well Oanny, dont see much of you these days.

The way that doorman was acting I thought I was barred!

Aye, he's keen.

Keen! Oanny rubbed his hands together, exhaled a puff of smoke. How's business? he asked.

Aw no bad no bad, surviving.

Good.

Heh Oanny, called Billy Hendrie, ever hear anything of the Ghoul these days?

Some of the company laughed. In the background Victor could be seen, he stood several yards to the side of Fat Stanley and to the rear of the main poker table. Oanny chuckled: The Ghoul eh! What a man yon was!

You're no kidding! laughed Hendrie.

Last I heard he was up in the 'rigs.

That's what I heard as well, said the Ragman. The Shetlands? Oanny nodded.

I wonder if he's still into the Crown & Anchor? asked Hendrie.

What! Oanny pulled a face and the company laughed. He glanced at the Ragman and said, Mind that fucking pitch-and-toss game he set up down in Bellshill? The heavy squad ran him out of town!

The laughter again. But after a moment the Ragman answered, I dont think it was Bellshill but.

Tommy Rollo called, Naw I think you're right, I think it was somewhere else.

It was Blantyre, said Alec.

Blantyre, aye.

Oanny nodded. Blantyre, he said, that's right. A team of heavyweight boxers they sent after him. Fucking lynched him if they'd caught him!

Heh . . . Billy Hendrie glanced swiftly at the kitchen door and whispered: Mind that time he tried to get a faro bank going in here?

Millar and his brother were supposed to be away off on holiday, grinned the Ragman.

Oanny chuckled, I'd forgot all about that!

The Ragman turned to those in the company who looked as if

they had never heard about the business and he continued, No kidding ye, there was about a dozen of us, all in here one Tuesday dinnertime – dinnertime, aye! Anyway, the Ghoul's got everything set up and he's running this fucking I think man it might've been a grand bank, eh Billy?

Must've been. Maybe even one and a half.

Oanny was nodding and grinning and he said, And then the fucking door opens . . .

And in they come, said the Ragman, the two of them.

Didnt know what the hell was going on! whispered Oanny.

Naw, said the Ragman, the two of them with their mouths hanging wide open!

And then the Ghoul, said Oanny, he just gives them both a wave: how's it going, he says, sit down, yous're just in time!

The Ragman laughed loudly and so too did Oanny and Billy Hendrie. Others chuckled and smiled. And the Ragman added, You'd have to have seen it to really appreciate it. Really funny but!

Tommy Rollo called, Heh there was that other time . . .

Oanny was aware of Alec's brief signal and he nodded. Victor and Fat Stanley were already approaching the exit. Oanny gave a cheery wave to Ellen whom he saw for the first time now, sitting on her own reading a magazine. Both he and Alec bade their cheerios to the rest and minutes later were along the lane with the other two.

It was still only half past three in the morning. A taxi for hire was stationary at the traffic lights ahead but none of the four suggested taking it though it was almost a mile from the club to The Edwardian. They walked quickly, speaking sporadically. Alec giving Oanny a brief run-down on how the game had been. He had managed to double their money but overall he was a bit disappointed. At one time there used to be a lot of cash around Millar's club. Nowadays people seemed more interested in throwing it away on roulette and blackjack. Where they now headed was like that, The Edwardian, but the bonus here was its private members' room, different from other ordinary casinos.

Oanny was first to enter and he pushed open the glass door in a nonchalant manner. Three men in evening suits were inside the lobby, two were in their early twenties and the other looked in his forties. Alec stepped to the small table on which lay the large signing-in book. Is big James in? he asked.

The oldest doorman gazed at him. The other two doormen were watching Oanny, Fat Stanley and Victor.

Tell him Alec's here and wee Oanny and that. Alec sniffed and added, I was on the blower about twenty minutes ago.

The doorman relaxed and replied, I doubt if the four of yous'll get signed in.

Alec made no comment. He withdrew a new packet of cigarettes and broke the seal, crushed the cellophane wrapping and dropped it into a wastepaper bucket. The doorman had gone. When he came back he flicked open the pages of the signing-in book and got the four of them to enter in their names and also their addresses. Alec nodded to Oanny and the two of them were followed by Fat Stanley and Victor. They strolled through the casino, going the longer way round to the lounge. The place was crowded, both sexes; a lot of the women looked to be wearing very expensive outfits. Quite a few Chinese were about, all ages. They continued into the lounge where a dozen or so people were sitting on the red velvet-backed chairs.

Alec took out the *Daily Record* and began reading immediately. Fat Stanley and Victor glanced about. Oanny grinned, They dont bite.

What? said Fat Stanley.

Oanny was still grinning; he nodded at the girls.

Aw naw, said Fat Stanley. I wasnt . . .

Although the girls wore long evening gowns they obviously worked for the casino. Their dresses were low cut at the front and the back and they had long slits up the sides. They carried trays of cups and saucers and plates and also of glasses. Oanny cleared his throat, about to say something but Alec shut the newspaper abruptly and got to his feet, he palmed a few notes to Oanny and murmured, See yous later.

The three nodded.

I'll eh . . . Alec paused, smiling at a man who was standing over by the door into the casino, and he strolled across, folding the newspaper and sticking it into his coat pocket. The man wore an evening suit and he smiled at Alec and shook him by the hand.

Oanny squinted over and waved: Tell big James I was asking for him!

Right you are Oanny, said the man.

Oanny glanced sideways at Fat Stanley and Victor, he whispered: That's wee James, his boy. He raised his eyebrows and slapped his hands together and winked: What d'yous want to drink then?

Fat Stanley smiled.

I'm serious. Oanny indicated the tiny enclosed bar. What d'yous want?

Eh . . . a bottle of beer maybe? if eh . . .

Fine. Oanny sniffed. Victor?

Eh a pint of lager?

Oanny nodded and called to one of the girls. Hey miss; could I have a pint of lager and two bottles of beer, and a wee vodka and lemonade. He grinned and added: I've got to take that vodka otherwise the lemonade goes to my head!

The girl's smile became apologetic. You need to get a meal before you can get a drink, she said.

Aw good, good. Oanny rubbed his hands together and said to Fat Stanley: Okay big yin, steak, egg and chips eh? Fancy it?

The girl was apologetic again. I think they've stopped serving now. It's past 4 o'clock.

Aw God.

I'll go and see but. The girl smiled.

Aye hen we'd appreciate that. Oanny sighed, shaking his head, gazing after the girl in an absent-minded manner.

Nice place, said Fat Stanley. The decor and that, it's nice.

Aye, said Victor.

Fat Stanley nodded. After a moment he said to Oanny, Is it a while since you've been here?

Ages. It's all changed.

Some money around though eh!

I dont know so much, said Oanny, some of the cunts sitting ben there'll hang about all night just playing that roulette for pennies.

Victor shrugged.

Fair enough, said Oanny, I'm no saying there's no money about, I'm just saying it might surprise you, that's all, that's all I'm saying. I mind once me and Alec landed in London – we'd been down at Goodwood with a couple of the boys . . . He paused as the girl appeared. She was still looking apologetic.

I'm sorry, she said then she pointed to an alcove nearby the cloakroom. You can get sandwiches in there.

Eh . . . Oanny tapped the girl on the elbow as she turned to leave. Can we still get something to drink?

Well, tea or coffee.

Aw aye. What is there no chance of eh a wee half or something?

The girl hesitated for a second; she shook her head, and added, Okay?

Fat Stanley smiled at her.

But if you just go over there somebody'll see to you for sandwiches.

Once she had gone Oanny sniffed and muttered, Those and such as those.

Och naw, said Fat Stanley, I dont think so Oanny.

Aye you better fucking believe it big yin!

Victor shook his head slightly.

You kidding? frowned Oanny.

It's no up to her, said Victor.

I'm no saying it is up to her. She could've put the word in but, that's what I'm saying.

Fat Stanley nodded. He smiled. Being honest, I dont really feel like a drink anyway.

That's no the point.

A coffee would do me, said Victor.

Aye plus the lassie was saying about sandwiches, added Fat Stanley. Eh Oanny? Is that no what she said, about sandwiches?

Oanny looked at him then he looked away.

Then Victor rose and muttered about needing a pish and went off to find the gents toilet.

Oanny sighed and patted the pockets of his jacket and coat but the halfbottle had been finished before leaving the club. He opened his cigarettes, took one out and left one beside where Victor was sitting, then said to Fat Stanley, Do you want one?

Naw.

Oanny nodded and got up. He lighted the cigarette while strolling to the alcove at the far end of the room, stuck the packet into his pocket. Another girl was behind the counter, reading a book with hard covers. She continued reading as Oanny stood there. He grinned eventually. That must be a good book! he said.

Oh, sorry.

Naw, it's alright!

Are you wanting something? The girl got up from the seat.

A wee niece of mine, he said, she was like you – nose always stuck inside a book!

The girl smiled.

What kind of sandwiches have you got then?

Well, there's only lettuce and tomato left now.

Lettuce and tomato . . .

We had roast beef and gammon earlier on.

Oanny shrugged. The lettuce and tomato'll do fine hen. It's for three. Plus two coffees and a tea – have you got tea?

Yes.

Thank God for that!

She returned with the stuff on a tray and Oanny applied the milk and sugar from the jug and bowl on the counter. He pulled out the small wad of notes.

There's no charge, said the girl.

What?

For a meal you would have to pay but sandwiches and coffee come free of charge.

Aw aye, I see. Thanks hen . . . Oanny started separating the saucers and putting the cups onto them, then he manoeuvered things about on the tray.

Can you manage? she asked.

Aye – I'm no decrepit altogether!

I wasnt meaning that. It's just that if you leave the saucers the way they were then everything'll fit till you get to the table.

Of course, aye. Oanny took the cups back off the saucers and returned the things back onto the tray. He nodded. He noticed a medium-sized bowl to the side of the counter. There was quite a lot of money inside it. Before lifting the tray he peeled two singles from the small wad and he put them in beside the rest. It was probably tips people left because the sandwiches came free. He hummed a tune while carrying the tray back to the table. The lassie was nice. But so bloody young! She hardly seemed old enough to be out at this time never mind working in a bloody casino. And these dresses they were wearing, hers was too tight, and the tops of her tits could actually be seen. It was a wonder the punters ever remembered to pick up their winnings! Not that there would be much winnings in a place like this. Take away the lassies and what did you have, one big con from top to bottom.

What you laughing at?

What?

Fat Stanley grinned whilst in the middle of munching a sandwich, a sliver of lettuce at the corner of his mouth.

Just thinking about something, replied Oanny. He gestured at the sandwich. No kidding ye but that's what Ellen should be doing I mean a lot of cunts dont fancy a bowl of fucking soup but give them a sandwich and a cup of tea and that . . . He shrugged.

I agree with you Oanny.

Plus you're killing two birds with one stone, you're cutting out the fucking riff-raff. That's what fucking draws them, the soup, they think it's the Salvation Army! Songs of fucking Praise they'll be giving us next!

Fat Stanley and Victor both grinned.

Victor stuck the last portion of his sandwich into his mouth and he munched it with his mouth shut, glancing about the room, and when he finished it he wiped his lips.

Still hungry? asked Oanny.

Who me – naw.

The lassie'd give us another couple of sandwiches.

I'm no bothered.

Oanny nodded. What about yourself Stanley?

Fat Stanley shrugged. I'm no bothered either.

Mm. Ah well. Oanny sipped at his tea, half of his sandwich still remaining on the plate. He took out his cigarettes and gave one to Victor, offered one to Fat Stanley who moved to take one, then hesitated.

Eh, d'you mind? he asked.

Course no, fuck sake here, help yourself . . . Oanny screwed his face up to avoid getting smoke in his eyes while getting his cigarette alight. Tell you something, he said, Rollo's place is getting really bad. I mind the time if you cleaned the fucking school you were talking about a monkey, and that was on a bad night.

Somebody else won as well but, apart from Alec, said Victor.

Still and all, two hundred quid, it's not much. Oanny nodded in the direction of the private members' room. And I'll tell yous something else, he said, half the cunts ben in that casino, they'll no even know there's a game of poker going on! And that's the way they want it, the house. Because poker's like chemmy, it's a punters' game. That's how you dont see a chemmy table in here cause they dont fucking allow it that's how.

No percentage, muttered Victor.

No enough of one, aye. Oanny nodded after a moment.

Fat Stanley yawned. Well . . . he said, think I'll go and have a looksee. Eh Victor?

Aye.

What about yourself Oanny?

Nah. Did Alec take that *Record* with him?

Aye.

Tch. Oanny shook his head but added: Maybe get a loan of

[110]

one off somebody. Here, he said. And he withdrew the small wad and handed it to Victor who nodded slightly, sticking it into his trouser pocket.

*

Oanny had not seen the pair enter. He glanced around the lounge. Nobody else was sitting down. Fat Stanley said, They're wanting to shut up shop.

Are they?

It's a case of hint hint.

Ah well. Oanny yawned and lifted his cigarettes and matches from the table.

That roulette! Fat Stanley grinned. No kidding ye Oanny it's hell of a fast so it is. You could lose a fortune.

Dont tell me yous fell for it!

It was blackjack I played, said Victor.

Just as deadly. It's no like fucking pontoons you know!

Victor frowned.

Oanny was opening the cigarette packet and shaking his head. He glanced at Victor as he started getting to his feet. You might know but a lot of cunts dont. They turn a blackjack and think they can take the fucking bank! I mind one time in Newcastle . . .

I know the difference.

Oanny gazed at him.

We were winning a few bob at the beginning, said Fat Stanley. Hey but see these Chinese! No kidding ye Oanny punting in scores so they were. Some of them must've been losing a bloody fortune!

Mugs! Oanny sniffed noisily. Fucking house games!

Victor cleared his throat, and he moved in the direction of the exit. Fat Stanley followed, pausing now and again to stay within a stride of Oanny. Before they arrived within earshot of the doormen Oanny tapped Fat Stanley on the side of the arm. Hey big yin, he whispered, did somebody actually say they were going to shut? I mean direct, did somebody actually tell you?

Aye.

Aw.

One of the younger doormen stood by the glass door with Victor. When he saw the other two approach he unlocked it and held it open for them.

Raining? said Oanny.

Aye, replied the doorman.

Were yous busy?

Eh, no bad.

Oanny nodded. Is this you finished for the night then?

Aye.

You'll no be sorry!

The doorman nodded. Fat Stanley and Victor were out on the pavement. The other two doormen were standing by the table with the signing-in book.

Oanny sniffed, rubbed his hands together. Aye, he said.

After a moment the doorman said, Goodnight.

The key was turned in the lock behind him. Oanny continued onto the pavement; he muttered, Bloody cold eh!

Fat Stanley nodded. He had his bunnet on now and the collar of his coat was upturned. Victor had his shoulders hunched and he shivered. Fucking freezing! he grunted and then he shuddered and spat out onto the street.

Oanny stood for a moment. He shrugged his shoulders a few times and kept his feet moving on the spot. Finally he gave a loud shiver, slapped his hands together and crossed to the opposite pavement, the other pair following. He stepped into a shop doorway and tried the doorhandle. Shut! he said.

Fat Stanley smiled briefly. He and Victor huddled in out the rain.

Oanny brought out the cigarettes, gave one to himself and Victor, one as an afterthought to Fat Stanley. Might as well take it, he added, it's the last!

Fat Stanley shrugged.

[112]

Just then the door of The Edwardian was unlocked, and the sound of cheery voices. A group of young men and women, dressed in ordinary clothes: employees – probably they had lockers to keep their evening wear in. Umbrellas were raised then they all headed along towards the high-rise car park. The door was locked behind them.

Wonder when it'll finish! said Fat Stanley.

Oanny waited a short time before answering. D'you mean the poker?

I was just wondering.

Oanny nodded.

Maybe we should've asked one of the guys on the door.

Oanny shrugged. They'll no know. It's poker Stanley, it finishes when it finishes – it's no like the club; big James and them I mean you're talking about dough, it could go on for hours!

That right?

Aye, fuck. Course. Oanny sniffed and he said, See when they told yous they were shutting, could yous no've asked if we could wait on a wee bit?

Aye . . . Fat Stanley nodded. Right enough . . .

They wouldnt've let us, muttered Victor.

Only one way of finding out.

Well you should've fucking asked then!

I'm no blaming you, said Oanny.

Aye I fucking know you're no! Hh! Victor shook his head and cleared his throat, spat onto the pavement.

Touchy bastard, grunted Oanny.

What d'you mean touchy bastard? Victor glared at him. Then he strolled to the edge of the pavement and looked for a moment at the sky. The rain had eased a little. He glared back at Oanny and shook his head again.

What's up with you? asked Oanny.

Victor spat into the gutter.

What's up with that cunt? said Oanny to Fat Stanley and he dragged deeply on the cigarette and blew the smoke harshly out the corner of his mouth.

Victor was staring at him. Oanny returned the stare. Then Victor said, You're an old man.

What's that supposed to mean?

Victor shook his head.

Eh? What's that fucking supposed to mean, I'm an old man?

Ah! Victor turned away from him.

Eh? said Oanny to Fat Stanley.

Never bother, muttered Fat Stanley.

I dont even know what he's fucking talking about!

Never bother.

Aye but I dont even know what he's fucking talking about Stanley, know what I mean!

Fat Stanley shrugged slightly. Victor was exhaling smoke, gazing in the direction away from the car park. For some minutes neither of the three spoke. Eventually Victor returned into the doorway, taking up a position close to the front.

Minutes after they had finished the cigarettes the glass door opened again, and the two younger doormen appeared and they could be heard quite distinctly, saying cheerio to somebody else – the oldest doorman probably. Then one of them noticed Oanny, Fat Stanley and Victor and he whispered something and the other one looked over. The pair continued along towards the car park and one of them laughed.

No point asking them anything! muttered Oanny. He stared after them. You wonder how they ever get a fucking job like that dont you . . .

The three of them continued sheltering in the doorway. It was Fat Stanley who broke the silence. He said: Is that the rain off?

Oanny made no answer.

Still fucking drizzling, muttered Victor.

What time does that café in the Central Station open?

Soon. How?

Aw nothing. I was just wondering . . . Fat Stanley shrugged. You any money?

Nah – couple of coppers just.

Victor nodded.

Enough for a tea, I suppose. Fat Stanley glanced at him: You skint?

Aye.

Fat Stanley glanced at Oanny but Oanny was gazing off out the doorway and seemed not to notice. And he said to Victor, Naw I was just wondering about maybe taking a wee walk or something, just to pass the time, stretch the legs and that . . ?

Victor nodded very slightly.

Then Oanny moved suddenly. I'm away, he said.

What?

I'm away home.

How d'you mean?

Ach! Oanny shook his head. This is fucking murder! He sidled past Fat Stanley, out onto the pavement. Yous two waiting on?

Victor looked at him.

Are yous?

How what're you doing? asked Fat Stanley.

I told you, I'm going home. It's a long hike and I might as well start now.

Aye but Oanny I mean . . .

Oanny shrugged. What's the fucking difference, he said. Either we win or we get fucking beat. Wait here and we'll wait forever.

Aye but what about Alec and that?

Oanny shook his head and he walked off, away from the direction of the car park, his shoulders hunched up and rounded. The other two watched him go, their heads poking out from the doorway.

THIS MAN FOR
FUCK SAKE

THIS MAN for fuck sake it was terrible seeing him walk down the edge of the pavement. If he'd wanted litter we would've given him it. The trouble is we didn't know it at the time. So all we could do was watch his progress and infer. And even under normal circumstances this is never satisfactory: it has to be readily understood the types of difficulty we laboured under. Then that rolling manoeuvre he performed while nearing the points of reference. It all looked to be going so fucking straightforward. How can you blame us? You can't, you can't fucking blame us.

HALF AN HOUR
BEFORE HE DIED

ABOUT HALF an hour before he died Mr Millar woke up, aware that he might start seeing things from out the different shapes in the bedroom, especially all these clothes hanging on the pegs on the door, their suddenly being transformed into ghastly kinds of bodies, perhaps hovering in mid air. It was not a good feeling; and having reflected on it for quite a few minutes he began dragging himself up onto his elbows to peer about the place. And his wrists felt really strange, as if they were bloodless or something, bereft of blood maybe, no blood at all to course through the veins. For a wee while he became convinced he was losing his sanity altogether, but no, it was not that, not that precisely; what it was, he saw another possibility, and it was to do with crossing the edge into a sort of madness he had to describe as 'proper' – a proper madness. And as soon as he recognized the distinction he began to feel better, definitely. Then came the crashing of a big lorry, articulated by the sound of it. Yes, it always had been a liability this, living right on top of such a busy bloody road. He was resting on his elbows still, considering all of it, how it had been so noisy, at all hours of the day and night. Terrible. He felt like shouting on the wife to come ben so's he could tell her about it, about how he felt about it, but he was feeling far too tired and he had to lie back down.

IN WITH THE DOCTOR

By ONE of those all-time flukes I landed head of the queue at the doctor's surgery. Somebody nudged me on the elbow eventually and pointed to the wee green light above the door. I laid down the magazine and walked across. The doctor opened it and said, You first this morning?

Yes sir, I says.

Yes sir! It was really incredible I could have said such a thing; I dont think I've called anybody sir in years. But the doctor took it in his stride, as if it was normal procedure; he ushered me inside, waiting to shut the door behind me. Then he walked side by side with me, leaving me at the patient's chair while he continued on round the desk to sit on his own one. He was quite a worried looking wee guy and it occurred to me he probably liked the drink too much. His face scarlet and his hair was prematurely white. He had on a white dustcoat, the kind hospital orderlies usually wear, but underneath it he was wearing an expensive three-piece suit. He sat watching me and frowned.

What's up? I says.

Aw nothing, nothing at all. Fancy a coffee?

Aye, ta, that'd be great. I sniffed and looked at the carpet while he rose to fill an electric kettle across at the sink. When he noticed me glance over he nodded. Aye, he says, this job, it's worse than you think. He grinned suddenly, he reached to plug in the kettle, then returned to the chair. I was reading that yin of Kafka's last night, 'The Country Doctor' – you read it?

Eh aye, I says.

Gives me the fucking willies . . . He shook his head: What about yourself?

Well, naw, no really.

It doesnt bother you!

Eh, no really.

He smiled. In this job you sometimes fall into the trap of thinking everybody's a doctor.

Pardon?

Naw, he says, you start talking to folk as if they're doctors.

Aw aye.

He frowned and turned to gaze at the electric kettle, he began muttering unintelligibly. Then he says, Probably I stuck in too much water and jammed the fucking thing! He shook his head and sighed loudly but it sounded a wee bit false. He got up off his seat and went to the window, he raised it and put his head out, and he whistled: Whsshhle whhssht!

The next thing the young lassie who works in the snackbar appeared. Her name was Brenda and she was roundabout 18, 19. Blonde-haired, but sometimes a bit sharp-tongued for my liking. He says to her, A piece on sausage hen, and a cup of coffee. Then he glanced at me: What about yourself?

Naw, no thanks.

He shrugged. Hey I hope it's ready the now Brenda!

Aye it's ready the now! she says.

Ah you're a lifesaver, a lifesaver!

So they tell me, she says.

He left the window ajar while she was away. The snackbar was parked permanently in the waste ground next to the surgery and it wasnt long till she reappeared. When she gives him the stuff she says, You can hand me the money in later on.

Aye alright.

I could hardly believe my ears. And I was thinking to myself, Aye ya bastard! if you werent a doctor! Frankly, I was beginning to get annoyed. Here he was having a teabreak and ben the room a pile of folk was sitting there waiting. And then another thing started annoying me as well. How come he was taking me into his confidence like this? At best it seemed as if he was making a hell of a lot of assumptions about me, and I didnt like it very much.

The kettle started boiling. He says to me: You sure you dont fancy a coffee?

Positive. Look eh I'm in cause of my back . . .

He nodded; he sniffed, then he took a bite of his piece. What is it sore? he says.

Sore? I says, It's fucking killing me!

Hh! He continued chewing the food, gazing at me occasionally; he was waiting for me to say something else. I shrugged: I think maybe it's caused by the damp.

He nodded. His attention wandered to the window then he sat to the front and glanced upwards and sideways, and indicated a framed certificate hanging on the wall. I was a mature student at Uni, he says. And he fingered the lapels of his dustcoat. I came late to this . . . I started only about three years ago. He shook his head and sighed. Ah Christ, it has to be said; to a fairly big extent you've got to describe this as a young man's job.

Mmm.

Aye, he says, truly, a young man's job.

Well, right enough, it needs a lot of training.

Naw but it's no just that. He grimaced at me and stared at his piece; he bit a mouthful and chewed, then drank a mouthful of coffee. He sighed again and he says: You married?

Eh, yes and no.

Separated?

I shrugged.

Ah – same as myself, I'm divorced. Hh! He smiled: Up at Uni I got involved with this lassie and *she* found out, the missis. Bang – out the door. More or less dumped the fucking suitcase out in the middle of the street man fucking terrible. Never seen her since! No even at all these family kind of business things. It's funny, when I dont go to one she does and when I do go to one she doesnt. And we never get in touch beforehand. It's a kind of telepathy or some fucking thing! He grinned at me: This auld uncle of mine, having a laugh with me, he says he never knows whether he's coming or going, is he going to see me or is he going to see her! Makes him dizzy he says!

I nodded.

Then there's the weans.

Aw. Aye.

You know what I'm talking about?

Aye.

Two I've got; how about yourself?

Four.

Four! Christ, aye, you do know what I'm talking about!

I shrugged.

But my two, he says, my two – aye, they're fine, they're alright. He began chuckling: Aye, they're alright.

I nodded.

Nice weans. I miss no seeing them. He frowned suddenly and leaned forwards. What was I talking about there?

Eh . . .

He carried on staring at me, waiting for me to remember. To be honest, I was kidding on I didnt know because I was hoping if he never found out he would get ahead with the job in hand. But he started getting fucking really strained and you could see he was really intent on finding out so I says: Look eh, I think it was something to do with women.

Aw aye Christ aye so it was. He nodded . . . Naw, I was just going to say, this job man, the way you feel at the end of the day it's well nigh fucking impossible I mean if you're wanting to meet the fair sex. You're just – you're knackered, simple as that; you just dont want to go out anywhere. I mean I've got this colleague and he was telling me I should join one of these singles clubs. What he was saying, he was saying it would just save all the sweat of that initial carry on, the introductions and so forth.

He paused there, looking at me, awaiting my reaction. Then he says: I'm no sure but, to be honest, whether I fancy the idea. You hear these stories . . .

And he paused again, watching me. Eventually I nodded.

Okay, he says, so it's your back.

Well aye, sometimes it gets really achy.

Mmm . . . aches and pains, aches and pains . . . He lapsed into the sort of silence that lets you see he was miles away. There was one wee bit of bread left on his serviette and his fingers just picked it up and let it fall, picked it up and let it fall. Then he snorted and shook his head, he smiled at me: Kafka! From what I hear he was setting out to write this straightforward Chekov type doctor yarn. And what happens! Naw, he laughed briefly. I've had my bellyful of country fucking doctors!

Mm.

Aye, Christ, I was down in Galloway for a bit of my time. And I'll tell you something man I dont want to see another blade of grass. It was funny at first, all the gossip and the rest of it; then after a while you got used to it. Used to it! And I mean once you're fucking used to it you're . . .! Hh!

He shook his head and pursed his lips, dabbed at his mouth with the serviette, swallowed the last of his coffee. He gestured at the door: Many waiting?

Eh, quite a few. There might be more now right enough.

He sighed. To tell you straight, he says, they deserve better than me.

I watched him when he said it but he seemed to have spoken without any trace of irony whatsoever so I decided to reply in the same way. Look, I says, it isnt that so much; what it is, I think, really, is just that you dont seem to have the interest, I mean no really, no the way you should.

Mmm.

Well, you dont – Christ!

Naw you're right, I know. He glanced at the electric kettle. Think I'll have another coffee. What about yourself?

Eh aye, okay, fine.

Good. Heh I mean if you want a piece or something . . .? He indicated the window.

Naw, I says, it's no that long since I ate my breakfast.

I mean hh! He shook his head and laughed briefly, gazed away over my head to someplace, one hand balanced on the handle of the kettle and the other in his dustcoat pocket. To be frank with you, I only went to Uni to get involved in the ideas, metaphysics and so on, the history of the intellect, the past and the future and – aw Christ, fuck knows what else, no point talking, no point talking. Them out there in that waiting room man I mean, really, they dont understand, they dont, they dont understand. And it's no fucking for me to tell them, is it!

He patted himself on the chest to emphasize the point, then he came walking back round to sit down on his chair facing me. I nodded in reply to him but I was non-committal; there was a certain amount of elitism showing in his talk and I didnt appreciate it, not one little bit. And no just the thing itself but the way he was lumping me in the same boat as him. I felt like saying: What about them ben there man they're fucking sitting suffering!

And me and that lassie too, he was saying, me and that lassie. No kidding ye man we were just really interested in yapping on the gether – about all sorts of things, Kepler and Copernicus, and auld fucking Tycho! and we were relating it all to the painters of the period. Really interesting I mean, really. I was enjoying it Christ I've got to admit it. But that's how I fucking went there in the first place I mean – hh! Hey . . . He frowned at me: You ever read that *History of the Conflict Between Religion and Science* by John William Draper?

Eh aye, aye.

Well I'll tell you something for nothing, I think that's a great book . . . And he jabbed his finger at me as if his suspicions had been confirmed but he was still saying it anyway and I could go and take a fuck to myself.

I didnt respond except to nod vaguely. But I kept my gaze matching his. After a few moments there was a rap at the door and he went to answer it immediately. He was scowling. He said loudly: Yes?

Eh, I was just wanting that prescription renewed . . . It was a male voice.

Mm yes yes, yes, well I'm busy the now so you'll just have to wait your turn like everybody else.

Then he closed the door. He paused there for a wee while. And then he went over to the kettle and began examining it. He had forgotten to switch it on. This is why it hadnt boiled. He reached to the switch in such a way that I knew he was trying not to let me see. He gazed up at a pictorial calendar on the wall.

After a moment he turned to me: You know something, he says, a few of them still act surprised because I'm weer than the average.

Honest?

Aye, he says, smiling.

Well, I suppose that's because they're used to doctors being this and that, because they've got certain expectations about what doctors should and should not be.

Exactly. Aye. They think doctors're like the fucking polis, you've got to be 6 feet tall to get in!

I laughed with him. I says, Aye but it's probably a class thing.

Probably, aye. He frowned and glanced back at the electric kettle. Then he sniffed. What d'you work at yourself?

I'm on the broo the now.

Aw are you!

Nearly eighteen month.

What! Jesus Christ! And he stared at me, a frown beginning to appear on his face.

What's up? I says.

Pardon?

Naw I mean how come you're so surprised? Is it because I've read cunts like Kafka and John William Draper?

Naw naw, not at all, not at all.

I didnt believe him.

Naw, he says again, not at all, not at all, it's no that. It's your suit.

My suit! You kidding?

Naw, I mean, the cloth.

Ah well, aye, but I mean it's an auld yin man Christ I mean . . . There's a lot of cunts walking about with better yins than this and they're on the broo as well.

So?

So! What d'you mean fucking so?

He stared at me.

Your fucking inference, I says after a few moments, it shows you're no really in touch with what's going on.

He nodded and felt the kettle.

Look, I says, if you want to know what I really think . . . I think you're an elitist wee bastard – your attitudes.

My attitudes!

Aye your attitudes. Especially considering you were a mature student and the rest of it.

Hh! He shook his head at me, grinning sarcastically. Well, he says, that's a fucking good yin right enough. I mean dont tell me this is linked to that hoary auld fucking misconception that the vast majority of mature students are all good fucking socialists.

What?

A load of shite that – Christ, you want to have seen the cunts I met up there! He made a face at me then laughed briefly: Tell me this, he says, how come you called me sir when you walked in that door? Was it because I'm a doctor?

Naw it wasnt because you were a doctor.

Are you sure?

Naw I'm no fucking sure.

Ah.

Well how can I be I mean Christ – anyway, I was trying to figure that yin out myself, earlier on. And I dont know, I dont honestly know. I was figuring it was because you're a doctor but that cant be right cause I've met stacks of yous in my time, stacks of yous. I mean I *never* call any cunt sir!

Mm . . . The kettle began to boil at long last but he just switched it off and came back round to sit down on his chair, he was frowning at something and he looked at me, then smiled: Okay, he says, these folk ben the waiting room there, I dont see you rushing to let them in.

Pardon?

I said I dont see you rushing to let them in.

Aw well that's no fair, that's just no fair. Fuck sake I mean you've no even seen me yet!

Mmm . . . He nodded. Sore back you said?

Aye, sore back. And it's fucking genuine and all so it is.

I didnt say it wasnt.

Naw, I know, but look it really is sore I mean . . .

Okay, he says, sorry. I apologize – for the wee dig and that.

Ah well. I shrugged. Aye and fair enough, I says, I'm sitting here chatting to you when there's a lot of folk waiting to be seen and eh . . . There again but, maybe that's cause you're a doctor after all, relating it for instance to the way I said sir.

Expectations – aye, you're right, what a doctor should and should not be. That was one of the things in *The Country Doctor* I thought Kafka got terrific.

Pardon?

Ah, sorry, sorry, you'll no really know.

I nodded. Then I says, But what I was meaning there was you, being the doctor, holding the position of power, you've got to dismiss me, else I'll wind up being here for the rest of my days!

He laughed and stood up and came round to me. Just open your jacket, he says, and pull your shirt out your trousers, and your vest if you've got one on.

I did as he said and I also leaned forwards a little so's he could see properly. He used a stethoscope, and then began tapping about with something that felt like a steel mallet; and it was quite bloody sore when he kept it tapping on the same spot. Then he says, Have you got a lumpy mattress?

Even though I couldnt see his face I knew he must have been smiling, that he had been cracking a wee joke. And he says: Naw, I dont want to disappoint you!

I didnt say anything back for a minute. There was no point losing my temper. I heard him sniff and he began putting the stethoscope higher up my spine. Breathe in, he says.

I did as he told me a couple of times and when he'd finished I says: Look, believe it or not, it is genuine; I did come in here to find out if there was anything up with my back.

Aw I know, I know, it's just . . . He came round from behind me and put the stethoscope on the side of the desk. In my experience there's a lot of folk love to get told bad news about their health, it means they can lie down and die in peace, without being bothered by any cunt.

Pardon?

He only smiled in answer.

Naw, what d'you say there?

He shook his head but was still smiling. It was a really smug kind of smile and I didnt like it one little bit. I'll tell you something, I says, you're a smug wee bastard. I dont like the way you think you understand all.

Ah I know. He nodded. It is a bad habit I've picked up. He yawned and stuck his hands into his trouser pockets and he strolled to the window, swaggering slightly; and he gazed out for some time. Then he glanced round at me and squinted at his wristwatch. It's a digital, he says, you cant always see what time it is. Fucking useless as far as I'm concerned.

He continued looking at me; till it dawned on me what he was after. O pardon me, I says, you've finished.

Aye . . . He yawned again and turned back to the window.

I was actually out the door before I realized the fucking situation, crossing the floor to the exit, tucking in my vest and shirt. Hey wait a minute, I says to myself, you're no letting the cunt away with that are you? Back I went – and I was feeling as fucking annoyed as ever I did in a long time. He was standing there just inside his doorway, ushering in the next patient. Hey you, I says, wait a wee minute, I've got something to say.

You've missed your turn, he whispers.

I have not missed my turn.

Aye you have.

Naw I've no. You dismissed me before I was ready, playing your wee class games.

I was not playing any wee class games.

Aye you were.

I was not. He frowned at me and then he glared to the side of where I was standing, as though he had spotted folk trying to peer in from the waiting-room.

And the other person who was to go in to see him said: Eh doctor, excuse me . . .

The doctor shook his head. Sorry, he says, sorry, you'll just need to . . . And he grabbed me by the wrist and took me inside, shutting the door.

I removed his hand.

He was already halfway round to his seat. Okay, he was

saying, I've got no time for this sort of carry on. Just state your problem.

There isn't any problem. There's just facts, facts – statements of fact.

He nodded. He placed his elbow on the edge of his desk and dropped his chin to rest on the palm of his hand.

Okay, I says, it's all hell of a fucking boring, I know, I know. But what I really object to is the way you've made your assumptions about me, about what I am and what I believe man that's what I fucking object to, all these assumptions. But leave that aside; it's the way you've acted, no like a doctor at all. Christ sake I mean I shouldnt've had to sit here listening to all that crap when these poor cunts ben the waiting-room are getting ignored, and for all you know are literally dying – literally, dying!

He smiled and raised his head, straightened his shoulders and clasped his hands on the desk. Well, he says, you're letting me down now. I didnt expect you to come away with a chestnut like that for fuck sake I mean we're all literally dying.

Aw aye, very good.

Naw but . . . He grinned. I truly believed you had a genuine interest in the whys and wherefores of this game, that's how I've been yapping on. I mean . . . He leaned forwards: D'you think I go about offering every cunt a coffee?

You've no even fucking gave me it yet!

He frowned slightly.

I mean you offered me one two or three times but you never got round to actually fucking giving me it.

O, sorry.

It doesnt matter I mean I was only fucking taking it for politeness man Christ I wasnt even really bothered. Anyhow, I dont want this to detract from my main point and that is you, lumping me in the same boat as yourself. As far as I'm concerned you're an elitist wee shite and I fucking resent getting linked to you, to your beliefs. Okay? And the sooner we get a new doctor here the better.

Aye, and so say all of us.

Ah well you would say that wouldnt ye.

Maybe. He shrugged. It doesnt mean it's no the case. Actually I only came back to this city out a sense of duty. I hate the fucking dump to be perfectly frank about it. It was some sort of filial obligation, I wanted to impress my father – and he's fucking dead! That's the joke!

Pardon? What d'you mean?

He was dead. I was wanting to impress him and he was dead. How do you impress somebody that's dead?

You mean you knew he was dead like?

Aye. Just – one of these daft things you do. Too many fucking Hollywood movies! Naw, Christ . . . He got up and strolled to the window. Take a look out there, he says, it's a fucking disgrace. Here I am trying to run a doctor's surgery and I can hardly get fucking moving for dirt and dust and dods of garbage man blowing in the fucking door every time it gets opened for something I mean Christ sake man you're talking about that lot ben there!

And he was gesticulating at the door now with his voice raised quite high: Just tell me this, how come they dont go out there and build a fucking barricade!

What?

A barricade. They could fucking erect a barricade man to stop all the garbage blowing in the door.

I stared at him, then added: You should go and join BUPA ya cunt!

Aw thanks, thanks a lot.

Well no wonder.

Hh! He smiled. You know something? Chekov didnt even practise medicine; I mean no really.

Aye he did.

Naw he never!

He fucking did.

He didnt, I'm telling you, no really. I mean I dont even envy him because he was a brilliant writer I just fucking envy him because he got engrossed in ideas.

I dont believe you.

You ever counted up the number of doctors who became

writers and artists, and musicians? Well there's been a hell of a lot, a hell of a lot.

Okay, fine, so you think it's better being one of them than the poor cunt who has to go about curing the sick.

He was about to reply but stopped himself and he says instead: The question doesnt even interest me. At one time it did but no now, no any longer. The way I see it I have to survive as best I can and sometimes that's bound to mean doing things that upset cunts like you.

Things like sitting about gabbing when you've a waiting-room stowed out with patients.

Pardon?

You – when people're waiting to see you man you dont even fucking bother acknowledging them hardly, their existence, you dont even bother, you're quite happy just sitting here fucking complaining to me.

Who's complaining?

You are ya cunt ye. Since I came in here, you've done nothing else. You hate your job and you hate the surgery and you hate the fucking city and you wish you could spend the rest of your days just farting about gabbing like a bourgeois fucking intellectual. Well I'll tell you something, I think you've got a big chip on your shoulder and that's it, end of story.

Aw thanks, thanks a bit.

Naw, no kidding but, you're wee – at least, weer than the average – and you're a bit older than your contemporaries, the ones you went to Uni with. And you wear the wrong clothes and you drink too fucking much and your hair's prematurely white. And your wife's fucking threw you out the house for messing about with a lassie and you dont get seeing the weans as much as you'd like. And aye, also, from what I read into the situation, your sex life is nil, absolutely nil.

I stopped there but I continued looking at him. I felt it was necessary to do this because I also felt I had gone over the score in what I had said to him. But I couldnt take anything back. It was said, and that was that.

He smiled, then he put his right hand up to cover his face, as if he was trying not to break down in front of me. In fact it wasnt that at all. He looked at me very seriously and he says, I doubt if you've truly understood a single thing I've said.

Hh – well I think the very opposite. I think I understand only too well, only too fucking well.

Aw well then there's nothing more to be said.

Exactly.

If you would just tell the next patient to come ben on your way out . . .

Naw, will I fuck, do it yourself.

He smiled. I knew you'd say that, this is why I said it; in fact I've got a wee light I switch on, so you dont have to say fuck all – okay?

Aye, aye, great, that's great with me.

Good, glad to hear it . . . He nodded then sniffed and glanced down at his desk.

After a moment I says: So what've you dismissed me or what? It's hard to tell.

He looked at me in an odd way, and I knew it was what to do next was the problem.

THAT OTHER

THE PEOPLE filed into the Memorial Tower in some consternation for the culprit was still at the gate, still shrieking that horrific blasphemy.

And all the while the foolish inconsistency prevailed.

Of those involved only two individuals could even hope to be aware of its singular significance. Yet the people were now spiralling upwards, blinking.

MORE COMPLAINTS
FROM THE AMERICAN
CORRESPONDENT

JESUS CHRIST man this tramping from city to city – terrible. No pavements man just these back gardens like you got to walk right down by the edge of the road man and them big fucking doberman pinchers they're coming charging straight at you. Then the ghettos for christ sake you got all them mothers lining the streets man they're tugging at your sleeves, hey you, gies a bite of your cheeseburger. Murder polis.

WHERE BUT WHAT

AND THAT chair I had wasnt even comfy. To have tried telling her
but. Honest, she wasnt fucking interested. She preferred no to
hear. No to hear, that was her game. No to even listen. And she
didnt even kid on she was listening. She didnt bother, she didnt
even bother. I was fucking browned off I mean, worse; worse
than that. I felt like – I dont know. I'm no sure, I'm no really sure.
Something but; I felt like something, I'm no sure.

But I just carried right on sitting there, getting more and more
uncomfortable. Sometimes I couldnt even be bothered going
to the cludgie. I mean sitting there needing, just sitting there
needing, saying Fuck it, Fuck the cludgie, I'm no going, cant be
annoyed. So I dont know what like a state it is, my belly, inside it,
I dont know.

Who cares.

She did in a way I suppose but was it genuine? Naw, I dont think
so. I dont think you could really say it was, that it was genuine. It
didnt worry me but; no really. It might've at one time but that was
a long time ago. I'll tell you something; there was this mate of
mine Billy, Billy Adams. No a bad cunt. I'd known him for years.
Years! me and him'd been mates for. As long as we knew each
other, I would say, we'd been mates. So it was as long as that, but
that was a while ago.

What was I on about? Fuck knows. That back of mine too, killing
me. I used to say to her, That back of mine's fucking killing me so

it is – murder! All she did but, nodded her head, nodded her fucking head.

Another thing I did right enough I drank that tea; I drank that tea! Fucking stacks of the stuff. Till it was coming out my ears. I used to drink coffee but then I started getting this terrible heartburn so I stopped. Funny thing too about it, when I was smoking, I never used to get it; well I did right enough but it was from the actual smoking, the actual smoking I got it, no the coffee.

Yet how do I know. I dont really. Maybe it was the fucking coffee after all!

Who cares.

And you couldnt tell her anything either neither you could cause she wouldnt listen, she wouldnt listen, she wasnt interested. She could just walk past you sometimes as well, when you were talking; just fucking walk past you. You could hardly credit it. I would just sit there but, saying nothing. Say nothing, I'd say to myself, just sit there, dont fucking say a word, cause you'll regret it, just fucking sit there. And she'd walk past, walk right past, where you were sitting.

Make you laugh so it would.

Then that fucking telly! She'd have it blaring! Fucking blaring. I never watched it. Never! I never fucking watched it. Load of shite. I just used to sit there.

Lassies right enough, sometimes I used to think of lassies. Couldnt help myself. I'd just be sitting there then all of a sudden I'm on a fucking beach! Or maybe just even walking down the road, a country lane, in the middle of summer. Anything. And there's this lassie, what's she doing? she's just I dont know, just fucking walking maybe or something like that. And underneath her dress, a frock, underneath it, she's no wearing fuck all – nothing, just her frock. And that's no really got anything to do with it either because what I was thinking about I was just, it was the cloth, the way her skin just touched it, the actual cloth, the dress, you could just imagine it, the way her skin just touched it.

What I liked but was the minis. She used to get onto me about it, as if I was doing something. But I wasnt doing anything. I was just fucking looking. And even then sometimes you werent even fucking looking, cause you got used to it. You'd hardly credit that but it's true; when you think back; the way the minis were, and now they're gone, and you try and mind what like it was and you cant, no really, you cant. Sometimes as well you're seeing them on the box, old news programmes or that, and you sit back on your seat, Fuck sake, but you still cant mind, no really, what like it was, the way they were, in real life, what they actually looked like, seeing a lassie walking down the street.

Where but what! I would just be sitting there, in a wee daze, a daydream. Where but what? Sudden, I would just think it.

Naw, me and Billy, we were mates for years. Anyhow, aye, I always liked his missus. Nice looking so she was. When the minis were in she used to wear hers halfway up her arse. It annoyed him as well, it was funny. He kidded on he didnt mind but he fucking did, he did mind, he just kidded on he didnt. Sitting in the boozer maybe and in she'd come looking for him. See his face! A fucking picture. Made you laugh so it did, just seeing him. A cracking looking wee bird but, his missus. I mind too this fellow telling him that. Heh Bill, he says, quite the thing, That missus of yours, cracking looking wee bird. And Billy's face! A fucking picture. The thing about her too, his wife, she never took any fucking notice. I mean the boozer, it'd be full of cunts, all staring at her, drooling – she never fucking noticed. No like mine. She'd have fucking noticed. Nothing surer. Makes you fucking angry

[136]

as well, you've got to admit it. It annoys you. I used to, get annoyed; I used to get fucking annoyed, with her, the wife, she made me fucking angry. I used to get really fucking browned off – worse, worse, I mean worse than that, really fucking angry, it fucking

THE GUY WITH THE CRUTCH

A GANGRENOUS patch on his right leg had resulted in amputation. The people at the hospital gave him a new one which he got used to quicker than most folk in the same predicament but something happened to this new limb and now he no longer had it. For a while he moved around as best he could, making do with a walking stick of sorts; but it was not easy and he was a guy who liked travelling about the place. One morning somebody found a broken crutch and gave him it and somebody else made a cross-spar and nailed it properly down for him. This meant he was back mobile again and he used to tell folk the crutch was as adequate as anything. But eventually he stopped telling them that and soon he stopped telling them anything at all. From then on, whenever I caught sight of him, he was carrying a plastic shopper that contained most of his possessions; usually he was trudging to places over stretches of waste ground, although trudging is the wrong word because of having the crutch and so on he used to move in a rigorous and quite quick swinging motion.

UNDECIPHERED TREMORS

IN THE ensuing scramble the body will melt
into undeciphered tremors, undeciphered in consequence of its having been laid to rest some time
prior to the call. And the 'call' here must not be
regarded as figurative; it will have proceeded
from whence great difficulty is experienced in
matters of prediction. You must also recall the
state of non well-being which exists beforehand.
It is certainly the case that one has to exercise
caution in hazarding a judgment but nevertheless, nevertheless, I would say if you feel the need
to leap then by all means leap.

HE SHOULDNT'VE been at school. He was past fifteen, the same age as his da when he started work and he was ready, he knew he was ready. School was so terrible, beyond talking about, so terrible. In the history class he sat to the side of the room just keeping out of everything, not wanting to be bothered by any of them. None of it was funny at all, none of it, he just wanted away and out of it. A thing he did was stare at the desk, at a certain bit on the surface, maybe an initial, a drawing, or just a stain or blemish in the wood, just stare at it, trying to concentrate the mind right out and away. It was supposed to be possible to transfer your mind away to some different place altogether. His da told him criminals could do it, guys in jail, they could more or less transfer their mind away onto a different level; and old people did it as well, staring back into the past. Maybe some folk did it into the future like they said. Psychic powers. The line drifts out from your mind and you go onto a different level, another plane. The fourth dimension, you go through a time-warp, enter into a totally new world where everything's totally different.

Mister Chambers!

Auld Doughball was looking down at him.

Mister Chambers! Are you with us? Have you kindly consented to rejoin the fold? Mister Chambers, would you be so courteous as to indicate . . .

What was he on about? Auld Doughball – this great big plook thing on the side of his neck and it wobbled when he spoke, the vibrations from his chin and his jaws.

He just shouldnt've been at school and that was that, that was just really it, it was plain, plain, he shouldnt've been there. His da had started as an apprentice at this age. In less than a year he would be old enough to get married. Old enough to get married. Mr and Mrs Chambers. I shall take this woman as my lawful wedded wife. Tracy McCall! She really didnt fancy him but. She was in a different world. There were lies as well about her getting groped but they were lies. It made your belly turn over to even think about it. That was what they did but, the way they spoke about you. They did it with everybody. They just seemed to pick on a person and then that was that and you couldnt do anything about it. Mainly it was the lassies. They were saying about Tracy down the club you could just feel her tit and she would let you, she would kid on she wanted you to stop but didnt. They did it about anybody. The best thing was to kid on just that it didnt matter, you didnt hear it or something, just kid on you didnt hear anything and you didnt know anything about it. Lassies were like that in a way, they could start acting as if they didnt know a thing you were talking about. And it was best, it was really best.

Mister Chambers?

Yes Mister McDougall.

Do you have a grandfather?

Gary looked at him.

Does Mister Chambers have a grandfather? Class?

Auld Doughball. What was he on about with that stupid big plook on the side of his neck, he had a cheek to even speak. That sarcasm, it was really terrible. Sometimes you felt like fucking punching him right on the mouth the way he did it to you. A lot of it was the name, Mister Chambers. Other teachers as well, they loved to say it, just to say it in that really sarcastic way.

Did you have a grandfather. What was that supposed to mean? It was history about the 2nd World War right enough so that's probably what it was about, if he had a grandfather that was in it. 15 was a good age to start work. That was when his da started. And it wasnt just Gary thinking he was ready because so did his maw; and his da as well; the pair of them. He was actually bigger than his da – it was terrible saying it but he was. What age was his grandfather when he started? Maybe only fourteen. What his da was saying the other night, what was it? what his da was saying the other night, about nowadays the boys are all bigger but they've got to be younger. What was that? What did that mean? It was about them being bigger and having to stay on at school longer, to do with them no growing up or something because they dont do any work and just hang about and all that. His great-grandfather was thirteen. Thirteen years of age and out working six days a week. There was a photo of him as a boy and he was wearing a bunnet and his jacket was really tight. You could actually get married at thirteen in different parts of the world even just now. There was that new boy as well in 3c who got Lesley Denham pregnant. He was just turned fourteen and he didnt tell anybody, he just kept it to himself. A wee baby boy the lassie had and then the two of them got put into different schools. That would suit Gary, it'd be really brilliant, just getting sent to a different school away from everything. Except maybe he would end up in the same place as that guy who was after him. It was a stupid thing. In the Amusements and then just out of nothing and he had to get off his mark right away, and he was just on his own but the other guy had a couple of mates and it would've been trouble. Gary didnt want to fight him. It was stupid. He didnt like fighting anyway. Except sometimes, sometimes there was that tingle.

The desks!

Auld Doughball sitting on the edge of his stool, making a big show of watching the time then calling: Ten, nine, eight, seven, six, five, four, three, two, late as usual . . . Now just walk, just walk . . .

RRrrrinnggggg.

Hey Chanty! It was Smit.

Gary glared at him and he whispered, Shut your fucking mouth you.

Smit laughed.

Gary's face had gone red and he punched Smit hard on the shoulder. I told you before, dont you fucking call me that.

Aw come on you! Smit had stepped back and was rubbing his shoulder.

Give us a fag! said Gary.

I've no got any . . . Smit was still wincing and rubbing the shoulder.

Fucking liar! Gary turned away from him, continued along the corridor and down the stairs, banging against the tiled wall with his left shoulder on each successive step. The rest of the class were ahead now, a few of the guys going fast toward the back of the toilets for a quick drag. Gary glanced behind.

Smit stopped walking at once and called: You going for a smoke?

I thought you didnt have any fags!

I've no.

Fucking liar! Gary grabbed him by the wrist. Who's got them then?

Big Hammy, he's got twenty.

Twenty?

He might give us one.

How do you know he's got twenty?

I saw them.

Liar!

I'm no; honest.

Gary strode on through the swing doors and out across the playground, Smit coming several paces behind him. It was mobbed at the back of the toilets. Between there and the back of the school wall there was a gap of about 6 feet. On top of the wall were layers and layers of black grease which the janitors put down to stop people climbing over. Gary pushed his way through the different groups, seeing Big Hammy and the guys about halfway along. Smit was already in at a group and a guy was letting him have a drag but without leaving go the fag so that Smit wasnt even able to get a proper hold on it. Gary got in nearer to Big Hammy and he jerked his head at the cigarette he was smoking: Eh Hammy, any chance of a fag?

A fag! Big Hammy grinned, giving a look of surprise, but got him one out, and added, Dont say I'm no good to you.

You still owe me a million!

That'll be fucking right!

Gary borrowed another guy's cigarette to get a light for his own. Smit was in the background now, peering over somebody's shoulder and making a sign which Gary kidded on he didnt see, and he said to Big Hammy: Were you out last night?

Nah.

Did you watch the game on the telly?

Big Hammy shook his head briefly. Then he smiled and poked one of the boys next to Gary. If it's your fucking birthday the morrow how come you're no having a party? Eh? Big Hammy laughed at the others: I bet ye he hardly even gets a fucking bevy!

You kidding! said the guy.

We'll see, said Big Hammy.

Gary was blowing out smoke, he shut his eyes for a split second, getting that lightheaded feeling. Somebody else was saying something about the football match being played tonight, and another guy was nipping his cigarette and sticking it away and then one by one the others were finishing their smokes. On the way back he tagged behind a bit, traversing the playground in a sort of arc and making it last into the science block. Smit was by the foot of the staircase and he called. You're going to be late!

Gary didnt acknowledge him. Smit waited and when the other passed him by to walk upstairs he whispered, You dogging it this afternoon Gary?

But Gary didnt acknowledge this either. He continued walking. It was pointless encouraging Smit or you never got rid of him. At one time he spoke ordinary to him but it wasnt worth it because all he did was talk nonstop and as well as that he was always there, you couldnt get rid of him. Even at the house; he used to come up for Gary at 8 o'clock in the morning. A right idiot. He wasnt really bad, not totally bad, it was just Gary couldnt be bothered having to listen to people, it got on your nerves. And then as well having them beside you all the time, sitting at the same desk for instance, really terrible, an uncomfortable feeling, no being able to move about, having to watch your elbows, keeping them in, and your knees, having to keep them in as well in case they banged into them. Sometimes just hearing them breathe was enough. You were working away and it was silence and then you heard them breathing, and sometimes their nose, you wanted to tell them to blow their nose. Even lassies, their noses sometimes, you could hear them, no blowing them till the very last minute. It was a wonder how they did that. How did they no just blow them straight away? Unless they didnt have a hanky. And no having pockets either a lot of them, just their bags full of stuff. Sometimes you kicked it and you'd see all the piles of stuff come tumbling out, and packets of pads. That was a thing he would have hated, being a lassie, terrible. Getting periods, the blood coming out; it was caused by eggs, once they were pregnant they were fertilized. Just thinking about it was enough. And some husbands stayed in to watch the birth as well. You saw the baby covered in a jelly stuff, the face all wrinkled and purple looking and crying away unless it wasnt right and had to get smacked first by the doctor.

One of chemistry and dinner. That was a mistake, taking chemistry. He shouldnt've done it, it was even worse than music. Music was the daftest thing of the lot but too late now to drop it. There was nothing he could do except just stick it out and just think about it as a subject he was going to fail. It meant it was one less thing to worry about. He had enough on his plate. And the way they were expecting as well you'd be staying in and studying at night-time, it was beyond talking about, it wasnt even funny. That thing you did you just found something to concentrate on, anything, a wee stain or a name or anything, just so's you could concentrate your mind right away, you're running through the middle with the ball at your feet and the big defender comes sliding in and you tap it on and run round the other side and pick it up again and stop dead and let the next one go sliding by, and you're on now and just at the eighteen-yard line; there's the goalie, he's jumping from side to side and now coming rushing out with the hands up and all set to dive at your feet and then he does it and you hit the ball with a lot of swerve and it just creeps in at the far post; too easy, too easy, and you turn and give a wee wave to the crowd, not showing off about it and you just stroll back for the re-start, shaking hands a couple of times, the guys patting you on the back. And what else you've got you've got a boat, a cabin cruiser you can sail anywhere you like or a big yacht or what else, a corner kick and you're hovering about on the eighteen-yard line and when the cross comes over you meet it first time on the volley and see it go bulleting into the top righthand corner of the net; what a goal! a cracker! the keeper had no chance! no chance. And what was bad as well was how if you didnt get into the school team you were an idiot, that was you and you'd be as well just chucking it altogether. Sometimes you had to kid on you didnt even feel like playing, as if you didnt even feel like playing and werent even really interested, and when you passed the gym and saw the names on the noticeboard, always having to look just to fucking see what it was, that was terrible, it was something that was really really terrible. And his da was disappointed. You couldnt explain either. This is what was bad about it. The way it worked, if you tried to explain it, how they picked the team. They didnt even really care who got put in and who got left out. It was like favourites, they just took the ones they liked and then left out the other ones, the ones they didnt like. It wasnt even that either; they just didnt really care, it was plain. They seemed to make up their mind you were rubbish and that was that and they would just more or less never see you again or else be sarcastic all the time, treating you like an idiot, the same as Doughball McDougall and even when you got a good mark in your test they acted like it was a kind of mistake and didnt take any notice. He was totally sick of it now. He just shouldnt've been there any longer. There again but, jobs. What was he going to work at? In a garage or something, that would be good. Some of the guys that did it got motors out for the weekend and they could just drive about the place. You got your licence at 17. A motor bike would be good as well and you didnt need to wait; it was really fast and nobody to bother you, just sitting on it yourself, unless maybe you had a lassie and you just shot off into the country for an outing, or down the seaside and the two of you going in for a swim. Even with Tracy, all you did was ask her and see and if it was a good sunny day she would say aye, or else naw, if she was going out with another guy. She was in a different world but, it was all older guys, some of them left school, and her and her mates went to the pub as well sometimes. It was easier when you were a lassie – everything. You just had to stand there and just wait. But if you were a boy you had to go out, it was more difficult, you couldnt just stand there, even knowing how to start, if you were a boy, you had to start, what did you do did you just feel the tit? These things you never seem to find out properly, you're never totally sure if it's right, if the lassie's thinking you're an idiot. In one book he got seeing the guy just straight away sticks his hand up her skirt and she's so surprised she just lets him, she just lets him do it. The very thought and you had to jam your eyes shut and switch off your brain or your hardon, you jammed shut the eyes because of the pants, thinking about that and a lassie like Lesley Denham, if you got stuck into her class in a different school, you had to shut off the eyes and switch off the brain and enter into a different dimension altogether, concentrating the mind like convicts did in their jail cells, the whole world linked inside their heads and they can control their thoughts to take them where they want. The old guys who've been in for life-sentences tell them how to do it, they pass it on from man to man because otherwise they'd all crack up, they'd go crazy.

The desklids were going up. It was good it was dinnertime and you got away for a while. Imagine a school where you had to spend the dinnerhour in the classroom, where you werent allowed out.

Mr Cowan was looking at him. Gary lifted the desklid and kidded on he was shifting stuff about. Smit was over by the door and most of the other boys had left already. And the lassies as well, nearly all of them standing up and lifting their bags and things. It was terrible. Gary got up and strode to the door and right out and down the corridor, not looking back the way. One thing he was going to do as well he was going to leave by the car park because it was strictly against school rules and you got that tingle.

Heh Gary!

It was Smit. He kept walking, striding across the playground towards the car park and soon there wasnt anybody else about and he felt as if the sun was about to shine and his nerves were twanging away and he felt it right down his spine, the voice shouting: You boy! Gary laughed aloud but there was nothing, nobody around at all, the teachers in the staffroom probably. Idiots. Their life was just a joke the way they got all worked up about wee things, petty things.

Far to the side and parallel he spotted Big Hammy and the rest walking along the track. They'd be heading for the chip shop. Where was Smit? If he was coming behind it would be really hopeless. But he was not going to turn round and see because that even made it worse. And if he was following Gary was going to knock fuck out him because he was fucking sick of it, getting followed about the place, people would think he was a poof or something, the both of them, because that was what happened, they just waited their chance, just so's they could start telling stories about you. They did it with everybody. If you could manage to kid on you didnt care, that you didnt really care what they said, that was the best thing.

He was approaching the last bit of the driveway now and he paused and moved his head sideways a fraction, and he whispered quite loudly: Smit! see if you're behind me, I'll fucking batter ye.

No answer. There was nothing. Gary was walking on again. As soon as he reached the gate he turned but there was nobody at all, there was nobody stretching right back into the car park, the space was totally empty. What a sight!

Hey Chanty!

Gary turned and started walking. It was Big Hammy had shouted on him; he'd be wanting to know if Gary was going to the chip shop or what was he doing, because he always liked to know what people were doing and he knew Gary might be dogging the afternoon. Some of them thought Gary was good because of the way he went about on his own, no really bothering about the rest and just going away and dogging it whenever he felt like it. There were places to hang out if you had dough but sometimes right enough he felt it would be better if somebody was there as well, along with him. Big Hammy and a couple of the others waved at him but he ignored them and kidded on he hadnt seen them and they shouted again, Hey Chanty! Gary – hey Gary!

He kept on walking.

The fish van was at the corner of his street. Three women were standing down from the step-up, talking together. One of them said, There's Gary.

Even Gary, he was getting sick of that. What was worse? Gary or Chanty or Mister Chambers? Or Chamby? Chanty Chamby.

He had the doorkey in his hand on arriving at his landing but he could see a light on in the lobby. His da was in. Usually he was at this time of the day but sometimes he wasnt, Thursdays and Fridays especially.

He shut the door, went into his own room immediately and changed his socks. Recently he'd been making a point of looking after his feet. He was reading about this guy John Brady who was an athlete and raced for England and something happened which led to his feet, something about his feet, no being right for running because of it, whatever it was, and he was under doctor's orders to stay away from all sports or games, and apparently it seems even if he had been taking regular care of them it would've been okay.

His da was at the kitchen table reading the newspaper, he glanced up to say: Alright Gary!

Hullo da.

If you fancy making scrambled eggs . . .

Nah, I'll just have some toast and cheese. You wanting anything?

Eh . . . His da frowned a moment. Ayé, he said, okay, I'll take a slice.

Gary pulled open the cupboard door for the loaf of bread. He felt like slamming the thing shut. That was what really fucking annoyed you when you came home, him just sitting there and you actually having to do the cooking. It was as if you just came home from school to make him his dinner. You would have been better off no bothering. He stuck the loaf back into the cupboard, went to the fridge. The margarine and cheese were next to each other. But he wasnt going to make anything now, fuck it, he wasnt going to make it, and he slammed shut the fridge door and stepped back to the cupboard. I'm just making a piece and jam, he said, I'm no bothering with toast and cheese.

Mm.

Will I make you one as well?

What . .? His da gazed at him over the top of the page.

D'you want a piece on jam? I'm no making toast and cheese.

His da frowned: A piece on jam?

I'm in a hurry so I'm no bothering with the toast.

Okay, aye. You making tea?

Naw.

His da nodded. Then he said, Something bothering you?

Gary shook his head, he swivelled the lid off the jar, began spreading the jam.

Stick the water on.

Gary filled the kettle and plugged it in without answering. He poured himself a mugful of milk, handed a piece to his da and started eating the first of the two he had made himself. He stood by the sink, staring out the window, the sky totally grey, a line of blackbirds sitting along the gutter of the roof opposite. Thirty-eight pence lay on the window sill. And that was it, he was definitely dogging it now. He waited for the kettle to boil then collected the coins with one hand while footering with the plug and the kettle with the other. Is it coffee you're wanting? he asked his da, and he slipped the coins into his pocket when the pages rustled. His da wasnt thick. The very opposite. It was just Gary knew how to work things. This beard his da had started recently and parts of it were whitish. Is it coffee? Gary asked.

See the 'Gers are playing the night!

Aye.

The Hibs!

Hibs?

Be a good game.

Aye . . . Gary felt his heart thumping and that feeling all over, nearly as if he was walking on a pile of cushions. He bit into the crust of his own slice and munched it, nodding in reply to the idea of Rangers and Hibs. Rangers and Hibs. He nodded, munching the bread, the coins in his pocket and what if his da knew they were there, if he knew but just wasnt saying anything. It was one of these things you could imagine, terrible. But he wasnt going to put them back because something would go wrong and he'd definitely get caught, unless he put them somewhere else, ben the living room maybe, on the mantelpiece.

His da was okay. No he wasnt, he was daft. Not an idiot but, just daft. Gary felt sorry for him, sitting about the house all day, and he had made that remark to the maw last week, Look at my beard! going white at 36 years of age! No even forty yet. But it wasnt funny, it never came out right and the maw as well, her face, you didnt know what she was thinking. The whole thing was rubbish. Hey Da!

Mm.

See granpa, what age was he when he left school?

Granpa . . . Same as me, fifteen.

Fifteen, I thought he was fourteen.

Naw, that was my granpa. Who you talking about?

My granpa, aye.

Mm, he was fifteen. My own granpa was fourteen.

Gary bit another mouthful of bread. Who was it was thirteen then?

Aw aye, that was my uncle, the one that got killed – well, he was my great uncle really, my granpa's brother, his big brother. We've got a photo of him when he was a wee boy.

Is that the one he's wearing a bunnet?

Gary's da nodded, smiling. That's the one, he said. You see him standing at a big wall; well that's the place he worked, it was a bottling factory down near Brigton Cross. I mind my granpa taking me and showing me the spot. He was just a boy when it happened and he used to tell me about it. That's your great grandfather . . . Gary's da laughed: They called him Wee Tam. He was a Clyde man, sometimes he took me with him to watch them when they were playing at home. That's your great grandfather, and your great uncle, that was his big brother – naw, your great great uncle, the wee boy that got killed; it gets complicated.

Gary had spooned the coffee into the cup; he poured in the boiling water, the milk, the sugar.

What was it you were asking? said his da, when Gary passed him the cup.

Nothing. I was just wondering but, if it was alright if I stayed off this afternoon.

How what's up?

Nothing.

His da nodded, he sipped at the coffee and reached for his tobacco tin. I'll tell you something Gary, he said, I think it's daft dogging school if you've no got a reason. I mean you'll never learn anything that way. You've got to try.

Alright, I'll go.

I'm no saying that.

Gary was back by the cupboard and lifting the mug of milk to gulp the rest of it down. The newspaper was rustling. His belly felt as if it was tied in knots; he wished he had a smoke, he could have a smoke. He glanced out the window and then into the sink, swallowed the last drips of milk and rinsed out the mug, upturned it on the draining board.

All I'm saying is it's best if there's a reason. What is it you've got on? said his da.

English and maths but it doesnt matter.

His da smiled.

Gary stared at him.

I used to hate them as well!

I dont hate them, said Gary. He turned and lifted the second slice of bread and jam, almost all of it remained, he opened the cupboard and threw it inside, shut the door. I'm away, he said.

You in the huff now?

What?

Nothing.

Gary sniffed.

His da munched the piece on jam, still looking at the newspaper.

I'm no in the huff . . . Gary stared at his da and continued to stand there by the cupboard, leaning his elbow on the edge of the worktop.

I cant just tell you to dog school you know.

Nobody's asking you to.

Fine then cause I'm no going to.

Gary opened and closed the cupboard door and he muttered, I wish maw still came home for dinner.

His da said nothing.

She used to make soup and that.

Gary! I've told you umpteen times, you can go to the bloody dinner-school whenever you like.

I dont want to go to the dinner-school.

His da looked at him.

Gary walked to the door into the lobby.

You going back to school?

Aye.

Fine.

He was out on the landing with the front door shut, before remembering about the thirty-eight pence. But he was glad he had lifted it. He thumped down the stairs and out through the close. Two lassies were across the street laughing at him. They were at St Joseph's Catholic school and were in 3rd year. One of them was supposed to fancy him or she had done when they were going to the club but probably she didnt now because he hadnt done anything. She was one of these lassies that looked really wee for her age and her legs were really thin plus as well she was always laughing all the time and it sounded daft. He glanced across and stopped walking for a count of three. He still had three quarters left of the fag Big Hammy had given him. He called over: Yous got a match at all?

They laughed and strode away with their arms linked together. That was actually a daft thing to do and showed the difference between them and somebody who was more grown up – anybody, no just Tracy, they would have said aye or naw or something but no just a silly laugh. That was how if he had done something, if he had met her after school, what would've happened? where would they've went? Imagine any of the guys seeing him! No chance. She was just too wee, or she acted too wee; weanish, too weanish. Tracy's figure was like a woman, it was how she got into pubs. She just didnt fancy him but. It was the truth and she had made it plain. She just didnt fancy him. You wondered how that happened. She didnt even seem to see him and sometimes he was staring right at her, it was funny. But that was the same with the rest of them, it was just older guys she was interested in.

Hey Chanty! It was Smit. He had appeared from a close.

Gary scowled at him: What you wanting ya wee bastard?

Any fags?

Gary continued walking.

Heh Gary that bird there, that Catholic, she fancies you.

Shut your fucking mouth.

Smit laughed. She's no got any diddies!

What did you say there! Gary had stopped dead and he grabbed Smit and punched him hard on the shoulder.

Oh ya bastard . . . Smit swung round with his boot and caught Gary just below the right knee.

Ya wee . . . Gary clenched his teeth and rubbed at it.

You shouldnt've fucking done that! shouted Smit.

Gary was glaring at him and his breath came harshly: I'm going to fucking batter you if ye keep annoying me – alright!

Smit stood where he was. And Gary lunged at him and got him by the neck and he bunched his left fist close to his face. Alright! he cried.

Take your hands off! shouted Smit.

A man in overalls was watching them from a shop doorway up ahead.

Gary let him go after a moment. I'm just warning you, he muttered.

Aye well just take your hands off!

Go and fucking leave us alone then! cried Gary.

Ya bastard, said Smit.

Gary stood with his hands on his hips then he cleared his throat and spat at the ground to the side of Smit and Smit moved off, taking the first steps back the way. Gary remained until a distance of about 30 yards separated them.

He went into the shop and bought a box of matches. Smit had disappeared when he came out. Freedom at last.

INCIDENT ON
A WINDSWEPT BEACH

A MAN walked out of the sea one February morning dressed in a boilersuit & bunnet, and wearing a tartan scarf which had been tucked crosswise under each oxter to be fastened by a safety-pin at a point roughly centre of his shoulder blades; from his neck swung a pair of heavy boots whose laces were knotted together. He brought what must have been a waterproof tobacco-pouch out from a pocket, because when he had rolled a smoke he lighted the thing using a kind of Zippo (also from the pouch) and puffed upon it with an obvious relish. It was an astonishing spectacle.

Hastening over to him I exclaimed: Christ Almighty jimmy, where've you come from?

Back there, he muttered oddly and made to proceed on his path.

At least let me give you a pair of socks! I said. Bu. he shook his head. No . . . I'm not supposed to.

A ROLLING MACHINE

SANDY HAD been leading me around all morning in a desire to impress – to interest me in him and in this place where he earned his living, also to show his workmates that here he was with his very own learner. He explained various workings and techniques of the machines and asked if I had any queries but not to worry if I didnt because at this stage it was unlikely though I would soon become familiar with it all, just so long as I took it easy and watched everything closely. Gradually he was building to the climax of his own machine. Here I was to learn initially. Up and down he strode patting its parts and referring to it as her and she as if it was a bus or an old-fashioned sailing ship. She wont let you down Jimmy is the sort of stuff he was giving me. The machine was approximately twenty-five feet in length and was always requiring attention from the black squad; but even so, it could produce the finest quality goods of the entire department when running to her true form. Placing me to the side in such a way that I could have an unrestricted view he kicked her off. He was trying hard not to look too pleased with himself. Every now and then he shifted stance to ensure I was studying his move-ments. His foot was going on the pedal while his right hand was holding the wooden peg-like instrument through which he played the coiled wire between the middle and forefingers of his left hand out onto the rolling section of the apparatus. At one point he turned to make a comment but a knot had appeared on the wire, jamming on the wooden instrument and ripping off the top end of his thumb while the machine continued the rolling operation and out of the fleshy mess spiralled a hair-thin substance like thread being unrolled from a bobbin somewhere inside the palm, and it was running parallel to the wire from the coil. Sandy's eyes were gazing at me in a kind of astonished embarrassment until eventually he collapsed, just a moment before one of his workmates elbowed me clear in order to reach the trip-safety-rail.

THE RED COCKATOOS

THAT MOMENT after sunrise I saw the troop of figures appear, then round the head of the loch, the Red Cockatoos. I was totally enraptured of the scene, unable to even reflect on how my own feelings were. The morning was so mild, so very mild and clear, perhaps the most mild and most clear of the entire summer. There too was the strange purity of air, almost an emanation from the pure loch water. If this scene could have reminded me of anything it could only have been of the Horsemen of Harris as witnessed by Martin Martin more than two hundred years ago. And yet, perhaps I speak only of the day itself, the actual atmosphere, the light and aural texture, for what could ever be likened to the figures I was now seeing? I was an intruder, and beholding a vision so awful that at once I myself had been transformed into victim. I could see them distinctly, the troop of almost thirty, the red circles of their faces, the unquiet, seeming to contain a frenzy. And a figure had moved too quickly and bumped into the figure in front and the laughter of the pair was immediate, and nervous too, scarcely controlled at all, revealing the anticipation of an event so horrible that hackles arose on the back of my neck, the hairs rising, on the back of my neck; and a shiver crossed my shoulders, I was having to fight hard to resist it, this terror. And were they now moving in single file? They were; rounding the head of the loch still, their hats prominent, and their old-fashioned frock-coats. I was seeing them from the rear, their voice-sounds muted but already having taken on a new air, a new sense of something, some unknown thing perhaps and yet known too, as though from the depth of a folk memory, the metamorphosis now reaching the later stages. When they vanished I had to jump onto my feet and twist and turn this way and that in my effort to find them; but they were there, they were there, only behind some foliage, not by intention hiding, being unaware of we watchers.

I relaxed and prepared to wait, sitting now with my elbows resting on my knees, gazing lochwards, away from the retreating figures. And gradually my mind had discovered its own concentration. I remembered Miller's tale of the loch wherein lies an island and on that island is a loch wherein lies an island and on that island is a loch wherein lies an island and so on and so forth to that ultimate island. And I envisaged the ancient female seer on that ultimate island's throne squinting at the world with – yes, her irreverent twinkle but also a coldness there too, for the fallibility, the presumption. When I arrived in the glade an elderly woman was there amongst us who did remind me of the ancient seer for she too had a coldness about her that might well have taken my breath away on a different occasion; and lurking there too was an amused expression which I did not like, I could not have liked. This elderly woman was a person set back a pace from the main body, preferring to allow others to take the floor.

But take the floor we did. There was a beautiful girl to the side, modest, her gaze downcast, to the grassy mounds on the edge of the area. She would be mine. Her hair had the sheen and her breasts the concealed manner I knew so well, her body lightly lined beneath the loose cotton dress, and the breeze to her, the lines of her knees and thighs. I could hold her so gently, my hands touching the small of her back, her forehead to my shoulder, dampening my shoulder. There is a life there, a life strong and not to be spent. I put my hands to the small of her back, my palms flatly now to her kidneys, a body of flesh and blood, the warmth of her breasts and the warmth of her breath through my shirt onto my shoulder. And too the others, the others being there too – for now she was thrusting me back from her and laughing quietly; but as excited a laugh as could ever be imagined, as ever could be imagined; and in the laughter a mischievousness there for me, a mischief, I would try to be catching her and always be missing her by a hairsbreadth. And the others dancing now, the figures of humans, men and women, from the young to the old, all dependent on such as myself and the elderly woman whom I could see seated beside an old man with a brosy complexion, his fine head of pure white hair, listening to her animated chatter with great attention, his hand to the crook of her elbow as though to steady her, to pacify her. Was the elderly woman like me?

But the girl wanted me. She urged me on, urged me on. And I was dancing her on a circle, a reel; and our laughter amidst the laughter of the others, the couples, indistinguishable. It was a rage. It was a fire. We were on fire. We were clinging together. I was holding her so tightly, to keep her now, to keep her safe forever. For it was time, it was the time. And my memory is of a total rapture: the memory of such a moment but without the moment's memory for I cannot recollect that moment, only of having had such a moment, of our total rapture, the girl with the dark hair and myself.

We were apart now, inches, inches and feet and then yards, and her hands upraised in a question, her frown being followed by a look of an almost sickening resignation; uncomprehending, she cannot comprehend why this is to be, why they are to be in this way, that she is here for this one day, this only day, forever, this poor Red Cockatoo. And I can stare and stare at her, the tears tucked behind my eyes now as they seem always to have been since first I glimpsed the troop at sunrise, my chest and throat of an acidulous dryness.

The others were with her. They were standing to the rear of us in their own grouping, fidgeting, muttering unintelligibly. But soon they were become silent and those who had been staring at the ground now raised their heads. We humans were the interlopers, myself and the elderly woman, the others. And we were having to stand there in our own isolation, watching this heartbreak, these poor Red Cockatoos, their moment having come and now gone, concealing nought from each other, not now, not any longer. And we must continue our watching as this further stage advanced, their thin arms stretching out to one another; and they cling hand to hand in a curious, orchestrated fashion, not looking to one another, as though a certain form of mutual recognition might destroy some very remote possibility of staying the process. And the process cannot be stayed. Even then were their hands tearing from each other as they fought to control their faces, and I searched for my girl but could not distinguish her, for the faces were now all of the uniform red circles, this bodily transformation seeming to induce a mental calm; but even so, there was an air of bewilderment amongst them, and a vague self-consciousness, their feet twitching uneasily, twitching uneasily. I had to turn my face away, glimpsing only the hurried movement of the elderly woman as she did likewise. But for an instant were we looking into the other's eyes? I do not know, for the screeching had begun and it was all to be over, within a brief few seconds these poor Red Cockatoos would cease to exist.

THE FAILURE

WHEREAS THE drop appeared to recede into black nothingness I deduced each side of the chasm to taper until they merged. Each falling object would eventually land. And if footholes were to exist then discovering them could scarcely be avoided. The black of the nothingness was only so from the top: light would be perceived at the bottom, a position from where even the tiniest of specks' would enable the black to be quashed. And should a problem arise, groping an ascent via the footholes would be fairly certain.

I jumped.

The sensation of the fall is indescribable.

Much later upon landing I faced black nothingness. I had been mistaken about the light. That speck was insufficient. I could distinguish nothing whatsoever. But it was impossible to concentrate for my boots were wedged into the sides and my knees were twisted unnaturally. My arms had been forced round onto my back, with my shoulders pressed forward. The entire position of my body was reminiscent of what the adept yogi may accomplish. I ached all over. Then I had become aware of how irresponsibly conceived my planning had been. It was as if somehow I had expected the bottom to be large enough to accommodate an average-sized, fully grown male.

For a lengthy period I attempted to dislodge myself but to no avail. I panicked. I clawed and clawed at the backs of my thighs in an effort to hoist up my legs until finally I was obliged to halt through sheer fatigue at the wrists and finger-joints. Sweat dripped from my every pore; and the echo consequent upon this was resounding. Beginning from the drips the noise developed into one continuous roar that increased as it rose and rose and rose before dying away out of the top. An awful realization was presenting itself to me: the more I tried and tried to dislodge my body the more firmly entrenched I would become. Think of the manner whereby a mouse seals its own fate within that most iniquitous of adhesives it has entered to search out that last scrap of food. Yes, an immediate reaction to a desperate situation may well be normal but it is rarely other than misguided. My own had resulted in a position of utter hopelessness. And the magnitude of my miscalculations seemed destined to overwhelm me. That failure to anticipate the absurdity of bottom.

No, not a mouse, nor yet a flea, could enter into that. Total nothingness. A space so minute only nothing gains entry. Not even the most supremely infinitesimal of organisms as witnessed through the finest of powerful microscopes can disturb the bottom, for here absolutely nothing exists but the point in itself, the vertex.

DUM VIVIMUS, VIVAMUS

THIS WHOLE business is getting on my nerves. I was ploughing my way through these St Machar legends when right in front of me appeared what can only be a reference to that bastard Brendan O'Diunne. I dont like calling him that. Up until recently I reckoned him the greatest Scotchman to ever live and the greatest Scotchman who ever could live, in a logical sense. If writing this a couple of years back I would probably have been beginning in a manner approaching the following:

> Ancient Schottisch Writtaris have chronicklt that which the Illustriss Buchanan has richtly acknowledgt "ane strange gamyn richt eneuch".

A load of shite. Pointless carrying on from an opening like this because it leads to greater expectations of consistency and coherence whereas the entire thing is an utter mishmash, a shambles. This is why I discontinued the project when I did. It also explains why the old George fellow finally, and not too reluctantly, allowed his own welter of research to 'slippit intill the muddis of auld annallis'. Of course he hesitated for ages but it has to be remembered the sort of person he was. And then as well, any writer as disciplined as that must readily – Ach. Who cares. And Boswell! Not to be spoken of in the same breath I know, but how come he fails to even rate it a mention? Especially when that English sidekick of his allows a reasonable sized paragraph to 'the peculiarly Scotch game'? It could be he just wasnt present while the shepherd was recounting the tale. Perhaps Johnson had refused him attendance, lest he made the shepherd so nervous he might have been unable to communicate. Or maybe it is simply the case he had gone off on his own to ferret a dinner invitation

from one of the local highland bigwigs. The point being that had
he been there in the bothy we could have found ourselves in the
possession of a genuine exposition of the game's mechanics.
As matters stand it would appear that either Johnson received a
full and proper oral account of the game which for some reason
best known to himself he neglected to record, or else he did not
receive an account at all, and I am inclined to plump for the latter.
The actual odds about the shepherd's having had any detailed
knowledge of the game's mechanics are very very long indeed.
And even if he did have such knowledge, so what? Does that
really suggest he would have felt the need to pass it on to the good
Doctor? Apart from anything else, as far as the shepherd was
concerned, the whole point of the carry on lies not so much in the
game itself but in its extraordinary and magnificent termination,
for without that there is almost nothing at all – and certainly no
rational explanation of how come the memory of an ancient game
should yet be lingering in the mind of a people. And that to me is
the crux of the problem. Other aspects are of interest but to regard
any as crucial seems a psychological nonsense. Obviously to gain
an understanding of how the game was played would be
interesting for its own sake, and I for one would travel a long
distance to find such a thing out, but that is as far as it goes. I used
to take it for granted that the old commentators were assuming a
working knowledge of the game's mechanics, but I now know
differently – and that's being kind about it. The simple fact of the
matter is that they didnt have a clue. It was always total guesswork
– the slippery slopes of inference, some of the more common
theories deriving from that astonishingly scientific premise that
games in antiquity were much more liable to be of a physical
nature. And even supposing that to be true, so what? Success at
physical games need not entail having the build of an ox. It is
certainly the case that by all accounts Brendan was a 'greit baist of
a man' but this type of stuff is banal and leads to all sorts of wild
conjecture, and I would prefer not to be involved in that. A quick
instance of what I'm talking about, a 'mathematician' of early last
century (whose name it is nicer not to mention though he seems to
have accomplished some pioneering work in the science of

phrenology) makes a grand case for O'Diunne's having been a weedy individual because of the startling rigidity of the game's rule-structure. Fine, is about all you can say to that. But it is a truism that the game's limits were rigidly defined. There again though, insofar as this concerns the nature of Brendan's skull, the guy makes the elementary error of confusing termination with inception, always a risk when somebody in that field strays beyond the somatic hedge. No wonder you start getting involved in discussions on the nature of the cranium! Too much. And yet to some extent he has to be given the benefit of the doubt; he was truly seeking after a disciplined approach and once that is begun every pathway, no matter how shady, seems an obligation. It would have been interesting to see his notes though, I have to confess. Better still but, seeing old George's. What I really would like to know is where his first written reference comes from. I have always thought it would turn out to be via the Achnasheen Monk which if true presents us with quite an irony. There again, I just dont have the patience any longer. I'm also beginning to believe those who handle it in a quasi-humorous way have got the right idea. But Buchanan couldnt manage that and neither can I. And why bother criticizing the likes of Achnasheen? Is it really an accident that he appears not to feel the need of dwelling at length on the famous exhortation? In fact, I'm beginning to think it might be a bit unhealthy to do so. In saying this I've got to remind myself there would be very little without it, at least nowadays. My own interest is well on the wane. Sometimes I just think, leave it to the linguists. But no. Definitely not. So much of it is just – Who cares. There again, I know that when Brendan leaves the field of play Achnasheen has him crying: Dum vivimus. It is all fine and good but the fascinating question here is not so much whether the 'vivamus' had already been dropped from the popular saying without affecting its sense but whether Latin was used at all. Did the Monk simply translate O'Diunne's utterance from the Gaelic? Yes, and it would be nice to know what old George's thoughts were on this specific point. Perhaps especially to know if he would have considered such thoughts as valid. Obviously too, it is worth bearing the matter in mind in regard to Boswell's absence

during the interview with the shepherd. And here I refer to his
sidekick's notorious rejection of the very possibility of Gaelic as a
literary form. My own gut reaction is to oppose the good Doctor
at all costs but on this particular issue I have to say no. I reckon
Achnashseen was recording what he saw as a fairly amusing albeit
minorish local legend and that he was recording it as roundly as he
could, in other words, no translation. I am well aware that it has
become a more controversial aspect than previously but I have to
stick with it at this late stage, otherwise – who cares about the
otherwise. I'm just sticking with it and that's that. And how in the
name of heaven anybody can accept that silly theory now being
pushed by those taking a lead from Ghrame and the Latheron X11
I dont know. It just seems to me daft. As far as I can make out it
hinges almost completely on the Abbot of Tain and his 'dulce est
desipire in loco'. And I know fine well that the existential mark of
the 'dum vivimus' has to appeal to one and all. But surely that is
the very strength of the argument? When O'Diunne leaves the
field of play he does so in such a manner that the game terminates,
never to be played again. I say this, that if he really had gone off in
the huff then he would have been met by scorn. It is as simple as
that and as basic as that. And never, not in ten thousand years,
could such a legend have come about. For one thing, the game
would have continued – if not on that selfsame day then the next
one, or the next one, but certainly at some future date. And to so
much as even suggest that the action might have been premeditated is a nonsense. No premeditated act could ever effect such a
consequence. Ordinary people just arent so readily impressed. It
had to be something else altogether. For what we are here dealing
with is very close to a sort of universal appreciation of an
absurdity; an immediate and absolute recognition of the validity
of one individual's action: a revelation. And revelations are by
definition irrational. According to Martin the final day's play
occurs somewhere in the Caithness region and although his
evidence is based on the same sources nobody raises any serious
objections. I think this is the correct approach and I have nothing
to criticize in it. Several months ago a Gaelic-speaking pal of mine
spent a few days in Barra and got speaking to a very old lady. Out

of it came the following, that her people hailed from a small island which has been formally uninhabited since the late seventeenth century, and that to the best of her knowledge the ancient Gaelic saying for 'fair play' on this island was always *cothrom na Dhiunne* and not 'cothrom na Fiunne', as it is elsewhere. Now at the time I was less interested in this than my pal because of course the great Finn had a cousin whose name was Dhiunn. Then this latest turn-up in these St Machar things. I'm still not going to get involved either. I feel like wrapping the lot up in a brown paper parcel and dropping it off the Kingston Bridge, except with my fucking luck it would land in a rowing boat. But fair enough I suppose.

THE WEAN AND THAT

BRIAN YAWNED; he had shifted his stance, taking the weight of his body onto the other foot. He squinted at the clock on the far wall then turned slightly to look at those queuing behind. And reaching into his jerkin pocket he brought out a cigarette packet and opened it, but put it back again, thrusting his hands into his jeans' pockets. He was whistling; he stopped it. He took the UB40 from his back pocket and gazed at the information on it. Then the man in front was preparing to step to the counter. Brian started whistling again and he followed him forward. And while the man was crouching to sign the receipt he peered over his shoulder as though trying to read his signature. Then he too had signed and was walking quite quickly out through the door and onto the pavement. His pace slackened. He strolled along, on the edge of the kerb, gazing to there and into the gutter.

Hey! Brian! Brian!

It was Gordon O'Donnell approaching, right arm extended as if set to shake hands with him; he patted Brian on the elbow: How you doing man?

Ah no bad Gordon, surviving.

I thought you were fucking asleep!

Ah! Brian grinned.

Gordon patted him on the elbow again. This broo eh! you meet all sorts. Heh, you have signed on I take it?

Aye.

Great stuff, we'll need to share pints.

Eh . . .

No ehs about it!

[169]

Naw I was just going back down the road Gordon.

Rubbish. I'll just be a minute . . . He made to walk away but paused when Brian gestured with his hands raised palms upward. And he smiled, No trouble old chap – they're paying me the giro across the counter these days.

Are they?

Hh, aye. Gordon shook his head. He nodded in the direction of the broo and began walking, Brian following. Aye, he said, a bit of bother with the posted yins they kept sending. Vanishing tricks! Cheeky bastards thought I was doing it myself too! I telt them straight: listen I says if you really want to apprehend the culprit away and get a grip of that wife of mine, she's been in and out of my pockets for years – no kidding ye man there's fuck all safe when she's about. Naw I mean if Í was wanting to go to the thieving games I wouldnt be wasting my time with daft fucking giros! No brains but, that's the trouble with these cunts.

He had pushed open the door and they walked to a small queue. Then he noticed somebody in a larger queue and he called, Hey Bill – how's life? You alright for a tenner till the morrow!

The man laughed. Is that all!

Make it a score if you like man I'm no fussy!

Aye it's okay for some!

What d'you mean!

The man laughed. Gordon gave an exaggerated wink then he nudged Brian slightly and winked in a more natural manner. He glanced about for several seconds. Then he said, So what you doing with yourself these days?

Brian shrugged.

The missus and that I mean, alright?

Aye.

Good. Good. It was Gordon's turn next and he stepped to the counter, producing his card with a flourish and passing it to the female clerk: How you doing honey!

The woman looked at her wristwatch before replying; she pushed the receipt to him. You're nearly an hour late Mr O'Donnell.

I know that, terrible – I couldnt get away from my work any earlier. Rush job on.

She smiled. You seem to think we dont know you're working on the sly.

On my weans' life now would I make a fraudulent claim? Gordon had his right hand over his heart.

The woman glanced at Brian and said, He thinks we dont take him seriously because he makes a joke about it, but we'll catch him one of these days.

Brian smiled. And Gordon said, It's one of these days for us all hen, one of these days for us all.

Oh dont be so morbid!

I'm no being morbid, he added as he leaned to sign his name.

They walked to the far corner and stood by the wall, close to where the cashier's window was. A youth was balancing on the edge of a radiator nearby. Gordon noticed him and crooked his right forefinger a couple of times. The youth came over slowly, hands in his pockets, and he muttered, Hiya Gordon.

How you doing young man.

Alright.

That's the game. What I want you to do is dish out the harrys.

Aw Gordon I've no got any, honest.

Dont tell lies.

I've only got a couple left.

Out with them.

Aw fuck sake man.

Gordon crooked the forefinger again, until the youth took out the packet. And he handed a cigarette to Gordon who passed it immediately to Brian; he gave another one to Gordon, took one for himself. Gordon flicked a lighter and when the three of them were smoking the youth said to him: Have you seen Wee Cally on your travels?

What? Gordon stared at him.

Naw Gordon I'm no kidding, have you?

What you talking about son? Gordon sniffed and dragged on the cigarette, blew the smoke sideways in the direction of the cashier's window.

Wee Cally.

Wee Cally. Gordon shook his head and he said to Brian: No kidding ye man this fucking younger generation, it's no real the way they carry on . . . He indicated the youth: The fucking young team he's talking about – hatchets arent good enough for them; one sniff of that barr's irn bru and they're away fucking about with shooters. A different world so it is, a different world.

Brian smiled.

I was just wanting to know if you'd seen him, said the youth.

Listen son, said Gordon, I dont see people like that – know what I'm talking about? Gordon dragged on the cigarette again and frowned suddenly, he gazed away to the big clock on the wall and shook his head.

Time is it? asked Brian.

Gordon made no answer. He stared at the male clerk working behind the counter. Heh, he called, what about the greengages? they no weighed in yet! Eh – fuck sake, the boy here's got his bloody work to go to!

The clerk looked at him.

The boy here . . . said Gordon, tapping himself on the chest.

The clerk continued to look at him for a moment, then dropped his gaze.

Gordon said to Brian, That's what I love about this place, the civility! He shook his head, took a folded newspaper from his side jacket pocket and started to read; but seconds later he folded it again and he stuck it back into the pocket and glanced at the clock, shaking his head and sighing loudly. Then he called to the clerk again: What's the score with the cashier at all! Is he away to the bloody Bahamas or what?

You'll just require to wait like everybody else, the clerk replied.

Oh, very pardon, I do apologies . . . Gordon winked at Brian, then stared at the clerk whose attention had returned to the person next in the queue he was assigned to.

The giro could only be cashed in a specific post office. It was more than a mile away, in the direction opposite to where Brian was going. When he mentioned this Gordon told him not to worry. Naw, said Brian, it's no that, it's just the wean and that, she comes home from school at dinnertime and I've got to be there I mean she's just six.

Six!

Six, aye.

Christ!

Brian looked at him.

I thought yours were aulder than that man, six!

Thanks a lot! said Brian.

Gordon grinned. Naw, I dont mean it the way it sounds.

They had paused at the traffic lights at the junction and now as the green showed Gordon continued walking immediately and Brian went alongside him, and began saying. Naw what it is Gordon, the wee yin, the lassie, she'll just no go near they school meals at all.

Can you blame her!

Aye I know but the trouble is I've got to be there and that I mean on the button, quarter past twelve.

Mm.

On the button.

Bags of time yet then eh.

Aw I know, I know, it's . . .

Brian! Fuck sake! Gordon had stopped walking. He shook his head, patted the other on the elbow. Will you stop your fucking worrying.

Aye but . . .

You can take a bus back down the road.

Brian nodded, then started to speak, but Gordon held up his right hand and said, The fare's taken care of.

Aw aye, aye . . . Brian sniffed. I wasnt meaning that.

They continued walking in silence for a time. Eventually Brian turned to say, This getting the giro across the counter, I wish to God I could get into it myself!

Aye well dont. Garbage so it is, you're better biting your nails. All it means is you're skint for the weekend. Fucking murder.

Still.

No stills about it.

Brian nodded, smiled. He had his cigarette packet out. There were two left. He gave one to Gordon and returned the packet to his jerkin pocket and took a half-smoked dowp from behind his right ear. And he struck a match against the grey sandstone tenement wall adjacent, shielding the flame in his cupped hands. I hate this smoking in the open air, he muttered while exhaling and chipping the dud match . . . Know how?

Gordon shrugged as they walked on.

The fucking wind, it smokes your fucking fags! Brian shook his head. Know what I mean, sometimes you're walking man and you've only had a couple of drags and the fucking thing's burnt right down to the tip.

Aye, said Gordon, glancing to the other side of the road.

The pub was at the corner of the next street along from the post office. Gordon and the barman knew each other. While the two were chatting quietly together Brian turned side on, gazing at the blank television screen, then at a big coloured poster on the wall nearby; a woman tennis player, standing scratching her bum, her skirt raised almost to her waist and not wearing any pants underneath. After a moment he looked away.

The barman was giving Gordon the change, and the two pints of lager were on the counter. Gordon lifted one and handed the other to Brian then led the way to one of the empty tables.

Once the first mouthful had been drunk Gordon said, So – no signs of a job I take it?

Nah, no yet – yourself?

Gordon shrugged.

Right enough, went on Brian, the wife's knocked it off, a wee part-time shot, nothing startling.

Good but.

In a boozer, said Brian. She helps out at dinnertime. Pub grub and that; it's a place up the town; hell of a busy with office workers and the rest of it. The manager says he'll take her full-time as soon as there's a vacancy.

Aw good, good.

Aye. Brian nodded, he took another mouthful of the lager. Thanks for this, he said.

Gordon frowned. Dont be daft . . . He raised his own glass and drank from it. Then he tore the cellophane off the packet and withdrew two fags, and he chuckled: Heh Brian, mind the times we used to have in that fucking paper factory! Eh? No kidding ye man I dont think I've had a decent laugh since I dropped them the resignation.

That's one way of putting it!

They both laughed loudly. Gordon said, Hurry up and swallow it down; we'll have another yin.

Naw, ta. I better get down the road. It's the wean; quarter past twelve on the dot, without fail, every day of the week. I've got to be there.

Gordon glanced at the gantry clock. You've still got time for one more.

Nah . . . Brian sniffed.

Well a half pint then. Or a wee yin? a goldie – eh? I'm having one myself.

You twisting my arm!

Naw.

Alright then. Brian grinned.

Gordon chuckled. For an awful minute I thought you were losing your touch! Eh what you want water or something? lemonade?

The former.

The former! Gordon raised his eyebrows as he got up from the chair, and he did a sort of rapid tap-dance shuffle across to the bar.

He came back with two ¼ gills of whisky and a jug of water. And he returned to the bar, to collect two half pints of lager. When he placed them on the table he said, Just remember me in your will old chap.

Aw Christ Gordon, thanks.

Ah! Gordon's face screwed up and his teeth clenched, he inhaled sharply, making a rasping noise. He poured a drop of water into his whisky and pushed Brian the jug. Brian added a measure into his own whisky. They drank simultaneously, following it up with quick sips of the lager. Gordon wiped his mouth with the cuff of his coat sleeve, glancing round the interior of the bar. Then he said, So how's the horses treating you these days?

Well to be honest, I've no been getting too involved.

I know the feeling!

Aw naw, naw, it's no that. I just get fucking scunnered with it.

I dont blame you. These last couple of weeks! No kidding ye Brian see last Thursday? I'm standing there, got a right few quid going onto the last favourite. Inside the final furlong and it's three lengths clear; then this big fucking fifty-to-one shot comes and beats it on the post. Eh? Game's as bent as fuck man I'm no kidding ye, it's no real.

Brian was nodding. I know, I know – and see what gets me, the faces; you walk in the door and you see the faces, always the fucking same . . . Brian shook his head and he reached for his whisky, paused before drinking: Telling ye Gordon sometimes if I'm going to put a line on I just fucking take a walk, I get off my mark, away to another betting shop altogether. Then I go somewhere else, afterwards . . . Brian had paused. He shook his head and studied his fag for a moment, before stubbing it out in an ashtray.

Gordon muttered, Hh! Then he glanced to the side and added, A slash, I'll need to go for a slash.

Brian was footering with the cigarette packet when he returned. He said, I've only got the one left Gordon. He shrugged and took the one out, crumpled the packet and placed it in the ashtray. He struck a match down the side of his chair but it did not ignite: he scraped it along the floor. Gordon had a cigarette of his own, and he had his lighter out, but took a light from Brian's match instead; as he exhaled he said: Something just occurred to me there.

He sniffed and leaned forwards, his arms folded, resting the elbows on the table: I might be able to put a bit of business your way.

What?

Naw, it's just eh . . . He cleared his throat and drank lager, inhaled on the fag. He glanced sideways, lowered his voice while speaking: Big ears Brian. Big ears and big fucking mouths. Know what I mean?

Brian nodded.

See what I was thinking . . . Gordon stopped and shook his head.

Brian nodded again.

Naw, it's just . . . Gordon frowned then smiled, tapped himself on the chest. The boy here – you know what like it is Brian, I can hardly get walking. Sometimes I've just got to fucking step out the door and the busies are there waiting; wanting to know where I'm going what I'm doing. Murder man I'm no fucking kidding ye. Anything up and round they come at all hours, chapping the door and waking the weans – mental so it is, the wife goes off her head about it. And no wonder, I mean . . . Naw Brian I'm no kidding ye, the way they carry on, it's just no fucking real.

Aye.

A lot of difficulties as well man because of it, you with me?

Brian nodded.

Naw, said Gordon. He sniffed and frowned a moment, dragged on the cigarette; screwing his face up before blowing out the smoke. Take the other night, just as a for instance; we got a wee turn, a wee turn. Trouble is it should've been a fucking lot better than that. Gordon sat back on the chair. He sat forwards again and leaned closer to the other: I mean somebody like yourself Brian, you could've done a nice bit of business, a nice bit of business. And no sweat. None. I'm no kidding ye.

Brian nodded.

Gordon sniffed and continued: See what it was man we've got a load – okay? And we've got to get fucking shot of the stuff at the double, at the double Brian, no fucking hanging about – you with me? So what happens? Hh! Cut-price fucking discount store – What Every Woman Wants man I'm no kidding ye, mental. Whereas, whereas, if we've got time. If we've got time Brian, I mean, if we've got time to fucking hang about then Christ, Christ sake. I mean a couple of days – that's all! A couple of fucking days!

Gordon snorted and shook his head.

Brian nodded. And if we could've done that we were laughing.

Aye.

See Brian somebody like you, somebody like yourself. Correct me if I'm wrong, but somebody like yourself man I mean! Gordon shook his head, he smiled.

If I was hiding a load or something?

Exactly. Exactly. And fuck sake it's no even a matter of hiding cause it's no as if any cunt's going to come round chapping your door. Know what I mean Brian I mean you could dump the gear on the kitchen fucking table and nobody'd be any the fucking wiser!

Brian grinned.

Gordon was chuckling, swirling the remaining drop of whisky round in the tumbler.

After a few moments silence Brian lifted his glass of lager and stared at what was left.

Then Gordon said, A dozen cardboard boxes Brian. You could've papped them straight into the wardrobe and shut the door. A couple of days later and that'd be that, you're past the post; sitting there with the feet up, a nice few quid in the tail.

Brian nodded, he smiled briefly.

I'm serious.

Aye.

Gordon was looking at him. I'm no kidding ye, he said.

Aw I know I know, I'm no eh . . . Brian sniffed. He upturned his whisky glass above the lager glass, watching the drop roll down into it. He puffed on his cigarette, looked across to the gantry clock. Then Gordon moved; he rose from the chair and reached for the empties: Just time for another yin eh!

O naw, Christ . . .

Och!

Naw. Naw Gordon honest! Brian was shaking his head and holding his hands aloft. I wish I could, he said.

Ah come on! Gordon grinned.

Naw, honest.

A slight pause, and Gordon said, You sure?

Wish I could.

Mm. Gordon nodded. He sat back down, then yawned and stretched his arms, flexing his shoulder blades. He looked at Brian. Brian shrugged and made as though to say something but Gordon leaned closer and said: I'm no being cheeky Brian but I think you're fucking daft, no to consider it I mean. That's what I mean, Christ, you dont look as if you're going to even consider it.

Brian glanced at the ashtray a moment, then his gaze returned to Gordon who said: Are you?

What . . .

Are you? Consider it – are you going to consider it?

Course.

Gordon continued to look at him.

Course I'm going to consider it.

Gordon nodded.

Brian swallowed the last drops from the lager glass. He paused, before saying: I'll need to be hitting the road, the wean and that . . . Heh Gordon, thanks for the drink and that I mean, Christ . . .

No trouble.

Brian sniffed. He stood to his feet: Course I'm going to consider it I mean, obviously . . .

Gordon shrugged. No fucking problem Brian dont worry about it.

Brian nodded. Well, see ye eh?

Right.

Seconds later and Brian was pushing his way through the exit. On the pavement outside he hesitated, then set off, walking quickly.

EVEN IN COMMUNAL PITCHES

I HAD arrived at the following conclusion: even in communal pitches people will claim their portions of space; he who sits in the left-hand corner of one room will expect to obtain the equivalent corner in every room. This is something I cannot go but I felt obliged to conform to standard practice. It was a kind of community I was living in. A veryrichman owned the property. He allowed folk to live in it at minimal rents; the reason was to do with Y being equal to C plus S or I. It was quite noisy but no worse for that, for somebody like myself, just in from country travels. A party had been in progress for the two days I was here; it seemed to move from room to room; those desirous of sleep but without permanent quarters were having to grab a spot here and there, preferably keeping a room ahead all the time. In its own way that was fine and a nice camaraderie always seemed about to exist, although for some reason people only spoke to me in reply to questions about tea and coffee and where was the bathroom etc. It didnt annoy me, I could just lie on the floor and listen to their conversations. Next to me a guy kept going on about medieval conventicles on the southern tip of England; he was with another guy who was having to conceal yawns. Then I noticed they were irritated by my presence. What's up? I said. But they ignored the question. At this stage I would definitely have been entitled to get annoyed, but I didnt, I was too tired, far too tired; all I wanted to do was sleep. But could I get a sleep! Could I fuck. Then this woman; up she comes: Are you John Myatt?

Who's that? I says.

Never mind, came the reply, and she moved off on her stocking soles.

That was the kind of place it was. There was this other woman who was friendly, but I made a blunder by introducing the business of that conclusion I had arrived at. And she looked right through me. I was beginning to think: When did you last change your socks?

Gradually it dawned on me they were waiting for something; it was a bloke, he turned out to be a kind of Master of Ceremonies. A get-together had been organized in a semi-official way so that for this night at least, the party would be taking on a structured form. You were expected to do a turn. Somebody shoved a bunnet under my nose, he was looking for a donation, presumably for a carry-out. I was skint unfortunately but when I explained he got all fucking annoyed and went off in a huff. Eventually I saw he was sitting not far from me, about six or seven spaces away, and he was pointing me out to his neighbours in a really underhand manner. Who cares.

The entertainment began with a series of monologues, one of which was delivered by the guy who knew about medieval conventicles. It was so totally boring you werent sure if you had missed the overall irony, but when you looked about you could see no-one at all was grinning, it was meant by him as dead serious. Other speakers were concerned with recent events in the world of politics. A woman with a big hat got up and sang a song and this was the best so far. But then another woman got up and she recited poetry. Well, it has to be said that she was not brilliant although I dont know but something in the way she did it plus the good hand she got at the end made me think it was all her own stuff she was reading.

Meanwhile the carry-out arrived, such as it was, and it was being guarded jealously; even so but it was finished in what seemed like a matter of moments and everybody began looking at each other as if secretly laying the blame on certain members of the company for drinking more than their fair share. I wasnt involved; I had taken some of the drink but without overdoing it. I was more concerned with retaining the portion of space. And with a bit of luck I would manage to snatch a couple of hours' kip. A guy got up on the floor with a guitar; and then a lassie joined him and everything was fine and going good till they started on these songs with choruses and we were all to join in; Farewell to the Trusty Rover and so on. What made it hopeless was the way if you werent joining in you felt it was being noted. The only ones okay were couples, it being assumed as valid that your attention could be total elsewhere so long as it was being concentrated on your partner. But not too much later a couple of folk began smoking dope and passing the joints about, then out came the plates of grub – grated carrots and turnips and cabbage, with wee dods of cheese and onion. And that was fine because although the quantities werent up to scratch the actual health-factor made you feel satisfied.

Then one by one people were getting up from the floor, making the move to a new room, a few having a laugh and trying to get everybody to do one of these snake-dances where you hold the person's waist to the front and somebody holds yours to the back. I had grabbed my stuff immediately and without making it too obvious was keeping into the wall and bypassing folk, heading out of the room and onto the landing where the vanguard had made it already, glancing at each other for signs of where to go, whom to follow, whether it was best to say fuck it and just shoot off in the offchance you would get to the correct room under your own steam. I waited a couple of seconds, not looking at anybody, then strode to the staircase and went on up to the next landing. There were scuffling noises behind but I didnt look back. I didnt mind at all if people were following me; I just didnt want to give the impression I knew where the fuck I was going, cause I didnt, I was just bashing on, hoping for the best. In situations like this the proper method of action often seems to trigger itself off on you without any deliberate thinking beforehand and sometimes I really go for it, setting all the conditions and so on. I wasnt wrong. On the next landing the door on the far side seemed familiar; it was the bathroom. I had been in using it earlier. It was a good bathroom, very spacious; to an L-shape design and I have the feeling it had been used as a small bedroom in years gone by. When I closed and snibbed the door I could hear the sounds of a couple of folk outside on the landing, as if they had been following me and had now realized it was a wild goose chase. Obviously I was a bit sorry for whoever it was but in a sense this was it about claiming your portion of space and I was only fitting in with the conventional wisdom of the place.

I sat down on the toilet and began thinking about the whole carry on, in particular the woman who had recited the poetry; but that other woman kept butting in, her who wanted to know if I was John Myatt. I always find it really irritating when something like that happens. Another thing: it was so long since I had slept with a woman. Aye, gradually that was creeping up on me as well, and I dont know but sometimes you can enter terrible fits of depression for no apparent reason. And this other kind of daydream was beginning to butt in: there I was bashing my way into room after room and then by a fluke I would find myself in this wee closet where the elderly owner would be raking about in his moneyboxes. Aw christ, I dont know, I began opening the bathroom door and was walking downstairs in this really slow slow step by step by step way, with noises of folk coming from somewhere, and muffled laughter as well. And just at that moment came an explosion in my head and I knew there was a change in me, a change in me for keeps. Something had happened and my life had altered in a way that might never have appeared significant to an onlooker, but as far as I was concerned, having to live this life, I knew it could never hope to be the same again, and I started to smile.

AN OLD STORY

SHE'D BEEN going about in this depressed state for ages so I should've known something was up. But I didnt. You dont always see what's in front of your nose. I've been sitting about the house that long. You wind up in a daze. You dont see things properly, even with the weans, the weans especially. There again but she's no a wean. No now. She's a young woman. Ach, I dont want to tell this story.

But you cant say that. Obviously the story has to get told.

Mm, aye, I know what you mean.

Fine then.

Mmm.

Okay, so about your story . . .

Aye.

It concerns a lassie, right? And she's in this depressed state, because of her boyfriend probably – eh?

I dont want to tell it.

But you've got to tell it. You've got to tell it. Unless . . . if it's no really a story at all.

Oh aye christ it's a story, dont worry about that.

                    Dear
                  o dear o
                 dear. And
                yet she must
               have been near
              about 30 years
               of age. But
                a certain
                  pair
               of legs have
               the following
              shape: slim over
             the knees with the
            sloped move down to
           the ankles which arent
          thick. She was wearing a
         miniskirt, and orange hair
        with rollers stuck in; about
      5'6"   in her red heels. And
      this   voice of an amazing
      kind   of hoarseness when
      first   I heard her in the
      shop   at the corner while
      she   asked for a pound
      of   brown sugar and 20
      of   your kingsize tips
      and   a box of cadbury's
      as   well Archie if you
         dont mind. And pushing
          out through the door
           she let it swing back
            as if leaving it for
            me. Against the wall
             of her close she
              was leaning as I
              walked by clutch-
              ing my golden vir-
              ginia. And at 23
              years of age I was
             going through a bad
      patch with the
              wife but
              I did go
              on past.
              A couple
              of days
              later I
              saw her
              in the
              street
              bawling
      at   some
      old timer:
      Ya   manky
      auld swine
      ye!   You
      still owe
      two   quid
      from last
              week.

A HUNTER

PETER RETURNED home shortly after closing time with a carry-out. The room was cold and bleak. He shuddered as he stooped to light the gas-fire. Not an enjoyable evening, the pub had been packed and he had only stayed through a combination of laziness and utter boredom. Of course that red-haired girl had stared at him over her partner's right shoulder for a while. Probably the landlord paid her a retainer to ensnare young and old men into staying and buying his lousy flat beer.

He sprawled on the comfy old leather armchair, kicked off his shoes and leaned to switch on the electric kettle. He had the beginnings of a headache or something. He would only be able to face a smoke after a coffee. Maybe he should have followed the red-haired girl home. Could have been genuine. Yes. Could have been.

He absentmindedly lit a cigarette but coughed so badly on the first drag that he stubbed it out, carefully, making sure it could be smoked again. Hell of a bad habit smoking. Causes cancer, bronchitis and several other diseases of the lungs, heart and throat. Drink too of course. Liver trouble. Plus your bladder. And alcoholism. And what about the gut you get if you bevy too much beer! Gambling as well. Good God Almighty! Some women say they'd rather be married to an alcoholic than a gambler. A fact. The nerves get it. Watch a gambler's hands, how they keep twitching all the time whenever he makes a bet. Hear his heart thump as they race well inside the final furlong. An alky sometimes will tell you he is trapped, no way out, but a gambler! He says he does not gamble. Yes.

The kettle was boiling. Peter reached down to switch if off. He

[187]

picked out a can of Guinness from the brown paper carrier bag. Hell with the coffee, he had the taste now. Pity none of the lads had been in earlier. Maybe have chipped in for a good sized carry-out, made a bit of a night of it, invited a couple of women back.

He peeled the stopper from the top of the can and took a long slug. Bitter! Sometimes Guinness could taste hell of a bitter. Should have bought some lager instead. No, not lager, too bloody gassy. And even worse for the liver so they say. Better off with a few cans of pale ale. Still, save money with the Guinness. Never drink too much cause of the taste.

He rose and went through to the toilet. As he began urinating he lurched forward but managed to support himself by clutching onto the pipe leading to the cistern. He pissed over his left sock. It felt warm and surprisingly pleasant.

As he returned to his armchair he accidentally kicked over the can of Guinness and had to open a new one. He lit a cigarette and then noticed the one he had begun earlier. He smiled up at the ceiling but then he started in surprise. Scratching? What is this scratching? The mouse? Oh no. Surely not? That bastard is dead. Killed a week ago with a rolled up *Sporting Life*. The bastard. Definitely a scratching. Under the bed in the recess. Must have been two of them.

Peter lay back on the chair with his eyes closed, nursing the cold tin of beer. The scratching began once more. God, to be deaf. He slowly opened his eyes and placed the beer up onto the mantelpiece. He grinned malevolently. This bastard shall join his comrade. *Sporting Life!* Call to arms. Consider yourself conscripted once again.

He dropped down to his knees on the floor and blinked into the shadows beneath the bed. His heart jumped. A strange harsh taste hit the roof of his mouth. He gulped. He bounded back into the chair and stretched his feet out onto the coffee table.

Jesus Christ Almighty. How many? How many? How many more? He leaned over, tucking his trouser bottoms into his socks like a cyclist then knelt back down on the floor. He watched hypnotized as half a dozen mice went scuttling and leapfrogging around the wall and far leg of the bed. His flesh crawled. His scalp itched. The blood thundered and thumped through his heart and into his temples. Perhaps the hebee jebees were upon him. Maybe the shaking pink elephants would attack next. On five pints and a half a can of Guinness? No. Surely not.

Again Peter returned to the chair where he lit a cigarette. He noticed one still smouldering on the ashtray with quite a lot to be smoked. Whose? The other stubbed-out unsmoked fag lay beside it. He broke it into two pieces and played with the loose strands of tobacco, then lay back, smoking peacefully for a few minutes. He moved his head nearer the edge of the chair and glanced over, and watched the tiny mice cavort in circles roundabout the front side of the bed. He started counting them. He stopped at seven and began a recount. He stopped again. Ten? A dozen? How many? Christ! How many in a litter? Could it be a new litter? He ran a clammy hand through his hair. His scalp felt oily and was almost unbearably itchy. Perhaps if . . . What?

He returned to the toilet, shutting the kitchen door on the way. He turned on the tap of the wash-hand basin and washed his head in the ice-cold water. Much better. Much much better. He paused in the lobby and pulled on his old heavy boots leaving his trouser bottoms inside his socks. To battle! To battle with the bastards! Onward! The glorious struggle.

From the cool of the lobby into the now-warm kitchen. He gazed at the floor beneath the bed and then at his armchair and quickly he jumped onto the bed and lay across it with his head over the side looking under. They appeared to be playing hide-and-seek. He crawled to the corner where the action was in progress and peered down. He could make out their shapes in the shadows here quite easily. One now seemed to be crawling up the leg of the bed with its back against the wall for support. Jesus! Oh Jesus.

He sat up, cross-legged with his right hand ready to wield the *Sporting Life*. He waited patiently, staring down at the edge of the bed.

Bastards. Okay, come on then. Come on then you creepy little bastards. Me and this paper. Come on you bastards.

He sat there waiting. He thought he heard the crawler fall back but lacked the courage to look. Perhaps they had started crawling up the legs at the opposite side of the bed, the ones behind him? Jesus Christ! He could feel their presence. He felt them there right behind his back. Then suddenly he relaxed. His mouth gaped open as the tension and strain eased from his limbs and body. He breathed in and then out, swivelled his head around. Nothing! Nothing at all.

He looked down over the bed and saw a mouse go hurtling across the floor towards the cooker and the pantry. No grub there anyway! Ha ha ha you bastard, nothing there.

God. Oh God. A shape under the candlewick bedspread moved steadily in his direction. He stared glassy-eyed for about ten seconds then screamed. He flew off the bed, picked up the carry-out, cigarettes and matches and bolted into the lobby slamming the door behind him. He leaned against the wall gasping and spluttering saliva down his chin. The *Sporting Life*? Must have dropped it in the rush. He looked about the place then noticed the container of blue paraffin. He grabbed it up and smiled slyly. He opened the kitchen door gently and slowly sprinkled the paraffin over towards the floor at the bed then lit a match and carefully threw it. The carpet burst into flames.

'Ha you little bastards!' he screamed. 'Ha ha now you bunch of bastards!' Then he locked himself into the toilet.

The firemen found him there half an hour later after breaking the door in. He stood with one foot in the pan and the other balanced on the seat. He appeared to have been plunging each one in alternately and pulling the plug every so often. He punched his chest when they told him that everything in the kitchen was destroyed.

SUNDAY PAPERS

TOMMY HAD lain awake for almost ten minutes before the alarm finally shattered the early Sunday morning peace. He switched it off and jumped out of bed immediately, dressing in seconds. He opened the bedroom door, padded along the lobby into the kitchenette. A plate of cornflakes lay beside a bottle of milk and bowl of sugar from which he poured and sprinkled.

When he had finished eating the door creaked open and his mother blinked around it: 'Are you up?' she asked.

'Aye mum. Had my cornflakes.' He could not see her eyes.

'Washed yet?'

'Aye mum, it's a smashing day outside.'

'Well you better watch yourself. There's an orange somewhere.'

'Aye mum.'

'It's yes.'

He nodded and stood up, screeching the chair backwards.

'Sshh . . .' whispered his mother, 'you'll waken your dad.'

'Sorry,' whispered Tommy. 'See you later mum.'

'At eight?'

'Don't know,' he said, stooping to pick up the canvas paper-bag.

'John's always in at eight for something to eat,' said his mother.

'Okay!' He swung the bag onto his shoulder the way his brother did.

'Don't say okay,' said his mother frowning a little, eyes open now, becoming accustomed to the morning light.

'Sorry mum.'

'Alright. You better go now. Cheerio!'

'Cheerio!' he called as she disappeared into the dark curtain-drawn bedroom.

Immediately her head reappeared around the door: 'SHH!'

'What's going on,' grunted a hoarse voice from the depth.

'Sorry mum!' Tommy could hear his father coughing as the bedroom door closed. He washed his face before quietly opening the outside door. He stepped out onto the landing and kicked over an empty milk-bottle but managed to snatch it up before the echo had died away. A dog barked somewhere. Hurrying downstairs not daring to whistle he jumped the last half flight of steps then halted, hardly breathing, wondering if he could have wakened the neighbours by the smack of his sandshoes on the solid concrete.

Out the close he clattered down the remaining steps to the pavement, not caring how much noise he made now that he was out in the open. Crossing the road he leaned against the spiked wooden fence looking far across the valley. So clear. He could see the Old Kilpatricks and that Old Camel's Hump linking them with the Campsies. He whistled as loudly as he could with two fingers, laughing as the echoes pierced across the burn and over to Southdeen. He turned and waved the paper-bag round and round over his head; then he began trotting along the road, swinging it at every passing lamp-post. He kept forgetting the time and day. It was so bright. He felt so good.

At the top of Bellsyde Hill he slowed down and stared at the view. What hills away over there? The Renfrews maybe. Or it could still be the Old Kilpatricks? Rather than use the tarred pathway he ran downhill across the grass embankment. He had seen nobody since leaving the house more than ten minutes ago. A truck nearly killed him as he came dashing out onto Drumchapel Road from the blind-spot exit.

The truck jammed to a halt and the driver peered out the window. 'Wee bastard!' he roared. 'You daft wee bastard!'

But Tommy never stopped running. He flew on down Garscadden Road and up through the goods' entrance into Drumchapel Railway Station. The paper-hut stood by itself on the adjacent waste ground, parked beside it were a couple of cars. Half a dozen bicycles were propped against the wooden hut walls. He pushed open the door. The thick blue air made his eyes smart. The place was crowded. It seemed as if everybody was shouting, swearing and joking. Tommy joined at the end of the queue of boys waiting to receive their papers. The boy standing in front of him was a man with a beard. Tommy gazed at him. Behind the wide counter three men assisted by two youths were distributing the Sunday newspapers. The big man and the thin man were laughing uproariously at something the crew-cut man was saying. Some of the boys were also grinning and it was obviously very funny.

Each boy's bag was being packed tight with newspapers and one large boy had so many that he needed two bags. When Tommy's turn came he stepped forwards and cried: 'Six run!'

'Six run?' repeated the crew-cut man gaping at him.

'Aye!'

'Where's MacKenzie?'

'He's away camping. I'm his wee brother.'

'What's that?' called the thin man.

'Says he's MacKenzie's wee brother,' said the crew-cut man over his shoulder.

'Hell of a wee!' frowned the big man.

'What age are you kid?' asked the crew-cut man.

'Twelve and a half. I've been round with my brother before. Three times.'

'Ach he'll be okay,' said the crew-cut man when the big man's eyes widened.

'MacKenzie be back next Sunday?" asked the thin man.

'Aye,' replied Tommy. 'He's only away for a week. He's down at Arran with the B.B.'

The thin man nodded to the other two.

'Aye okay,' agreed the big man.

'Right then Wee MacKenzie, pass me your bag!' The crew-cut man began packing in *Post*, *Express* and *Mail*; as he worked he called out to the two youths who collected other newspapers from the shelves which ran along the length of the wall behind them. When the bag was filled and all the newspapers in order the man bumped the bag down twice on the counter and told Tommy to listen. 'Right son,' he said, 'they're all in order.' He counted on his fingers. '*Post*, *Express*, *Mail*. That's easy to remember eh? Then *People*, *World*, *Pictorial*, *Reynolds* and *Empire*. Okay?'

Tommy hesitated and the crew-cut man repeated it. Tommy nodded and he continued: '*Telegraph*, *Observer* and *Times*. You got that?'

'Aye.'

'Right kid, then off you go, and we close at two remember.'

'At two?'

'Aye, two. Remember!'

'But John's always home before eleven.'

'Aye that's John kid.' The crew-cut man grinned. 'Anyhow, take it away.' He pushed the bag along the counter and Tommy walked after it. One of the youths held the strap out and he ducked his right arm and head through. The youth helped him to manoeuvre it to the edge of the counter and then he looked down at him rather worriedly.

'Okay son?' he asked.

Tommy nodded and straining he heaved it off from the counter. The bag of papers plummeted to the floor like a boulder, carrying him with it. Everybody in the hut roared with laughter as he lay there unable to extricate himself. Eventually the thin man cried, 'Give him a hand!'

Three boys jumped forward. They freed him and hoisted the bag back up onto the counter. Tommy gazed at the men. After a moment the thin man said to the crew-cut man, 'Well Jimmy, what do you think now?'

'Ach the kid'll be okay.'

'Give him a weer run,' suggested the big man, 'that six is a big bastard. Somebody else can do it.'

'No mister,' said Tommy, 'I can do it. I've helped my brother before.'

The crew-cut man nodded then smiled. 'Right Wee MacKenzie. Put the strap over one shoulder just. The left's the best. Don't put

[194]

your head under either, that's how that happened. It's a question of balance. Just the one shoulder now. Okay?'

Tommy nodded, pulled the strap on, and the crew-cut man pushed the bag to the edge of the counter. 'Ready?'

'Aye.'

'Right you are kid, take it away.'

Tommy breathed in deeply and stepped away from the counter, bending almost horizontal beneath the weight. He struggled to the door, seeing only the way as far as his feet.

'Open it!' shouted the thin man.

As the door banged shut behind him he could hear the big man say: 'Jesus Christ!'

Tommy reached the top of Garscadden Road and turned into Drumchapel Road by the white church. His chest felt tight under the burden and the strap cut right into his shoulder but he was not staggering so often now. It was getting on for 5.30 a.m. When he looked up he saw the blue bus standing at Dalsetter Terminus. About fifty yards from it he looked again, in time to see the driver climb up into the cabin. Tommy tried to run but his knees banged together. The engine revved. He half trotted in a kind of jerking motion. The bus seemed to roll up the small incline to the junction. Fifteen yards now and Tommy was moving faster on the downhill towards it. An oil-tanker passing caused the bus to stay a moment and Tommy went lunging forwards and grabbed at the pole on the rear platform. The bus turned into the main road and he swung aboard with his right foot on the very edge, managing to drag on his left, but he could not pull up the bag. The weight strained on his shoulder. It was pulling him backwards as the bus gathered speed. Nobody was downstairs. His chest felt tighter and his neck was getting really sore. The strap slipped, it slipped down, catching in the crook of his elbow. He clenched his teeth and hung onto the pole.

Then a cold hand clutched him.

'PULL!' screamed the old conductress.

He gasped with the effort. She wrenched him up onto the platform where he stood trembling, the paper-bag slumped between his legs, unable to speak.

'Bloody wee fool!' she cried. 'Get inside before you fall off!' She helped him and the bag up the step and he collapsed onto the long side-seat with the bag staying on the floor. 'I don't know what your mother's thinking about!' she said.

He got the money out of his trouser pocket and said politely, 'Tuppny-half please.'

At the foot of Achamore Road he got down off the platform first and then got the paper-bag strap over his left shoulder again and he dragged it off. He heard the ding ding as the conductress rang the bell for the driver. On the steep climb up to Kilmuir Drive he started by resting every twenty or so yards but by the time he had reached halfway it was every eight to ten yards. Finally he stopped and staggered into the first close and he straightened up and the bag crashed to the concrete floor. He waited a moment but nobody came out to see what had happened. A lot of the papers had shifted inside the bag and he heaved it up and bumped it down a bit, trying to get them settled back, but they did not move. His body felt strange. He began doing a funny sort of walk about the close, as if he was in slow motion. He touched himself on the shoulder, his left arm hanging down. Then he walked to the foot of the stairs and sat on the second bottom one. He got up and picked out a *Sunday Post* but it stuck halfway it was so tightly wedged; when he tugged, the pages ripped. Eventually he manoeuvered it out and he read the football reports sitting on the step. Then he did the same with the *Sunday Mail*. A long time later he returned the *Reynolds News* and stood up, rubbing his ice-cold bottom.

He completed the first close in five minutes then dragged the bag along the pavement to the next. At the faraway flat on the top landing, as he pushed through the rolled up *Post*, *Mail* and *World*, the dog jumped up snapping and yelping and he jammed three fingers in the letter-flap. He sucked them walking downstairs. At the third close he left the newspapers sticking halfway out. At the fourth he dragged the bag on to a point between it and the fifth and he delivered both sets of papers at once. He was down to about two to three minutes a close now.

About three quarters of the way through the delivery he noticed the dairy had opened at the wee block of shops. Some of his customers had paid him at the same time as he was giving in the papers so he had enough for an individual fruit pie and a pint of milk. In the newsagents he bought a packet of five Capstan and a book of matches. After the snack and a smoke he raced around the rest of Kilmuir and finished the first part. He had twelve *Sunday Mail* extra and was short of eight *Sunday Post* plus he had different bits of the *Observer* and the *Times*.

On the long road home he had to hide up a close at one point when he saw Mrs Johnstone the Sunday school teacher passing by on her way to church. As soon as he got into the house he rushed into the bathroom. He brushed his teeth to get rid of the smell of smoke then he sat down to toast and egg. His father was still in bed. At about this time John would usually have finished the run completely and be in the process of cashing in down at the paper-hut. His mother did not make any comments about it. Shortly after eleven he made the return journey to Kilmuir Drive and began collecting the money. There were also some outstanding sums to collect which John had left notes on. One family owed nine weeks' money. Tommy had delivered papers to them in error, against his brother's instructions and they never answered the door when he rang and rang the bell. Other people were not in either. Some of them he managed to get in when he went back but by the end of it all he still had a few to collect. He got a bus back to Dalsetter Terminus. The conductor told him it was quarter past three.

He walked slowly up to the junction at the white church. He had money in three of his four jeans' pockets. One of the ones at the front had a hole in it. In the other front one he had a pile of pennies and ha'pennies and threepenny bits; all his tips. In the two back pockets he was carrying the sixpences, shillings, two-bob bits and half crowns. He had the 10/- notes folded inside the Capstan packet which he held in his left hand. There were three fags and a dowp left in it.

The three men were alone in the hut. They were sitting up on the counter smoking and drinking lemonade. The big man stood down. 'You made it!' he cried.

Tommy looked at him but did not reply.

'Right,' said the crew-cut man coming over with a wooden tray, 'pour the cash on and we'll get it counted.'

Both men stacked and quickly double-checked the money while the thin man marked up the pay-in chit for £7/5/4.

'Much did you say?' echoed the big man.

'Seven pound five and four.'

'Well he's only got four and a half here!'

'What?'

'Four and a half.'

'Christ sake!'

The crew-cut man shook his head. 'No more money kid?'

'No. Just my tips.'

'Your tips!'

'His tips,' said the big man.

The thin man smiled. 'Get them out,' he said.

Tommy hesitated but then he lifted out all the change from his right front pocket, dumped it onto the counter. The crew-cut man counted it rapidly. 'Twenty-two and seven,' he said, 'plus it's a twenty-five bob run.'

The thin man nodded.

'Seven and nine short,' said the crew-cut man. He looked at Tommy. 'You're seven and nine short kid.'

Tommy frowned.

'You still got money to collect?'

'Aye.'

The crew-cut man nodded. 'Good, you'll get it through the week then eh?'

'Aye.' Tommy gazed across at the big man who had taken the wooden tray of money over to a desk. The thin man was also over there and writing into a large thick book.

'Okay kid,' said the crew-cut man, 'that's us locking up now . . .' He lifted a key from a hook on the wall and came to the counter, vaulted across it, landing with a thump nearby the door.

He opened the door, ushering Tommy out. 'MacKenzie'll be back new week eh?'

'Aye.'

'Good, good.'

The thin man called, 'Is he looking for a run?'

The crew-cut man nodded and said, 'You looking for a run yourself?'

'Aye!'

'Okay then son, as soon as one falls vacant I'll tell your brother, eh? How's that?'

'Great, that's great mister.'

'Right you are,' answered the crew-cut man and he shut the door behind him. Tommy heard the key turning in the lock.

His mother opened the door when he arrived home. She cried, 'It's nearly four o'clock Tommy where've you been? What happened?'

'Nothing mum, I was just late, honest.'

'Just late!'

'Aye, honest.'

'Tch! Away and take off these old trousers then and I'll make you a piece on cheese! And go and wash yourself in the bathroom you're filthy! Look at your face! Where did you get dirt like that?'

When he came through to the living room after his piece was on a plate on the sideboard and there was a cup of milk. His father was sitting on his armchair reading the *Mail* and drinking tea, a cigarette smouldering on the ashtray. 'How did you get on?' he asked over his spectacles.

'Okay dad.'

'What a time he took!' said his mother.

'Any problems?' asked his father.

'Some but it was okay really. I've to collect people through the week.'

His father nodded.

'Were they not in to pay the money?' asked his mother.

'No, and I went back.'

'That's terrible.'

'The man said I might get a run soon. He'll tell John.'

His father nodded, his gaze returning to the paper.

'That's good son,' replied his mother.

Then his father murmured, 'See and save something.'

Tommy nodded, biting into the piece on cheese.

GETTING OUTSIDE

I'LL TELL you something: when I stepped outside that door I was alone, and I mean alone. And it was exactly what I had wanted, almost as if I'd been demanding it. And that was funny because it's not the kind of thing I would usually demand at all; usually I didnt demand anything remotely resembling being outside that door. But now. Christ. And another thing: I didnt even feel as if I was myself. What a bloody carry on it was. I stared down at my legs, at my trousers. I was wearing these corduroy things I mostly just wear to go about. These big bloody holes they have on the knee. So that as well. Christ, I began to think my voice would start erupting in one of these bloodcurdling screams of horror. But no. Did it hell, I was in good control of myself. I glanced down at my shoes and lifted my right foot, kidding on I was examining the shoelaces and that, to see if they were tied correctly. One of those stupid kind of things you do. It's as if you've got to show everybody that nothing's taking place out the ordinary. This is the kind of thing you're used to happening. It's a bit stupid. But the point to remember as well; I was being watched. It's the thing you might forget. So I just I think sniffed and whistled a wee bit, to kid on I was assuming I was totally alone. And I could almost hear them drawing the curtains aside to stare out. Okay but I thought: here I am alone and it's exactly what I wanted; it was what I'd been demanding if the truth's to be told. I'll tell you something as well: I'm not usually a brave person but at that very moment I thought Christ here you are now and what's happening but you're keeping on going, you're keeping on going, just as if you couldnt give a damn about who was watching. I'm not kidding you I felt as great as ever I've felt in my whole life, and that's a fact.

So much so I was beginning to think is this you that's doing it. But it bloody was me, it was. And then I was walking and I mean walking, just walking, with nobody there to say yay or nay. What a feeling thon was. I stopped a minute to look about. An error. Of course, an error. I bloody knew it as soon as I'd done it. And out they came.

Where you off to?

Eh – nowhere in particular.

Can we come with you?

You?

Well we feel like a breath of fresh air.

I looked straight at them when they said that. It was that kind of daft thing people can say which gives you nearly nothing to reply. So I just, what I did for a minute, I just stared down at my shoes and then I said, I dont know how long I'll be away for.

They nodded. And it was a bit of time before they spoke back. You'd prefer we didnt come with you. You want to go yourself.

Go myself?

Yes, you prefer to go yourself. You dont want us to come with you.

No, it's not that, it's just, it's not that, it's not that at all, it's something else.

They were watching me and not saying anything.

It's just I dont know how long I'll be away. I might be away a couple of hours there again I might be away till well past midnight.

Midnight?

Yes, midnight, it's not that late surely, midnight, it's not that late.

We're not saying it is.

Yes you are.

No we're not.

But you are, that's what you're saying.

We arent. We arent saying that at all. We're not caring at all what you do. Go by yourself if you like. If you had just bloody told us to begin with instead of this big smokescreen you've always got to draw this great big smokescreen.

I have not.

Yes you have. That's what you've done.

That's what I'd done. That's what they were saying: they were saying I'd drawn this great big smokescreen all so's I could get outside the door as if the whole bloody carry on was just in aid of that. I never said anything back to them. I just thought it was best waiting and I just kind of kidded on I didnt really know what they were meaning.

JOHN DEVINE

MY NAME is John Devine and I now discover that for the past while I've been going off my head. I mean that the realization has finally hit me. Before then I sort of thought about it every so often but not in a concrete sense. It was actually getting to the stage where I was joking about it with friends! It's alright I would say on committing some almighty clanger, I'm going off my head.

On umpteen occasions it has happened with my wife. Two nights ago for instance; I'm standing washing the dishes and I drops this big plate that gets used for serving cakes, I drops it onto the floor. It was no careless act. Not really. I had been preoccupied right enough and the thought was to do with the plate and in some way starting to look upon it not as a piece of crockery but as something to be taken care of. This is no metaphor; it hasnt got anything to do with parental responsibility. My wife heard the smash and she came ben to see what was up. Sorry, I said, I'm just going off my head. And I smiled.

ONE SUCH PREPARATION

THE INITIAL REBELLIOUS BEARING IS SEEMINGLY AN EFFECT OF THE UNIFORM'S IRRITATION OF WHICH AMPLE EVIDENCE IS ALREADY TO HAND. BUT THIS KNOWLEDGE MAY BE OFFSET BY THE POSSIBILITY OF BEING TOUCHED BY GLORY. AT THE STAGE WHERE THE INCLINE BECOMES STEEPER THE ONE IN QUESTION STARED STEADFASTLY TO THE FRONT. HIS BREATHING, HARSH AS BEFITS AN UNDERGOING OF THE EXTREME, NEVER BETRAYED THE LEAST HINT OF INTERIOR MONOLOGUE. THERE WAS NO SIGN OF A WISH TO PAUSE AND NOR WAS THERE ANY TO REDUCE OR TO INCREASE PACE. HIS CONTROL WAS APPROPRIATE. THE AIR OF RESIGNATION GOVERNING HIS MOVEMENT CONTAINED NO GUILT WHICH INDICATED AN AWARENESS OF OUTSIDE INFERENCE. IT WAS AT THIS PRECISE MARK THE SATISFACTION EMERGED IN THE PROCEEDINGS. HIS ARMS AROSE STIFFLY UNTIL THE FINGERTIPS WERE PARALLEL TO THE WAISTBAND. HIS GAZE HAD BEEN DIRECTED BELOW BUT HE CONTINUED STARING TO THE FRONT AS IF EXPECTING OR EXPERIENCING A REACTION. WHAT WAS THE NATURAL SUMMIT MIGHT WELL HAVE BEEN INTERPRETED AS OTHERWISE.

GREYHOUND FOR BREAKFAST

RONNIE HELD the dog on a short lead so it had to walk on the edge of the pavement next to the gutter. At a close near the corner of the street two women he knew were standing chatting. They paused, watching his approach. Hullo, he said. When they peered at the greyhound and back to him he grinned and raised his eyebrows; and he shrugged, continuing along and into the pub.

The barman stared while pouring the pint of heavy but made no comment. He took the money and returned the change, moved to serve somebody else. Ronnie gazed after him for a moment then lifted the pint and led the dog to where four mates of his were sitting playing Shoot Pontoon. He sat on a vacant chair, bending to tuck the leash beneath his right shoe. He swallowed about a quarter of the beer in the first go and then sighed. I needed that, he said, leaning sideways a little, to grasp the dog's ears; he patted its head. He manoeuvred his chair so he could watch two hands of cards being played. The game continued in silence. Soon the greyhound yawned and settled onto the floor, its big tongue lolloping out its mouth. Ronnie smiled and shook his head. He swallowed another large draught of the heavy beer.

Then McInnes cleared his throat. You looking after it for somebody? he asked without taking his gaze from the thirteen cards he was holding and sorting through. Ronnie did not reply. The other three were smiling; they were also sorting through their cards. He carried on watching the game until it ended and the cards were being shuffled for the next. And he yawned; but the yawn was a false one and he sniffed and glanced towards the bar. Jimmy Peters had taken a tobacco pouch from his pocket and started rolling a fag. Ronnie gestured at it. Jimmy passed him the pouch and he rolled one for himself. He was beginning to feel a bit annoyed but it was fucking pointless. He stuck the finished roll-up in his mouth and reached for a box of matches lying at the side of the table. Heh Ronnie, said Kelly, did you get it for a present?

What?

I'm saying did you get it for a present, the dog – a lot of owners and that, once their dogs have finished racing, they give them away as presents – supposed to make rare pets.

Aye. Ronnie nodded, inhaled on the cigarette.

I'm serious.

Aye, said Tam McColl, I heard that as well. Easy oasy kind of beasts, they get on good with weans.

Ronnie nodded. This is a good conversation, he said.

Well! Tam McColl grinned: You're no trying to tell us it's a fucking racer are you! McColl chuckled and shook his head: With withers like that!

Withers like that! What you talking about withers like that! Ronnie smiled: What do you know about fucking withers ya cunt!

The others laughed.

My auld man used to keep dogs.

Aye fucking chihuahuas!

Are you telling us you've bought it? asked Kelly.

Ronnie did not reply.

Are you?

Ronnie dragged on the cigarette, having to squeeze the end of it so he could get a proper draw. He exhaled the smoke away from where the greyhound was lying. Jimmy Peters was looking at him. Ronnie looked back. After a moment Jimmy Peters said, I mean are you actually going to race it?

Naw Jimmy I'm just going to take it for walks.

The other three laughed loudly. Ronnie shook his head at Peters. Then he gazed at the dog; he inhaled on the cigarette, but it had stopped burning.

Does Babs know yet? asked McInnes.

What?

Babs, does she know yet?

What about?

God sake Ronnie!

Ronnie reached for the box of matches again and he struck one, got the roll-up burning once more. He blew out the flame and replied, I've just no seen her since breakfast.

Tam McColl grinned. You're mad ya cunt, fucking mad.

How much was it? asked Kelly. Or are we no allowed to ask!

Ronnie lifted his beer and sipped at it.

Did it cost much?

Fuck sake, muttered Ronnie.

You no going to tell us? asked Kelly.

Ronnie shrugged. Eighty notes.

Eighty notes!

Ronnie looked at him.

Jimmy Peters had shifted roundabout on his seat and he leaned down and ruffled behind the dog's ears, making a funny face at it. The dog looked back at him. He said to Ronnie, Aye it's a pally big animal.

Ronnie nodded. Then he noticed Kelly's facial expression and he frowned.

Naw, replied Kelly, grinning. I was just thinking there – somebody asking what its form was: oh it's pally! a pally big dog! Fuck speed but it likes getting petted!

That's a good joke, said Ronnie.

The other four laughed.

Ronnie nodded. On you go, he said, nothing like a good fucking joke. He dragged on the roll-up but it had stopped burning once again. He shoved it into the ticket pocket inside his jacket then lifted his pint and drank down all that was left of the beer. The others were grinning at him. Fuck yous! he said and reached for the leash.

McInnes chuckled: Sit on your arse Ronnie for fuck sake!

Fuck off.

Can you no take a joke? said Jimmy Peters.

A joke! That's fucking beyond a joke.

Kelly laughed.

Aye, said Ronnie, on ye go ya fucking stupid bastard.

Kelly stopped laughing.

Heh you! said McInnes to Ronnie.

Ah well no fucking wonder!

Kelly was still looking at him. Ronnie looked back.

McInnes said, You're fucking out of order Ronnie.

I'm out of order!

Aye.

Me? Ronnie was tapping himself vigorously on the chest.

Aye, replied McInnes.

It was just a joke, said Jimmy Peters.

A joke? That was fucking beyond a joke. Ronnie shook his head at him; he withdrew the dowp from his inside ticket pocket and reached for the box of matches again; but he put it back untouched, returned the dowp to the ticket pocket, lifted the empty beer glass and studied it for a moment. He sniffed and returned it to the table.

The others resumed the game of Shoot Pontoon.

And after two or three minutes Tam McColl said, Heh Ronnie did you see that movie on the telly last night.

Naw.

We were just talking about it before you came in.

Mm. Ronnie made a show of listening to what McColl was saying, it was some sort of shite about cops and robbers that was beyond even talking about. Ronnie shook his head. It was unbelievable. He stared at the cards on the table then he stared in the direction of the bar, a few young guys were over at the jukebox.

Jimmy Peters was saying something to him now. What was it about, it was about fucking the football, going to the football. Ronnie squinted at him: What?

Three each, said Jimmy, what a game! Did you see it?

Ronnie shook his head. He glanced at the shelf in beneath the table, the four pint glasses there, dribbles of beer in each. It was fucking beyond belief.

That last goal! said Jimmy.

Ronnie nodded. He clapped the dog's head, grasped its ears,

tugging at them till at last it shook his hand away. He sniffed and muttered, I'll tell yous mob something: see if this fucking dog doesnt get me the holiday money I'll eat it for my fucking breakfast.

The others smiled briefly. And Kelly said, So you are going to race it?

Ronnie shrugged. He didnt feel like talking. It was time to leave. He felt like leaving. It would be good to be able to leave; right now. He reached to clap the dog, smoothed along its muzzle.

Heh Ronnie, said McInnes. Where you going to keep it?

Ronnie wrapped the leash round his hand and he nodded slightly, lifted the box of matches.

No in the house? grinned Tam McColl.

There was a silence.

You're fucking mad!

Whereabouts in the house? asked Jimmy Peters.

Ronnie struck the match and tilted his head while getting the roll-up burning; he exhaled smoke: The boy's room, he said. Just meantime. He's no here the now. He's away with a couple of his mates. Down to London . . . He sniffed and dragged on the dowp again.

The others had been sorting the cards out after a new deal.

We never knew he was going, said Ronnie, no till the last minute. One of his mates got a phone call or something so they had to move fast.

Move fast? said McInnes.

It was a job they were after. They had to move fast. Otherwise they wouldnt fucking get it.

Aw aye.

Ronnie shrugged.

Kelly glanced at the greyhound and said, What you going to call it? You got something fixed?

Eh . . . I dont know. The guy I got it off says it's up to me. The way it works, most of them's got two names, one for the kennel and one for when it races.

Kelly nodded. Has it definitely raced Ronnie I mean I'm no being cheeky?

Aye Christ it's qualified at Ashfield and it's won three out of ten at Carfin.

Honest?

Aye, fuck sake.

What'd they call it?

Ronnie sniffed. *Big Dan*.

Big Dan? Tam McColl was grinning.

What's up with that ya cunt ye they've got to call it something! Ronnie shook his head, and he glanced at Kelly: You heard of it?

Eh naw, no really.

Ronnie nodded.

I've never been to Carfin but; never I mean – have you?

Naw.

You sure it's won there? asked Jimmy Peters.

Aye Christ he showed me, the guy; it's down in black and white.

Whereabouts? asked Kelly.

Whereabouts? Ronnie squinted at him.

Where's it written down?

The fucking *Record*.

Aw.

Kelly said, You talking about the results like? On the page?

Ronnie looked at him without saying anything in reply. He lifted his empty beer glass and swirled the drop at the bottom about, put the glass to his mouth and attempted to drink, but the drop got lost somewhere along the way. He said, Plus I saw its form figures and that on a race-card.

Kelly nodded.

Both McInnes and McColl and now Jimmy Peters were looking at him. Ronnie said, In the name of fuck! What yous looking at!

Aye, well, muttered McInnes, Your boy's fucked off to England and you've went out and bought a dog.

What?

There was no further comment. Ronnie shook his head and added, For fuck sake I've been wanting to buy a dog for years.

[211]

Aye, well it's a wee bit funny how it's only the now you've managed it.

What?

Your boy goes off to England and you go out and buy a dog . . . McInnes stared at Ronnie.

Who was it you bought it off? asked Kelly.

What?

Who was it you bought it off?

Away and fuck yourself, muttered Ronnie and he stood to his feet and jerked at the leash, the greyhound getting quickly up off the floor; and he walked it straight out the pub, not looking back.

*

Once through the park gates he let more slack into the lead before continuing on up the slope, the big dog now trotting quite freely. But the exercise he was giving it just now wasnt necessary. He was only doing it because he needed time to think. Babs would not be pleased. That was an understatement. It was something he had managed to avoid thinking about. And he was right not to have. If he had he would probably never have bought it. It was a case of first things first, buy the dog and then start worrying.

It stopped for a piss. Ronnie could have done with one himself but he would have got arrested. When they resumed he watched it, its shoulders hunched, keeping to the grass verge, sniffing occasionally and looking to be taking an interest in everything that was going on. It was quite a clever beast, the way it paid attention to things. And as well the way it moved, he was appreciating that; definitely an athlete – sleek was the word he was looking for. It described the dog to a tee. Sleek. That way it gave a genuine impression of energy, real energy – power and strength, and speed of course. The thing was every inch a racer.

Leaving the path he crossed the wide expanse of grass,

heading down by the bowling greens. It was late spring/early summer, getting on to the middle of May, still a bit cold when the sky clouded; but just now it was fine, the sun shining. More than half of the bowling rinks were occupied. Ronnie paused by the big hedge, peering over, and recognizing a few faces. But he was not going to go in. He wasnt in the mood for more slagging. Sometimes you got sick of it, you werent able to fucking, just to cope with it, it was difficult. You felt as if you'd had enough of it.

Beyond the bowling greens lay the flowerbeds. A lot of prams and pushchairs were in the vicinity, and on the benches women mainly, with the wee toddlers staggering about here and there, looking as if they were going to fall and bang their heads on the paving. But they were always okay; it was fucking amazing. He took the leash in to have more control of the dog but it seemed not to notice anything, not to be in the least nervous, even when one of the toddlers made a lunge at it.

Along by the pond he spotted a bench where a middle-aged guy was seated alone in the centre, a folded newspaper and a plastic bag of messages beside him. He had a bunnet on his head, a fawn trenchcoat, a scarf; probably the same clothes he would have been wearing in January.

Ronnie sat down, he sighed. He was aware of a tension easing out of his shoulders and he deliberately made them droop so he could relax even more, feeling a sort of twinge at the top of his spine which made him shiver. He glanced at the middle-aged man and nodded. Nice day, eh?

The man's head twitched in agreement.

Ronnie brought the cigarette dowp out from his inside ticket pocket and he gestured with it. You got a light at all? he asked.

Dont smoke. I chucked it ten year ago.

Aw. Wise man.

The middle-aged guy nodded at the pond: I mind the day it was chokablok with boats – big yins; yachts and all kinds.

Ronnie looked at him.

Beauties. You'd be lucky to get sailing at all unless you were up early!

What?

Now it's paddle-boats for weans. Pathetic, bloody pathetic.

Aye . . . Ronnie looked away. It was models he was talking about. His attention was attracted to a couple of boys who were fooling about on one, a paddle-boat, right away out, rocking the thing from side to side until it looked like the water would go over the top. Their laughter was loud; it was yells more than anything, really noisy. Fucking terrible. Ronnie grunted and shook his head, glanced at the middle-aged man. And then he said, Look at them. Pair of bloody eedjits. They're going to wind up capsizing the thing – look at them! Christ Almighty!

The middle-aged man was staring off in the other direction altogether.

And the dog had started tugging at the leash. It was behind the bench and moving about, and now doing a shite, straining and doing a shite. Ronnie smiled and shook his head. Life just continued, it was fucking crazy how it went. He faced the front again, seeing the two boys, laughing and rocking the boat, one of them trying to paddle at the same time. But there were stacks of broken glass at the bottom of the pond, that was what they failed to realize. It wasnt just him being totally out of order and losing his temper with them. If one of them fell in he could really hurt himself, he could cut himself quite badly, that was what happened, something fucking silly, turning into something serious. Weans! He shook his head and glanced at the middle-aged guy. Weans! he said, Bloody awful!

The man nodded slightly and sniffed.

I've got three of them, said Ronnie, smiling: A boy and two lassies.

Mm.

Ronnie looked at him for a few moments, seeing something in his face that made him think he probably didnt know what he was talking about, that he didnt understand because he didnt have any kids of his own. They're a fucking problem at times, he said, weans. Bloody awful! He grinned and then sighed and after a brief look at the greyhound he got up and tugged on the leash, headed off towards the exit. And the middle-aged man hadnt even acknowledged him. A moaning-faced old bastard he had been anyway. It was funny how some folk ended up like that. All fucking screwed up and tight and not able to open out with people. Chucked smoking ten year ago. No wonder he was so fucking bad tempered! Ronnie had tried to chuck it twice and each time it was Babs told him he'd be as well starting again because he was making every cunt's life a misery! But if he had succeeded she would have been delighted. She only said it to give him the excuse for starting again, because she thought he was suffering. And she was right! He was fucking suffering! No half! And yet, there again, he could have put up with it; he was putting up with it. Maybe she should just have kept her mouth shut, if she had kept her mouth shut and let him fucking get on with it, if she had just let him get on with it then maybe he would have fucking knocked it off, he might've chucked it. But what was the point of making excuses? He was good at that. That was one thing he was always good at, making fucking excuses, he was smashing at that.

*

It was half past four. He saw the time through the window of a shop.

He had bypassed his own street and kept on towards the Cross. The traffic was heavy; lines of buses at the terminus. People who still had jobs. He led the greyhound on across the road and down by the newish housing development. The dog was probably getting quite tired now. He had it back on a short lead, it was walking where he wanted it to. It was a nice big thing. He liked it. There was something about it; it made him feel a bit sorry as well, a kind of courage in the way it walked, its head quite high. He was not scared to face Babs. Even though she had this habit of always being right!

It was just that he wanted to have things clear in his head first. So that he would have an answer; that's all. She was too good at arguing, Babs, too good at arguing. She was liable to make him totally speechless. This is because she was always right. She just had the knack of finding that one thing, that one thing he could never get the answer for. That one thing, it always seemed to be there. But the only way he ever found the fucking thing was once it came up, once she brought it up or it came out, sometimes it just came out, while the argument was happening, and that was him, stuck for words.

He had arrived at the pier. It was derelict. He stood by the railing peering through the spikes. The ferryboat went from here to Partick. Old memories right enough! Ronnie smiled. Although they werent all good. Fuck sake. They werent all good at all. And then these other memories. And the smells. And the journey twice a day six days a week. These smells but of the river, and the rubbish lapping at the side of the steps down, and at low tide the steps all greasy and slippery, the moss and the rest of it. Did folk fall in? It always looked like that. It always looked as if folk would fall in. Fucking dangerous – especially for auld people with walking sticks. Even just the rain, that made the steps slippery.

The greyhound was looking at him. It had tugged on the leash to make him notice. A big whitish dog with a lot of black markings. Now standing squarely, like a middleweight boxer; and its long thin tail curling down to between its hind legs. So placid. It was strange. Sometimes when you saw them at the track – especially after the race – they were fierce, really fierce; going for each other, fangs bared inside the wire muzzles. Even just now, seeing its shoulders and that barrel chest, the power there, so palpable, the power, it could have stepped right out the fucking jungle. And its walk, that sort of pad pad pad – athletic wasnt the word.

Ronnie felt in his pockets for a loose match but there was none. He hadnt a light! He smiled. But one of the obvious factors was money. It cost a fortune to keep a dog. And you had to look after it properly otherwise what was the fucking point? you'd be as well keeping a stupid wee pet, a poodle or something. Stew twice a day was what the guy had advised, unless of course it was running that night. If that was the case you gave it nothing, not till after the event, not unless you were wanting it to lose. In which case you fed it five minutes before the fucking *off!*

There were other things he would have to find out about. Although some of it he would really only find out at the actual track, when he was along there giving it a time trial on Sunday afternoons. He was looking forward to that, it would be quite good. And he would be keeping his ears open and his mouth shut. Maybe get to know a couple of folk, and they would keep him straight at the beginning. Which was one of the reasons he had been hoping that bastard Kelly would've got involved. Kelly knew guys who were into different things and as well as that he used to like going over to the track. Between the two of them they could start finding out the right ways of working it. There was a lot more to the game than fucking exercise. Kelly was a bastard.

Ronnie paused. He had been walking a wee while, as far as the town hall. He crossed at the zebra crossing, making for Copland Road. His tea would be ready right at this minute and Babs would be wondering. But it was still too early; he was not prepared enough. And his fucking feet were beginning to feel sore. And if *he* felt like that what about the dog? A sit down would have been nice. He did have the cash for one more pint; also over and above that he had enough for 10 smokes. Not buying the packet earlier had been intentional, for obvious reasons: he would maybe only have had 2 or 3 left by this time, plus if he had crashed them in the boozer for fuck sake he would've had fuck all, maybe just the same roll-up dowp! Now, if he watched himself, he could buy the 10 and even put one aside to wake up with the morrow morning, when Babs got the Family Allowance money – the giro wasnt due till next Wednesday.

The leash was jerking. The dog knew how to get his attention alright!

It was across the road: a guy walking three greyhounds at once, two from one fist and one from the other – them all looking well-groomed, taken care of. Sleek. Ronnie nodded. He called over: Nice day!

Aye!

As long as the rain keeps off!

Aye! When the man made to continue on Ronnie called:
You getting a turn?

The man shrugged. He indicated the dog walking alone: This yin goes the morrow night!

I'll keep my fingers crossed!

The man nodded.

Whereabouts? Ashfield?

But the other guy made no reply to this; instead he continued on with the three dogs without glancing back over to Ronnie. Ronnie shook his head but he grinned briefly. Typical dog owner! They were notorious for it. And any information they did give out had to be treated with caution; in fact you were probably better just to consider it as useless, as not worth bothering about.

He went into a wee shop and bought the 10 fags and a book of matches and he was puffing when he appeared on the pavement. Farther along there was another guy with a dog, an elderly man – he looked like an old age pensioner. That was another thing about this, how it could keep you active and fit, and still involved.

At one time this district had two greyhound stadia to itself. Ronnie had been well acquainted with the last that closed down. The White City. It had been a licensed track and he used to go quite regularly, even as a boy; him and his pals used to have this way of skipping in down by the dummy railway. It had been great, evenings like this, the sun shining and the rest of it. The other track was the Albion, a flapping gaff. Ronnie had been too young for that one but the old timers yapped about it still, how it was the best of the lot and all that sort of shite.

He just wasnt ready to go home yet, not yet, not quite; he would be soon. At least it wasnt raining; if it had been raining it would've been terrible, even for the sake of the dog just. Kelly was a disappointment. So was the other three. But it was hopeless dwelling on that; you had to do things for yourself in this life; nobody was going to do it for you. It was him that had bought the dog, and he would have to fucking take care of it, just take care of it, it was down to him. The lassies would give him a hand; they would like being able to take it out for walks and the rest of it. They wouldnt think he was daft, it was Babs just, she would think he was daft. Other people would think he was daft as well. Was he daft? Maybe he was daft; he was always fucking – what was he?

He could just go home for his tea. No, not yet. He couldnt get it right. He still needed to think things out. Where to keep the dog for instance. The boy's room. Could he keep it there? Would Babs accept it? Would she fuck. She would just fucking, she would laugh at him. Quite right as well. What did he actually go and buy it for? Stupid. That would be her first question too and he couldnt fucking answer it, her first fucking question, he wouldnt be able to answer it, he wouldnt be able to give a straight answer to it. Thirty-five years of age, soon to be thirty-six, married for nearly nineteen years, a son of eighteen – a fucking granpa he could be.

He needed time to think. He just needed time to think. And what was the fucking time anyway? it must've been after six. The tea would just go back in the oven; the tea would go back in the oven.

Ronnie jerked at the dog; he had wound the leash round his knuckles and was clenching his fist as he walked, and he transferred it to his left hand.

*

The same guy served him as at dinnertime but this occasion he did speak; he frowned and he muttered, They'll no like you bringing it in too much.

What?

The barman nodded, looking up from the pint he was pouring: A lot of folk bring in theirs as well Ronnie, know what I mean? Just ordinary pets I'm talking about – in other words, wee yins!

Dont give us that, replied Ronnie. What about these big fucking alsatians! You're feart to walk in here sometimes in case you step on a tail and get fucking swallowed.

The barman nodded, smiled slightly.

[219]

Ronnie sniffed; he glanced at the greyhound by his feet: He wouldnt hurt a flea.

The barman shrugged. I'm just telling you Ronnie, they'll complain.

Okay, I hear you . . . Ronnie sipped at the pint, awaiting his 2 pence change; when the barman passed it to him he dropped it through the slot of the huge bottle of charity money, and he went to the toilet. The dog was quite the thing on the floor when he came back.

He should have come to another pub. That would have been the best idea. He glanced about; a couple of curious stares at the dog. Fuck them all. The dog wouldnt harm a flea. It was just a big – Christ! it was just a big pet.

Across at the rearmost table Jimmy Peters and McInnes were sitting on their own. Ronnie arrived and put his pint down, tucked the leash beneath his right shoe heel, and he nodded towards the bar: According to that yin there's going to be all sorts of complaints about the dog.

That right? said Jimmy Peters.

Too wild or somefuckingthing! Ronnie grinned and sipped at the beer. You want to have seen it in the park as well, with all the wee weans! Ronnie grinned: I mean they were fucking poking it and everything and all it did was look at them, it didnt even notice.

The other two nodded.

I mean I've been with it all day and it's fucking . . . Ronnie stopped and shook his head, he grinned. He brought out his fags and gave to each: It's just won its first race!

Fucking must've! chuckled Jimmy Peters, taking the cigarette and looking at it.

But it didnt stretch to a pint! added McInnes.

Ronnie nodded. It was a wee race!

You've cheered up since this afternoon.

Me?

Me! said McInnes.

Well . . . Ronnie sniffed.

You were like a fucking bear with a sore head, said Jimmy Peters.

Ronnie sniffed; he glanced at the greyhound by his feet: He good . . . He smiled: No wonder, I came in for a pint and I got a fucking row!

Jimmy Peters chuckled.

McInnes said, Naw you didnt.

Aye I did, grinned Ronnie. I mean I fucking expected it right enough, the slagging.

It wasnt a slagging.

Aye it was.

McInnes pursed his lips.

Let's face it, said Ronnie, it was a slagging.

Eh . . . began Jimmy Peters. Ronnie looked at him and he shrugged.

Mind you, said Ronnie, I was expecting a wee bit of interest, just a wee bit.

Och come on, muttered McInnes.

Well, replied Ronnie, just a wee bit would've been fucking something; better than nothing. But naw; fuck all, just the four of yous trying to take the piss out me.

We werent trying to take the fucking piss out you! Jimmy Peters replied.

You were.

We fucking werent!

Aye you fucking were Jimmy – the two of yous were in it just as much as McColl and Kelly.

Jimmy Peters stared at him then looked away. But McInnes sniffed and leaned closer to Ronnie, and he said: I'll tell you something man you better screw the fucking nut cause the way it's going you're going to wind up bad news, bad news. I'm no fucking kidding ye either.

What?

McInnes sat back and grunted, That's all I'm saying.

What're you meaning but?

McInnes shook his head.

Eh?

I'm no saying anything more Ronnie; you fucking know what I'm meaning.

[221]

Ronnie continued to gaze at him, then he frowned at Jimmy Peters and reached for the beer, sipped at it and put it down, lifted it again and sipped some more, gulping it down this time. He inhaled on the cigarette and stared towards the clock. And his hand lowered onto the head of the greyhound, and he grasped its ears.

Dont take it personally for God sake, said McInnes.

Naw.

Jimmy Peters said, It's just you're fucking, you're under pressure and that. The young yin, have you heard from him? the boy.

Ronnie shrugged. Then he said, Look, you dont really think I went out and bought the dog because of that, the boy, because he's away; eh?

Naw, Christ.

Cause I've been wanting a dog for ages. Fuck sake.

Jimmy Peters nodded.

And I'm no the only one – Kelly, he's fucking been on about it more than me. Eh?

Aye.

Ronnie shook his head: I mean I've got to laugh at yous cunts. All talk. All fucking talk.

McInnes was looking at him. Ronnie looked back at him. McInnes said, This is you out of order again.

What?

This is you fucking out of order, again.

What d'you mean?

The way you go on . . . McInnes shook his head and stared at the floor.

Ronnie stared at him.

Aye, God sake, the way you go on!

What! Ronnie's face screwed into a glare.

Leave it.

Leave it?

McInnes looked at him then looked away. Jimmy Peters was looking away too. Ronnie sniffed and glanced at the dog, it was asleep, poor big fucking beast, sound asleep. Greyhounds were short-haired. The top of its head was really smooth. He reached to stroke it, it didnt feel like hair at all, more like a kind of material. He took a long draw on the cigarette, ground it out beneath his shoe on the floor.

Jimmy Peters said, I see the Celts're going to sign that Thomson?

Ronnie nodded.

No a bad player.

Aye.

No Celtic class, muttered McInnes.

It needed a feed as well, it was probably starving. That was another thing about greyhound owners, how they were really tight, they treated their dogs like racing machines, no sentiment. The guy he had bought it from probably never fed it because he knew he was selling it, so it was probably fucking starving.

That movie . . .

Ronnie frowned slightly, then nodded. What time does it start? he asked.

Jimmy Peters smiled. Naw, he said, I'm talking about that one that was on last night – fucking brilliant, did you see it?

Nah.

Were you out? asked McInnes.

What?

I was just asking if you were out, last night; you were no in here?

Naw.

McInnes nodded. Oh by the way, he said, that fucking *Hammurabi* won again!

What! You're kidding?

7 to 1.

For Christ sake!

7 to 1 . . . McInnes smiled, shaking his head. They're sending it to Royal Ascot.

Many's that it's won? Jimmy Peters asked.

Four.

Four on the trot, added Ronnie.

Jimmy Peters grinned. Pity you couldnt've bought a horse!

Ronnie looked at him.

Imagine coming in here with it! Peters laughed: Imagine the faces!

For fuck sake! Ronnie began chuckling.

McInnes was smiling.

A pint and a barrel of oats! cried Peters. Heh barman, a pint and a barrel of oats!

The three of them were laughing now. Gradually they stopped. Ronnie began stroking behind the dog's ears and it opened its eyes for a moment, made a movement in its mouth as if it was thirsty. It would be thirsty. When had it last had a drink? Ronnie hadnt given it one. And the guy he'd bought it from, probably he hadnt either. The truth of the matter is Ronnie was feeling bad. He probably shouldnt've bought the dog, if he wasnt going to look after it properly. It just wasnt fair. The lassies would help right enough. They were good, they helped. They would take it for walks. Babs would just – she wouldnt bother, she would be okay. He was just fucking, it was him, he was daft, stupid, coming home with a greyhound, it was out of order. Jimmy was talking. Ronnie nodded, acknowledging something; he didnt know what the fuck it was he was acknowledging but he was fucking acknowledging something! He smiled, he raised the pint to his lips and swallowed beer. Jimmy pushed the tobacco pouch towards him and he rolled himself a smoke. It was time to leave. He struck a match, lighting his own before offering the light to Jimmy; then he finished off the beer and wiped his mouth quickly. Okay, he said, lifting the leash. And he got to his feet.

You off? asked Jimmy Peters.

Aye.

I'll be heading that way myself, said McInnes, glancing towards the clock.

See you the morrow, said Jimmy.

Aye ... Ronnie gave a slight tug on the leash and the dog rose from the floor. And he left the pub quickly, in case McInnes came along the road with him. They both lived in the same street. He didnt want McInnes to know, that he wasnt going home just now. He wasnt going to go home just now, definitely not. He wasnt feeling right for it. That was it in a nutshell. What was that thing about Hamlet? Like a king. Something. Ronnie just felt fucking, he felt lousy. He hadnt been feeling as lousy as this before. Last night for instance he had been feeling good. He had made the phonecall and he knew he was the only one who had made any inquiries. And eighty quid as well; it was about exactly what he had saved up, almost the total sum. Everything just seemed spot on. And the guy himself seemed okay. If it was possible to trust a doggie-man! Ronnie grinned. They couldnt all be fucking rogues. Surely to fuck!

Heh Ronnie!

It was McInnes out from the pub and waving to him and coming along after him. Ronnie waved back and continued, and on round the next corner and he started walking fast, and then round the next corner, and away.

He liked McInnes, he wasnt fucking, it wasnt as if he was trying to avoid him, especially; he just didnt want to fucking speak to anybody, not anybody. Nobody. Fucking nobody. He didnt want to speak to any cunt at all. And not McInnes, a good pal, he didnt want to speak to the likes of him at all. And not fucking Babs either. Babs least of all. And the weans, he didnt want to speak to them, not to even see them, he couldnt face them; he actually couldnt face them. He couldnt face them, the wife and weans, that was it, in a fucking nutshell.

*

It was fucking really terrible. The truth of the matter is he was feeling really terrible. How the fuck was he feeling as terrible as this? And there was the big dog! So fucking placid. That was it about these animals, how placid they were and then when you see them at the track they're so fucking fierce, so fierce looking; fangs bared and fucking drooling, drooling at the mouth and ready to fucking – bite, kill, kill the hare except its a bundle of stupid fucking rags. Imagine being as easy conned as that! Letting yourself get lulled into it, racing round and round and fucking round just to catch this stupid fucking bundle of rags. It made you feel sorry for it. Dogs and all the rest of the animals. And people of course, they were no different – they seemed different but they werent; they seemed as if they were different but they werent; they really fucking werent, they just thought they were, it made you smile. Because there they were, running round and round trying to fucking catch it, a crock of gold, and did they ever catch it, did they fuck. The boy was like that, off to London; and what would happen to him, fuck all, nothing. He would just wind up getting a job somewhere and it would be fucking awful, and maybe he would just stay in London or else he'd come back. And if he stayed in London that'd be that and he probably'd hardly ever see them again. It was fucking strange. And Ronnie actually felt like doing himself in. It was a feeling he'd had, creeping up on him. He was actually feeling like doing himself in. What a thing. What a fucking thing. It was because he felt like a, well, because he felt like he'd fucking let them down, he'd let them down, it was because he felt like he'd let them all down, the whole lot, the lassies and Babs and the boy. Jesus, he'd really fucking let them down. What did he do it. What did he do it. What was the thing. There was water at the edges of his mouth, and he wiped it off along his left forefinger and it made him feel better. The dog still walking there, that courageous picture. Because it was going into the fucking unknown! That dog! Getting led by him and not knowing where in the name of fuck it's going. Stupid. And the fucking power, letting itself get led. It was funny how human beings came first, and even one of these wee weans in the park could walk up and take over the lead, and the dog would just let it probably, just let it, itself be led.

Ronnie was walking quickly now, the greyhound trotting to remain abreast of him.

It was maybe good to change speed like this so it kept more alert, especially with it being so tired – and hungry. The thing must have been starving. That was him walking it since fucking what? 10 o'clock in the morning for fuck sake! Poor bastard. Of

all the owners to get it gets him. Ach well. The tea in the oven.
Babs would have switched it off now and she'd be wondering
what the hell, how come he had got money; because she would
just assume he was in the pub and in the process of getting totally
paralytic. And a drink of water, it hadnt even had a drink of water.
For fuck sake. It was actually worrying; it was more than just, it
was more than just thinking it was thirsty it was actually thinking
it might be getting bad because of it, the dog might actually
become ill or something, because of the lack of water; it was
possible. What he could do was just throw it in the fucking Clyde!
then it'd get bags of water! That old joke about falling into the
river, you didnt drown, you died of diphtheria. It was true but
you couldnt see into it. Ronnie minded well as a boy when he used
to hang over the side and see if he could see any fish, and he
couldnt see anything it was so cloudy, so fucking mawkit. Christ!
And yet that smell, it was a great smell, and fresh and what else
could it be but the sea air, the smell of the sea. Yes. A fucking tang,
it was the sea. It was fucking – Jesus, it was fucking great; it was
just fucking great. And these other smells working in the leather-
works across in Partick, making football bladders and stuff like
that. What a fucking job; that twice-daily journey six days a week
and the rain pelting down, and the wind biting your ears going
across in the ferry; walking up the steps at the other side and then
the cobbles, that terrible monotony, the wooden fence, spar after
spar. The good bit about it was the race, every cunt racing each
other but kidding on they were just walking fast. Maybe they
were walking fast. Maybe he was the only person racing. Not at
all. Everybody was at it, seeing who'd be first to reach Dumbarton
Road. And anybody who ran was fucking cheating! Comical!
Ronnie laughed, shook his head. It was just so fucking comical.
Stupid. The greyhound was looking at him and it had tugged the
leash. It was going to do another shite. The guy must have fed it
after all otherwise there would've been nothing more to come out.
Poor bastard. It wasnt much of a shite right enough. *Big Dan*; it
was squeezing out this wee skinny shite. Maybe he would give it
another name. He could call it whatever he liked. *Shitey*! He could
call it *Shitey*. But that wouldnt be allowed, unless he changed its

spelling. *Iteysh*. Something like that. Or *Keech*! Outside of Glasgow nobody knew what the fuck it meant. *Big Keechy*. Ronnie shook his head, transferred the leash to his other hand and brought out the cigarette packet and matches. There were only two left. It was unbelievable how they went. Two before going into the pub; three in it; then this was the second since leaving. Which makes seven. He must've smoked another one somewhere else.

The dog was sitting at the gutter, staring down in the direction of the river. It was wondering what was happening. And Babs as well. And the lassies maybe; them thinking he was in the boozer.

The pier was derelict around here, it was a pity. At one time the steamers pulled in on their way down the Firth. And boats went to America, £5 for the one-way trip. When was that? That was fucking years ago. The turn of the century.

Ronnie peered through the fence; he tied the leash round a spike and rubbed his hands together. The wind coming down the Clyde; he moved his shoulders into a hunch. The cigarette packet and matches were back in his pocket again. He was going to save them for later. He didnt need a smoke just now. It was just habit. But he did need another pish. And he would have to wait a minute because there was a couple walking past, man and a woman with the arms linked. And the way they stared at the greyhound it was as if they thought it was there by itself. Ronnie stared after them and there was something in the way they walked that made him think they were wanting to look back but were doing their best not to. It was funny the way people were, how they acted, always so fucking self conscious and embarrassed about things. All they had to say was, Is this dog yours? And he would've said, Aye. And that would've fucking been it, end of story.

But people didnt do things like that. They didnt do things as simple as that. They had to do it in a devious sort of – they had to be devious, that was it, they just had to be fucking devious. That was it, that was human nature, they just had to be fucking devious. Even the boy – eighteen years of age and just as devious as the rest of them. All he had to do was tell them and that would've been that. But no; what he does is fuck off and then gives a phonecall from a fucking motorway cafe. And Babs is up to fucking high doh worrying about it. Unbelievable. Just like a fucking wee wean. Eighteen years of age! Ronnie had been his father at that age. Eighteen! Fuck sake. It's no that young. It's young, but no that young. Eighteen. Christ Almighty.

It was getting dark. What time was it? When he was in the pub it was 7. It was after that. Nearer 8, when he left. Probably it was 9, it'd be 9 now. And they'd think he would be really paralytic. It could even be after 9.

Heh Ronnie!

Christ! McInnes! McInnes had come after him. McInnes. Where was he? He wasnt here at all. It hadnt been a shout. But it was like a shout. As if somebody had shouted on him. An apparition. A fucking ghost! The docks was a creepy place but, deserted and fucking derelict. And this pier, how you could see the actual particles of coaldust lapping in on the surface of the water, onto the steps for fuck sake, if you wanted to commit suicide you'd choose a better place, you wouldnt want to fucking choke, if you wanted to fucking choke you'd do something else altogether, a bottle of fucking pills maybe.

What did he buy it for? He shouldnt've bought it.

Ach well. It was too late. He had it and that was that. Poor old bastard. Maybe he wouldnt race it at all, maybe he *would* just keep it as a pet, and fuck them. Bastards.

Here was somebody else coming. Another couple.

That was funny how the shout had happened, it sounding like a shout, from inside the head. And it was McInnes; it was his voice. It wasnt Babs for instance, if you'd expected that, because maybe to do with telepathy, her thinking he was about to do himself in or somefuckingthing and so trying to reach out to him, the way twins are supposed to.

She would maybe be worrying about him now. Would she? Aye, she would be, she would be worrying about him because he hadnt phoned. Fuck sake, of course she would; what was the fucking point of fucking, trying to fucking keep it away, of course she'd be fucking worrying about him. On top of the boy; on top of the boy she would now be worrying about him. And the lassies, they'd know something was up because they'd see the way she was looking; if they were watching the telly, they'd see she wasnt really seeing what was on, her attention would be fucking, it would be nowhere near it, wondering if the phone was going to ring; and the boy as well, if he was okay – London for fuck sake, what could happen down there, things were bad down there, weans on the street, having to sell themselves to get by, the things that were happening down there, down in London, to young lassies and boys, it wasnt fucking fair, it was just fucking terrible, it was so fucking terrible, it was just so fucking terrible you couldnt fucking man you fucking Jesus Christ trying to think about that it was Christ it was so fucking terrible, it was so bad. Ronnie had the cigarette packet in his hand and he opened it and took out one; when he was smoking he returned it and the book of matches to his pocket. He inhaled twice without exhaling, let it all out in a gasp. He leaned his shoulder against the fence, inhaled again, exhaling the smoke through his nostrils. He would just tell Babs something or other, what the fuck he didnt know, it didnt fucking matter; what did it matter, it didnt fucking matter.